"Why are you looking at me like that?"

"Like what?" he asked.

She blinked. "Like you want to kiss me."

"I've wanted to kiss you since you left my house that night. I can respect you enough to control myself, though."

Melanie's brows drew in. She closed her eyes and shook her head before focusing back on him. "I don't understand you."

"I'm a pretty simple guy." With a past he wasn't ready to share and a job he couldn't. "You know I'm attracted to you. But for now, we're going to get to know each other."

"I'm not doing a relationship."

Tanner lifted her hand to his lips and kissed her knuckles. "I'm not, either. At least not today."

Melanie tipped her head and narrowed her eyes. "Tanner, I can't. This baby has to be our focus. Not the attraction."

Unable to help himself, Tanner closed the distance between them and nipped at her lips. "The attraction is only going to get stronger, so fighting it is a waste of energy."

Silence enveloped them and Tanner wanted to know what she was thinking. That she hadn't eased back or pulled her hand from his was a good sign. He wasn't quite sure himself what he wanted with her, but he needed to start somewhere. Chemistry was a hell of a place . . .

Books by Jules Bennett

WRAPPED IN YOU

CAUGHT UP IN YOU

LOST IN YOU

STAY WITH ME

BE WITH ME

Published by Kensington Publishing Corporation

be with me

JULES
BENNETT

ZEBRA BOOKS
KENSINGTON PUBLISHING CORP.
http://www.kensingtonbooks.com

ZEBRA BOOKS are published by

Kensington Publishing Corp.
119 West 40th Street
New York, NY 10018

All Kensington titles, imprints, and distributed lines are available at special quantity discounts for bulk purchases for sales promotion, premiums, fund-raising, educational, or institutional use.

Special book excerpts or customized printings can also be created to fit specific needs. For details, write or phone the office of the Kensington Sales Manager: Attn.: Sales Department. Kensington Publishing Corp., 119 West 40th Street, New York, NY 10018. Phone: 1-800-221-2647.

Zebra and the Z logo Reg. U.S. Pat. & TM Off.

First Printing: November 2018
ISBN-13: 978-1-4201-4498-7
ISBN-10: 1-4201-4498-7

eISBN-13: 978-1-4201-4499-4
eISBN-10: 1-4201-4499-5

10 9 8 7 6 5 4 3 2 1

Printed in the United States of America

Chapter One

*You're allowed to scream, you're allowed to cry,
but you're never allowed to give up.*

—Mel's Motivational Blog

If there was ever a time for cocktails, it was now. On the flip side of that, Melanie Ramsey couldn't drink. Her drinking days were over . . . at least for the next seven months and two weeks, because this morning she'd had two thin blue lines staring her in the face.

Still, she found herself in the wine aisle of Quicky Mart choosing a bottle for her best friends because they were certainly going to need it when she broke the news to them.

What paired well with dropping a bomb like an unplanned pregnancy? Blush? Red?

Considering she'd had white the night of the greatest sexual experience of her life, which had landed her here, she chose the only white that was available from this dismal selection.

"Mel."

Her fingers curled tighter around the neck of the bottle. She knew that voice. She'd replayed over and over how he'd whispered it in her ear as he'd had her pressed against the door in the foyer of his house. For the past six weeks she'd done a remarkable job of dodging him after their one-night stand. What had she been thinking? She wasn't a one-night stand type of girl . . . then again, if they all were with men like Officer Tanner Roark, she might have to reconsider. Holy smokes that man knew how to pleasure a woman.

But playtime was over . . . and now they both would have to face the consequences.

However, now was not the time to tell Tanner that he was going to be a daddy. She was still grasping the life-changing fact herself.

After their night together she hadn't known how to handle a situation so foreign to her. Unfortunately, avoiding him had become her go-to method until she thought of something better.

Dodging Tanner had been quite a feat considering her best friend was marrying his cousin, but Melanie had been busy and apparently so had Tanner, because he'd done little more than text. Maybe he'd only wanted one night, too. She'd heard of his widespread reputation as Haven's most sought-after bachelor.

Melanie had thought for certain they'd been on the same page. She'd only wanted a safe man, someone she could have fun with, and prove to herself that she was in charge of her life and if she wanted to have a fling, then she sure as hell would.

Tanner was a ladies' man. Oh, he might not exploit his bedroom talents, but Melanie had been in town long enough to see how women looked at him, what they whispered through hushed gossip at the Curl Up and Dye salon.

She'd been so certain she was ready to take full control

of her life, including taking a lover of her choice, and afterwards she would go on her way.

The irony of running into Tanner only hours after her world had tilted on its axis wasn't lost on her. She firmly believed in fate and signs.

Melanie pulled in a breath and pasted a convincing smile on her face—at least she hoped it was convincing. For the first time in two years, her nerve and courage faltered. She'd been shaken from the solid foundation she'd recently rebuilt for herself.

But she wasn't going to fall. Never again. This moment might shake her stability, but that was life, and she'd discovered long ago as a child growing up in poverty that the more obstacles life threw in your path, the stronger you were from dodging them.

She'd developed a strength she'd never thought possible.

Clutching her cheap wine, Melanie spun around. "Hey, Tanner."

Try as she might for a casual greeting, her heart sped up and her mouth nearly watered at the sight of him in uniform. She took in his navy uniform, how well his broad frame filled out every piece of that material, and the aviators he had tucked into the top V just above a glossy black button.

The knots in her stomach tightened. He was just as sexy and intriguing as she'd remembered . . . damn it. She'd been hoping her imagination had just conjured up how amazing they'd been together. But one look at him now only had each and every touch rushing back in glorious detail. The tingling she'd felt from his simple touches, the tickling from his warm breath along her bare skin, the passionate way he commanded her.

"What are you doing here?"

Dark eyes raked over her, giving her chills and even

more flashes of their night. He had *dark and sultry* down without even trying.

After her less than storybook marriage ended, it had taken her a hell of a long time to get up the courage to approach another man. For reasons she couldn't comprehend, Tanner had been the only man in the past couple years to interest her in any way. And by interest, she meant he drove her absolutely crazy with a want she barely recognized.

"I just stopped in to grab a sandwich," he explained. "I didn't see your car out front."

Yeah, her silver Beemer had stood out in this tiny town of minivans and pickup trucks. Haven was a far cry from Atlanta.

Melanie swallowed. She'd sold her car recently to help her best friend, Olivia Daniels, with her goal of renovating the small-town airport. Besides, ridding herself of the last shred of material things from her ex and assisting such a good cause all in the same whack had been so rewarding, so freeing.

If Neville Prescott knew where his precious BMW SUV had gone, he'd somehow spin things to the media that he was helping those less fortunate. Egotistical jerk of a politician.

Not that she'd ever wanted anything he'd given her, but when Melanie had left, she'd taken the only car she had. She'd been owed that much, to say the least.

Since selling her car she'd used the little in her savings and bought a gently used two-door sporty model. By gently used, she meant the seat didn't move and she had to shove a pillow behind her back to reach the pedals, but it ran and got her from point A to point B. Oh, the horn might sound like a cat whose tail got run over, but other than that the car was in tip-top shape. Plus, she'd purchased a nice bike for exercise and roaming around the quaint town, so it was still a win.

Considering her childhood and teen years, having a less-than-impressive vehicle actually felt right at home. But her marriage and her childhood were not areas she wanted to explore now—or ever, really.

"Oh, I'm driving something else now."

That's right. The black heap in the lot, with a rusty bumper and a shorted out horn, was all hers.

Tanner propped his hands on his hips and scanned both directions of the aisle before zeroing back in on her. "You've dodged me for weeks."

She'd rather talk about the sad excuse for a car than get into why she'd avoided him. In her defense, he'd not been around much, either. "I've been busy."

Not a total lie. She'd been working on all of the permits and discussing renovations for the airport Olivia was revamping with the help of her fiancé, Jax Morgan. Her law degree was coming in handy in ways she never would've guessed a few years ago.

To turn a small-town airport into a grand, high-concept business that would draw high-dollar clients took time and patience and a hell of a lot of paperwork and funds.

Celebrities were rolling through like clockwork to film in and around Haven, Georgia. Savannah, only a short twenty-minute ride away, had definitely become a hot spot for filmmakers. Melanie planned on making sure her friends were legally covered and protected in their endeavor. She wanted this next chapter in Olivia's life to be successful and a tribute to her late father and former owner of the airport.

"Too busy to talk to me after you slept with me and left the second your clothes were straightened out?"

That would be because their clothes never fully came

off. They'd been too hot, too hurried to worry about getting completely naked.

Heat flooded her, as well as a nice dose of guilt. "Keep your voice down," she whispered through gritted teeth. The last thing she needed was people in the Quicky Mart to hear the fairly new girl in town was getting it on with the hottest bachelor officer. Well, she *had* gotten it on, they weren't doing anything now.

Except the memories that kept replaying in her mind like a silent movie.

Tanner took a half step forward and tipped his head down as he lowered his voice. "I know we didn't agree on anything beyond that night. Hell, we didn't even talk much. But, considering our circle of friends, I didn't take you for the type that would brush me aside."

She hadn't, not exactly. She'd been completely out of her element when they'd torn each other's clothes off in a frenzy. Melanie had gotten swept up in the moment, in the man. She'd gone into the one-night stand with her eyes wide open, teetering on the edge of fear and exhilaration all rolled into one giant ball of emotion.

Then afterward, she'd had no words. How could she know what to say or do when she'd experienced something she'd never done before? The instant retreat had been the coward's way out, and she'd prided herself on becoming stronger than the woman she used to be. But she just couldn't face him. Not until she knew where her head was where he was concerned, because Tanner Roark made her feel things she shouldn't, things she'd never felt before.

After her failed marriage . . .

No. Just no. She didn't trust her judgment—especially now. Besides, the one-night stand and the changed dynamics of their friendship weren't of the utmost importance at this point.

"I've just been busy," she repeated. "Livie is planning a cookout and bonfire soon, though. Friday, I believe. I'll see you there?"

Tanner's brows drew in. "Is everything okay, Mel? You seem, I don't know, jittery."

Jittery? More like scared out of her mind and no clue what to do next. Her life was one giant roller coaster, and she'd really like to slow down and hop off the emotional ride.

"I'm fine," she lied with a smile.

He eyed her once again. Tanner wasn't stupid and he wasn't buying her quick brush-off. Today of all days was not the time to get into this discussion. Delivering baby-daddy news in the middle of a gas station/convenience store was teetering too close to the lifestyle she'd tried to escape when she'd married Neville. She'd thought he was the way out of her impoverished life. She'd thought he would take her down the path to make something of herself and maybe make her parents proud.

She'd wanted their approval; she'd wanted to be proud of herself, too. None of that happened. Hindsight only proved she would've been better off in that trailer park working her ass off, with her scholarships to get through school, and then moving on to a law firm like she'd first planned. Thankfully, she'd been smart in school, had graduated early, had pushed through college before marrying. After that, though, her life had fallen apart.

Melanie had quickly discovered she was going to have to be her own ticket out of hell.

Too many emotions threatened to overtake her. She just wanted to get the wine and get out. There was no way she could go empty-handed to Livie and Jade and tell her two best friends about this pregnancy. Melanie needed a buffer, and wine, no matter how cheap, was always the answer . . . unless you were pregnant.

"Mel."

She jerked from her thoughts. Neville hated when anyone called her Mel—which was precisely why she'd named her successful blog *Mel's Motivations*.

Her ex had claimed that he'd taken her from the slums and she needed to remember that. Her name was Melanie, she was his wife, and his appearances mattered, so by default hers did, too. Considering she was a branch of him, she needed to always have those pretenses in place. Perfect clothes, perfect hair, always smiling with just the right responses when she was allowed to speak.

She'd failed in so many areas. Smiling in public had been so difficult when behind closed doors she'd been living a nightmare. Some wouldn't understand because she'd had money, cars, a big house. But none of that had ever mattered to her. Not once did she ever care about material things. She just wanted to be with a man who loved her.

Neville had been the complete opposite. He'd hated quite a bit about her, looking back. She'd mistook his attention when they first met for affection. She'd thought the grass was greener on the other side when her parents urged her to jump at the possibility of a life with such a powerful, charming man. Little did they all know . . .

Unfortunately, Melanie couldn't change the past, and her future required all of her attention at the moment.

"I'm running late." She gripped the bottle with both hands as if drawing strength from the inanimate object. "We'll talk at the cookout."

Again, probably not the best place to inform him he was going to be a dad. She'd have to tell him soon. Before Friday, because she wasn't going to be able to keep the secret from her friends. She needed them now more than ever, and it wasn't fair to let them in on the secret when Tanner was so unaware.

Melanie despised secrets and lies and swore never to be that person. Right now, though, she needed to gather her thoughts, her fears, her nerves, and figure out the best time and way to tell him.

Tanner propped his hands on his hips as he took a half step closer. Her body instantly tingled. Despite everything she'd been through, even what she dealt with now, Tanner Roark was one impressive man and demanded attention. Oh, he didn't do so with words or fists.

Tanner's strength and power had her captivated, though she'd fought it for months until six weeks ago, when she'd given in. She'd gone to Taps for a girls' night out with Livie and Jade. A little flirty banter led to a little more, then to a harmless dance . . . well, she'd thought it had been harmless.

Being torso to torso with Tanner hadn't been harmless in any way whatsoever. That moment had awakened something inside her, something she hadn't even known she possessed. She would've been a fool to ignore the burst of emotions that had spiraled through her.

They'd gone from dancing to long glances to feather-light touches. Then she'd been in his house, plastered against his front door as he'd held her wrists above her head and given her a night that would fuel her fantasies for the rest of her life.

And right there in the Quicky Mart her body betrayed her and started heating all over again. Damn hormones were all over the place.

Everything about the man was dangerous. Not in the sense that her ex had been a danger. No, Tanner made her think too much about what she wanted, what she'd finally taken. He made her crazy with that devil-may-care attitude. And he was dangerous because those lips could drive a woman out of her mind with need.

But she had no idea how he'd react to the news of a baby. Sex was one thing, but entering into a bond that would forge them together for life was a whole other level. It was that *bound for life* thing that had Melanie more terrified than anything. She'd finally gotten control for the first time, but now everything she'd built for herself, every decision she'd made in the last two years, were threatened. Not because of the innocent baby, but because of the man who stood before her.

She would not fall prey to another man again. And once Tanner found out about the baby, Melanie feared he'd become all too hovering and controlling.

"I want to see you, Mel. I never chase women and I don't intend to start now." His lips thinned slightly, the muscle in his jaw clenched. "If I thought you didn't have a good time, then I'd back off, but I know you did. My shift ends at seven. You know where I live."

So many emotions curled low in her belly as Tanner left her standing alone holding a bottle of Quicky Mart's best white wine with a twist-off cap that money could buy.

Tanner had thrown out that invitation for one reason and one reason only.

What he didn't know was that the girl who had gone home with him over a month ago was not the same girl she was on an everyday basis. She'd been in town long enough to get to know him through their friends. From the get-go she and Tanner had butted heads, they'd argued, they'd ignored each other, and finally shared witty banter. But beneath all of their heated exchanges, the sexual tension had been brewing.

Melanie had fought the good fight until she hadn't

been able to deny herself another second. Wasn't that why she'd left Atlanta and her old life? Hadn't she wanted to be free to make her own decisions? Free to live as she wanted and not be ashamed of herself or her past? More importantly, free to be out from underneath such a controlling thumb. For once in her life, she was finally in charge . . . and she wasn't doing a very good job of things.

Turning to head to the register, and praying she wouldn't run into Tanner again, thoughts swirled through her head. What was she going to do? She obviously had to tell him about the baby, and he'd just presented her the perfect opportunity.

Melanie knew the type of man Tanner was. Which was exactly why she'd chosen to give in to her desires and have a one-night stand. He was safe, he wouldn't want a relationship. She'd been through enough hell to know that committing herself to another man might never happen and she was just fine on her own, thank you very much.

Oh, she still wanted that family with a devoted husband. She was just enough of a romantic to believe such faithful, loving men still existed, but she had also learned enough about herself to know she didn't have to have a man to be complete.

And trying to form any type of a relationship with the first man since her marriage, was not smart. Getting pregnant by a rebound guy wasn't either, yet here she was.

Melanie blew out a sigh and quickly paid for the wine. She headed out to her new-to-her car and brought the engine to life, then cranked up the A/C. Despite being the middle of November, Haven, Georgia, had delivered a warm afternoon with the sun shining bright. Of course the heat in her body wasn't only because of the unusual weather. Running into Tanner when she hadn't been prepared had set her body into all sorts of heated emotions.

Before they'd ever been introduced through their mutual friends, Tanner had pulled her over and given her a ticket. She'd hated him at that moment. Her life had been in a bad spot, she'd been struggling to find that strong woman within.

The similarities between her ex and him had been too close, her memories too raw. Even then, though, she hadn't been able to deny the instant attraction. Something about a man who put himself out there to protect others was so attractive, but she and Tanner weren't in a spot that led to happily ever after. They were friends at best.

Melanie drove through the main part of downtown Haven, past all the little specialty shops with colorful flowerpots outside their doors. Tourists milled about on the sidewalks, couples walked hand in hand, a family headed into the park with a picnic basket.

This is why she stayed. Even if Livie hadn't decided to settle down and enlist Melanie and Jade's help in renovating the airport, Melanie would've still planted roots. Haven was absolutely perfect. It was impossible to live here and not be happy, and she deserved happy, damn it.

Besides, where else did she have to go? Going back to Neville was a big *hell no*. They'd been divorced for two years, but now that he was gearing up to run for the senate, he was determined to get her back, to use her as his big publicity angle.

In his warped world, he'd have the paparazzi in his pocket to spin this as the happy couple coming back together as a united front—and he'd no doubt get her stylist back. Melanie's hair would have that perfectly coiffed look, her suits would be tailor-made in red, white, or blue, and she'd have to fake the smiles everywhere because you never knew where the media were hiding.

Melanie had changed every aspect of her life. While

she had her law degree, she'd quickly discovered that wasn't her passion. Over the past two years, she had become an extremely popular social media motivation speaker and blogger. Neville thought she was perfect to play the role of wife once again. He figured their united front and faux romantic reunion was something from a fairy tale.

That deranged man clearly had a different view of their marriage than she did if he thought for one second she'd ever go back to him. And being a politician's wife sounded like another level of hell she didn't want to get into. Being married to the mayor had been enough. A senator? No, thanks.

Even if Neville left her alone, being part of the big-city life, the fake smiles and the air kisses, all of that had been so depressing. She didn't want to be back in Atlanta. She'd choose her ratty childhood trailer park over the hoity-toity lifestyle she'd lived for years.

Haven had been exactly what she'd needed at precisely the right time. The name of the quaint town itself seemed to welcome her with open arms. Granted she hadn't liked the circumstances that brought them all to town.

Livie had lost her father and had come to try to sell his dilapidated airport. But she had ended up falling in love and getting engaged to Jax Morgan, who owned the other half of the airport.

Jade had come along because her personal and professional life sucked and she'd desperately needed the getaway. The three of them had formed a strong bond a few years ago and hadn't looked back. They were closer than sisters could ever be.

When Melanie first filed for divorce, she'd started training for a marathon. She'd wanted to prove to herself that she was strong, that she was able to do something so great with her body that had been beaten down for too long. But less than a mile from the finish line, she'd tripped and twisted her ankle. Livie and Jade had come along and flanked each side of her, carrying her to the end so she could finish.

Friendships and a bond deeper than sisters was instantly born.

So, yeah, there was nothing they wouldn't do for each other. When Livie was dealing with the loss of her father and the up-in-the-air decisions about the unwanted airport, they'd come right along with her.

Melanie thought she'd been strong by leaving Neville and pushing forward with her new life, but even since moving to Haven, she'd evolved so much more. Each day she became more and more determined to cling to the woman she'd become.

Thanks to her booming social media accounts and her popular blog, Melanie had reached so many women who were striving to become a better version of themselves. She'd taken time off from working as an attorney, focusing on herself and the airport renovations. At least with her law degree, she could guide Livie and Jax in the right direction and still do the work she loved with her online sites.

Now, though, she had a more pressing matter. Melanie came to a stop at a red light and settled a hand on her flat belly. She had so much rolling through her mind, so much she needed to sort through before she went to Tanner's house tonight.

How did one make this announcement? There was no good way to drop such a life-changing declaration. Tanner wasn't the type of man, in her opinion, that wanted a family. Not that she knew him really well, but she'd never heard mention of it. He seemed too content with where he was with his career and social life to entertain the idea of something familial.

To her knowledge, he hadn't dated since she'd been in town. Or at least he hadn't mentioned another woman.

Livie had discussed how Jax and Cash were divorced, but their cousin Tanner had vowed against marriage after seeing what those two had gone through. So Tanner obviously wasn't looking for long-term and was just fine living with his bachelor status.

What was Melanie even doing thinking about marriage? She certainly didn't want to venture into that territory again either, not until she was absolutely positive the man was worthy of her and her awesomeness. There was nothing wrong with loving yourself enough to wait on the best. That was something she'd had to work on since her divorce, but she was happy to admit she deserved love and devotion.

Yes, she was pregnant, but that didn't mean she had to marry Tanner. She'd prided herself on becoming independent since leaving Neville, and so far she'd excelled at it. There was no turning back for her.

Melanie headed out of town, toward the old home she shared with Jade now. Livie moved out, which was strange since they'd all been staying in her childhood home, but she now lived with Jax and his adorable little girl, Piper. They weren't only working on renovations for the airport, they were figuring out when to get married and living as one happy little family.

Melanie knew she needed to tell Tanner the truth tonight, then she could call a girls' meeting and break the news to her friends. The cheap wine should cushion the shocking blow. Now more than ever, she was going to need her friends to help guide her through this scary time. Not that they had any experience with pregnancies, but at the same time, they could at least hold her hand and give her that shoulder she would no doubt cry on at some point over the next several months.

Gripping the wheel tighter, Melanie formulated a plan in her head. At least if she was trying to prepare a speech she felt like she was doing something and moving forward instead of just settling in with her thoughts of fear and unknowns.

Worrying wasn't going to get her too far, but it was an inevitable by-product.

As she turned into the drive of the charming white two-story with wraparound porch, Melanie eyed the glowing clock on the dash. She had five hours to relax, stay calm, prepare a plan . . . and stare at the clock worrying about Tanner's reaction.

Chapter Two

*When life shuts a door . . . open it. It's a door.
That's how they work.*

—Mel's Motivational Blog

Tanner checked his phone as he headed to his truck. The text he'd been waiting on had yet to come through and each passing minute he grew more and more anxious.

Anxiety—a by-product of his occupation and the bane of his existence. He hated the quick heartbeats, the nerves that couldn't be suppressed. Unfortunately, since his days in the air force, he couldn't ignore the signs of his anxiety. He'd been too proud to talk to a counselor and definitely too stubborn to go to a doctor for medication. There was nothing wrong with people who did, but admitting weakness, especially in his line of work, simply wasn't how he wanted to go.

Work on the police force consumed his days. His secret project on the side consumed several nights each week. It was the night hours that caused him the most apprehension. A year of leading a double life was hard on his social time, but so damn rewarding he wasn't about to give it up.

Even his best friends and cousins, Jax and Cash, had no idea what he really did.

The last few hours of his day shift seemed to drag because all he could think of was this text regarding the undercover operation he'd been working on for the past few weeks. Aside from waiting on that message, a certain blonde with green eyes and a punch-to-the-gut smile also occupied a good chunk of real estate in his mind.

She was the first woman he'd approached in months. Not long ago his date card had been filled up and his evenings were all about himself. Not anymore.

Hadn't he vowed not to get too involved with a woman again? Getting his heart torn out once was enough. No matter how many years passed, the hole where his fiancée and child had lived still gaped and he couldn't let more hurt inside. So he'd gone on the defensive and only dated women who weren't his type, who wouldn't expect a ring or commitment.

When he dated, Tanner didn't go after a woman more than once. He never led a woman on, either. He always remained up-front and honest about his intentions.

His own personal hell aside, Tanner had seen enough from Cash, Jax, and even his own mother to know that marriage usually ended in disaster. Though his cousin Jax had found his perfect match with Livie Daniels. Those two did seem like they were made for each other and Tanner couldn't deny they would no doubt defy the odds and stay together.

Cash, hell, that poor man had been through it with his pill-addicted father and a wife who couldn't handle the ups and downs that came with addiction, so she left.

And his own mother had just remarried a few years ago to a guy who seemed to dote on her and worship the ground she walked on. Tanner's stepfather was one powerful man and always put his wife first with everything. Obviously those two were in love.

That wasn't the case for everybody, and he simply didn't want to take that chance. The nightmare he'd endured in his early twenties had scarred him for life. There was no way in hell he'd ever let his heart get that involved with a woman again, or ever attempt to start a family. His fiancée's unplanned pregnancy had thrown him for a loop, and just when he'd gotten used to the idea, embraced the fact he was going to be a father, his entire world had been ripped from him.

That whole incident at too young an age made him who he was today. He threw himself into his work, he devoted every waking hour to saving others. That way, there would be no time for heartache or personal attachment. Dating randomly was fine. Casual sex was fine, too. He was human, after all.

Tanner was well aware what people said about him being a player. The same words were thrown around when Jax was single, and Cash also had those rumors spreading around him.

Tanner wasn't going to waste his time defending himself to people whose opinions didn't matter. He had a heart to protect and his reasons didn't need to be shared. Everyone coped with life differently, and random hookups were how he dealt with his.

What mattered most to him were defending the weak, seeking justice, and living each day to the fullest. With his hectic schedule, he certainly did just that.

On the occasion he had free time lately, he went out, had a good time, and that was the end of it. His personal life really shouldn't be the concern of gossipmongers, but small towns and all that. He'd grown up here, he was well aware how people enjoyed chattering. If they were talking about him, at least they were leaving others alone.

So what if he'd dated quite a bit in his past? What was a single man supposed to do? Stay home? Those in town knew what he'd been through years ago, but they'd rather discuss the man he was now as opposed to the great loss he'd endured.

Tanner purposely didn't lead women on, but after that heated night with Melanie, damn if he didn't want more. Not a relationship, but definitely to see her again and not just with their group of friends.

There had been something so vulnerable, yet so feisty about her. She'd had a sadness in her eyes when she'd first come to town, yet she always tipped that defiant chin and never backed down from a verbal sparring match. That in and of itself had spoken volumes about her resiliency and strength. Damn if he wasn't instantly drawn to her because of her attitude.

When Tanner had discovered she had a successful blog site, he'd checked it out, then fell down the rabbit hole and started looking through her popular social media accounts. He'd been stunned to find out just how many people she inspired through her stories and motivation. The praise from her followers and the stories they shared proved how giving and loving Melanie truly was.

And his admiration had gone up another notch.

While he knew full well who her ex was, she'd never once mentioned that on her blog or any of her accounts. It was almost as if she'd started completely over.

Tanner actually didn't know her that well. Little bits of information came out here and there, but other than that one heated night, he'd never been alone with her to actually talk. She was closed off for the most part, didn't volunteer information unless she was asked. The quiet, reserved, yet dynamic woman had sparked his interest from day one and damn if that didn't confuse him even more because he'd never been this intrigued by a woman.

A while back, Jax had told Tanner that Melanie's ex was Neville Prescott, mayor of Atlanta. His cousin had also hinted about a less-than-perfect marriage she'd come from. But Tanner hadn't heard anything about her past from Melanie herself. He never asked and she never offered up the information. All of her social media and blogs discussed healthy lifestyles, eating habits, exercise, how to make every day count, and living life to its fullest. Clearly she wanted things regarding her marriage and divorce to be kept private, which was fine with him. He had his own demons he kept locked away. Didn't everyone?

Over the last few weeks, Tanner had been so swamped with the side project that he'd had little time to get in touch with Melanie. But he'd at least texted her, to which she had given some lame, brief reply.

Tanner slid behind the wheel of his truck and fired up the engine. His mind flashed to the narrow, darkened hallway at Taps where he'd followed Melanie. She'd flashed that heavy-lidded gaze over her shoulder and given him a wink. He'd followed like a moth to the proverbial flame, making sure no one had been looking. Those swaying hips had hypnotized him, her out-of-character flirting had pulled him in and left him hypnotized. Hell, he was still in a trance from that night well over a month ago.

Something had triggered this new attitude, and he wasn't going to question the new Melanie. He'd wanted her since he'd first laid eyes on her.

Tanner had taken her to the dance floor for a little fun, only to realize that the way her body moved against his was some sort of sin. It had to be. He'd needed her clothes off and a hell of a lot more privacy. Apparently she'd felt the same because they'd ended up in the dimly lit hallway.

One kiss rolled into the next, then hands had roamed beneath shirts, beneath her knee-length skirt.

Pushing aside the erotic thoughts of that night over a month ago, Tanner pulled out of the parking spot at the precinct. He'd been stunned when he'd run into her earlier at the convenience store, but there was no way he was going to let her slip by without a face-to-face.

He *should* stay clear of Melanie Ramsey. He knew full well that pursuing her wasn't the smartest. Her best friend and his cousin were getting married sometime soon, when they could fit it into their hectic lives. So, needless to say, their inner circle was rather small and tight.

Yet he'd basically demanded she come to his house tonight. What the hell had he been thinking? She'd tried brushing him off with the cookout, saying she'd see him there. She'd pushed aside the topic of her fancy car when he'd brought it up. Something was off with her, and he didn't know if it was their one fierce night together or something more that had her spooked. All he knew was he wanted to see her.

Damn it. He hadn't thought of another woman on a personal level since he'd met Melanie. Was it her mysterious past he was drawn to? That vulnerability she tried to hide only pulled him closer in an attempt to figure her out.

Call it an occupational hazard, but he lived to resolve anything that stumped him, and Melanie was one hell of a mystery.

Yes, he knew she wasn't into relationships—something they definitely had in common. From the minor nuggets of information Tanner had heard from his friends, Melanie had been through hell being married to Neville Prescott. The thought of someone as sweet, as passionate as Melanie married to that smarmy-looking politician made Tanner furious. Obviously she wanted a brand-new life because she no longer had the name Prescott.

The mayor seemed to be on the news quite a bit lately, flashing that toothy grin and waving. No doubt he was working up his campaign for next year. But Tanner had no use for someone who lived through pretenses or mistreated others.

And a woman being abused in any way had a rage boiling inside of him he couldn't describe. He'd lived through that with his mother, and now with the secret protection detail he'd been working on the past year. There was a special pocket in hell for anyone who mistreated a woman or child.

Tanner didn't know specifics of Melanie's past. That was her place to share and it wasn't like they were that close. He had no right to pry into her darkness when he refused to let light shine into his.

Perhaps that was just another element that drew him to her. He needed to keep an eye on her, he needed to know she was safe now. Hell, he just needed her, and he never needed anyone. Tanner wanted more time because the quickie against his front door only left him frustrated and aching for more.

One more time. Then maybe she'd be out of his system and they could go back to the friend zone with the rest of their little circle.

Since his house wasn't far from the station, Tanner's commute took less than ten minutes. He'd purchased a two-story bungalow when he'd gotten his job on the force, fresh from the academy. The selling points had been that the sellers were leaving the furnishings and they had a kick-ass fire pit in the backyard.

Since he was rarely home these days, other than to

crawl into bed and catch a few hours' sleep, the place wasn't dirty. And there were often nights he had to sleep in an unmarked car. So yeah, his house pretty much just looked staged because rarely was anything out of place.

For reasons he didn't want to venture into, Tanner wanted to make a good impression on Melanie. Which was absurd in the grand scheme of things. He wasn't inviting her over so she could grade him on his cleanliness or décor.

Just because she'd been married to a man with a heavily padded bank account, was used to having nice things, had recently driven a car that was more than his annual salary, that didn't mean Tanner had to live up to those standards.

He couldn't help but wonder what made her sell her Beemer, though. She seemed like a high-end type girl who liked to surround herself with the nicer things in life. Her clothes were always tasteful and had that pricey look. Her purses usually had those gold emblems that had some name that immediately made them expensive. He wouldn't know about such brands, but he could spot nice things when he saw them.

Tanner refused to be something he wasn't. He was a cop, living on a cop's salary and working undercover for next to nothing. He was just fine with his bank account because at the end of the day, he was only in both of those positions to help the helpless. Money was just paper.

Besides, he only wanted Melanie on a physical level. Well, that wasn't true. He wanted her, yes, but he wasn't going to use her. He admired her. Surely they could remain friends, right?

Sex complicated so many things, but he didn't want that with Melanie. How the hell could he get her out of his system and still remain friends? Maybe he couldn't, and that would be his problem. He couldn't do a relationship, couldn't even entertain the idea. He'd gone that route once. Then his life exploded and he'd never fully been pieced back together. He was a shell of the man he used to be, and had nothing to offer.

Tanner's cell vibrated in his pocket as he pulled into his drive. Adrenaline pumped through him as he hoped this was the message he'd been waiting on, to tell him about the next intervention appointment.

Haven's retired police captain had formed an elite group of current and former law enforcement and military personnel to help him carry out delicate jobs—namely getting abused women and children to safety.

They pulled strings, sometimes skirting the edge of the law in order to save those who couldn't help themselves.

Tanner was careful never to do anything that would affect his badge. If anything was questionable, his superior always pulled Tanner off that particular case and kept him in the dark.

Tanner pulled into his garage and put the truck in park before sliding his cell from his pocket. A quick glance gave him the information he'd been waiting on. The woman they were currently trying to save finally reached out to them, asking for help. She had a two-year-old and a five-month-old and was in desperate need of safety.

There was always a bit of relief when someone reached out. Each woman or child saved was just one more that had a chance at a better life.

Extracting children was always tricky, but with the mother's reassurance, they always managed to pull off the move without incident. Tanner had seen some of the ugliest, vilest things while working this job. Another reason he couldn't give it up. There were always people who needed saving, and if he stopped, he'd always wonder if he could've saved just one more.

Tanner recalled a time in his life when someone had stepped in to help his mother, to help him. He had no idea where he'd be today had his mother not gotten the assistance she'd needed.

After a quick reply, Tanner headed into his house through the access into the utility room. He wanted to get changed before Melanie showed up—and he had every reason to believe she would. It was a rarity to have an evening free, so he planned on making the most of it.

She may have offered up a forced smile earlier, but he'd caught that swift intake of breath, noted the pulse at the base of her throat that had kicked up. He'd had to turn and walk away before he did something even more out of character, like grip the back of her head and put his lips on hers. That would certainly get the town talking even more, but he wouldn't do that to Melanie and he wouldn't put his reputation on the line right in the middle of the damn Quicky Mart.

Why was it this woman intrigued him and had him losing his mind with want? Was it that she'd clearly been through hell with her ex, yet she seemed so strong, so resilient? She wasn't afraid to speak her mind and never backed down from his witty banter. She threw it right back at him, and damn if that wasn't sexier than her curvy shape and expressive eyes.

In the seven months she'd been in town, he'd already determined there were several layers to Melanie Ramsey, and he had the pressing need to unwrap each and every one of them.

When the hell had he turned into a masochist? Someone like Mel would want flowers and nice restaurants and commitment. She'd been hurt in the past and she wasn't a short-term-fling type of girl. He knew without a doubt that their night together was out of character for her, but he hadn't been about to turn her away. If she'd wanted to use him to get over whatever hell she battled, then use away.

Tanner changed from his uniform to a pair of running shorts and a gray T-shirt. If Melanie didn't show, he'd get in some boxing in his basement. He needed to let some of his frustrations out and pounding his heavy bag was always his go-to. Well, there were other, more primal ways, but boxing always did the trick, too.

After putting his gun away in the safe in his bedroom, Tanner headed downstairs. Maybe he'd go ahead and get a fire going in the pit. The evening had turned cooler, which made this the perfect night to sit out with a beer and relax.

Fall in Haven was his favorite time of year. Nice warm days, but evenings hanging by a fire with friends and a beer to just relax from the day. He desperately needed this downtime. He could always get in the boxing later.

Just as Tanner grabbed the matches from the drawer in his kitchen, his doorbell rang. He couldn't help the smile that spread across his face, or the arousal that pumped through him.

Looked like Melanie couldn't turn down his offer after all.

Tanner set the matches on the kitchen island and headed down the narrow hall toward the foyer. With a flick of the lock, he pulled the door wide and nearly snarled at the uninvited guest.

"What do you want?"

Cash stood on the other side of the door, hands shoved in the pockets of his jeans. His black T-shirt with gym logo stretched across his broad chest and outlined those ridiculous muscles he had. The tats only made him seem even more menacing, but Cash was one of the nicest guys Tanner knew. He just didn't want him here right now.

"Good evening to you, too, sunshine." Cash pushed past Tanner and stepped into the entryway. "I would've let myself in but it was locked."

"Because you weren't invited." Tanner closed the door and turned to face his cousin. "Again, what do you want?"

Cash raised one dark brow. "I take it you're expecting a woman and I'm in the way?"

"Something like that."

"Then I'll make it quick." Cash shoved his hands in his pockets. "I've got an issue at the gym and I'm going to need your help."

Intrigued, Tanner nodded. Family always came first. Always. "What's up?"

"A client overheard some chatter between two guys. The gist of what she heard was that these guys have been using my gym as a meeting place to deal drugs. I have no clue the type or if this is even true, but I need to know what actions I should be taking or if you just need to get involved."

Next to abusers, drugs got Tanner fired up and ready to spring into action. Unfortunately, they were everywhere now. Small towns weren't exempt from drugs or their dealers. If anything, they were the new stomping ground because too many people believed they were safe in rural America.

"You can't accuse anyone of anything without concrete proof," Tanner stated, already thinking how they could get to the actual truth. "Do you have the names of these guys? If they've been in trouble before, I'd recognize them and maybe we can go from there."

His doorbell rang before Cash could answer.

"Ah, the lady of the evening?" Cash asked as he reached around Tanner to grip the doorknob. "Who will be on the other side?"

Tanner stepped aside, knowing full well who'd be standing on his porch. He didn't want anyone to know he'd asked Melanie over. Nobody knew of their night together and out of respect for her, he intended to keep their secret locked away. That didn't mean he wasn't ready to revisit it in private with her, though.

Cash jerked the door open and a second later he let out a low chuckle before throwing a glance over his shoulder at Tanner.

"Well, well, well," Cash drawled out with a wide smile as he turned his attention back to Melanie. "Isn't this interesting?"

"I can come back."

Melanie started to turn, but Cash reached out and gripped her arm. "Come on in, darlin'. I was just heading out and I do believe my cousin was expecting you."

Tanner stepped back to make room for Melanie. She met his gaze and raised her brows. "I don't want to interrupt."

"You're not interrupting." Tanner would call Cash later and get the lowdown on the issues at the gym. "Cash is leaving."

Cash kept his eyes on Tanner and that damn mocking grin on his face. "Yes, I was just leaving."

Melanie frowned as she glanced to Cash. "I hope not because I'm here."

"Tanner said he was waiting on someone," Cash stated. Tanner flipped him the one-finger salute behind Melanie's back. "I can text him."

Cash leaned in and gave Melanie a kiss on her cheek. "See you both later."

Once he was gone, Tanner clicked the deadbolt back into place and turned his attention to Melanie . . . who wasn't smiling, wasn't even looking his way. She twisted the strap on the purse she had on her shoulder. Her other hand clutched the closure of her oversized cardigan. The Georgia weather had turned a bit chilly in the evenings, but that was to be expected in November.

But he didn't think the crisp fall air had anything to do with the way she held her sweater so tight against her chest.

Tanner made his career out of reading people and comprehending what they weren't saying. Something had Melanie terrified. Perhaps it was being back in his house, in the exact spot where they'd torn at each other's clothes.

But if she was that tense, why was she here? He hadn't seen her like this before. This Melanie was a far cry from the confident, brazen woman at the bar and the woman he'd come to know over the past several months. He'd never seen her anything but confident.

"You didn't have to come if you're that nervous."

The last thing he wanted was for her to be uncomfortable or feel pressured. He wanted her to see how this chemistry shouldn't be ignored, but he'd shut down everything if she thought for a second that he'd force her.

Melanie barely moved, other than her eyes, which finally met his. "Can we talk?"

Oh, hell. Those three words never preceded anything good. But what could she have to say that was so upsetting? She wasn't calling things off between them, it wasn't like they had a relationship.

Worst-case scenario, she'd decided not to sleep with him. And that would be tragic because they'd nearly set his front door ablaze when they'd finally given in to the inevitable. He'd discovered just how passionate sweet, quiet Melanie truly was.

If nothing else, maybe they'd just be friends. He was cool with that, too, because as sexy and sultry as Melanie was, she also intrigued him. Tanner found that he wanted to learn more about her and what brought her here . . . other than her friends.

Never before had he thought of just getting to know a woman for no apparent reason. Everything about Melanie fascinated him, though. She wasn't like any woman he'd ever met before.

On the flip side, if this didn't end in a friendship, their social gatherings would nosedive straight into awkward, and that was the last thing he wanted for his friends.

Deciding the entryway wasn't the best place to get into what was obviously going to be a serious conversation, Tanner gestured toward the living room. He wasn't used to playing host, but he wanted to do something to calm Melanie's obvious nerves. It was apparent she'd rather be anywhere else, so he was eager to uncover just what had her so *jittery*. Odd that that word slipped into his mind when it was the same one he'd used earlier, but it described her. She was definitely on edge about something.

"Come on in."

She gripped that purse tighter and licked her lips. "You need to know something first."

Tanner's heart kicked up. Something had seriously spooked her. Was it her ex? Had he threatened her? Tanner had no qualms about confronting bastard abusers.

Melanie's demeanor with Cash only moments ago had been completely different than now. So perhaps the issue was in fact with Tanner. His gut tightened. He sure as hell didn't want her afraid to be alone with him.

Aside from their narrow circle of friends, the town was too small to dodge each other completely. The last thing he wanted was to avoid the one woman who'd piqued his interest in months.

"What is it?" he asked.

Melanie met his eyes. Without blinking, she said, "I'm not here for sex."

Well, she was blunt if nothing else. Must be that attorney in her that didn't want to mess with the small talk or dance around the topic. He might not like what she had to say, but he appreciated her honesty, and she'd come here for a reason. He was more interested in what she *did* want.

"You look like you're ready to shatter." He took a step forward until he stood directly in front of her, but he used every ounce of control not to reach for her. "Is someone bothering you, Mel?"

"What? Oh, no. Nothing like that." She pulled in a shaky breath, then shook her head and glanced away. "This is harder than I thought."

Unable to ignore her obvious turmoil a moment longer, Tanner reached out and pushed a strand of honey-blond hair away from her cheek. He feathered his fingers along her creamy skin. Call it masochism, but he couldn't resist. Maybe if she realized he actually did care, she'd relax.

Bright eyes flared, desire stared back at him for the briefest of moments before she blinked it away and took a step back.

Apparently she'd wanted to remove herself from his touch. Tanner understood. He didn't like it, but he wasn't about to say anything to make her even more skittish. He respected women, and Melanie deserved for him to be completely attentive to what she came here for. Which meant he'd have to rein in those heated hormones.

"You know, I don't expect anything," he assured her. "Sure, I invited you over in hopes we'd pick up where we left off six weeks ago. I've been busy with work or I'd have asked you over sooner. But if you're not into—"

"I'm pregnant."

Chapter Three

Great things never come from comfort zones.
                                        —Mel's Motivational Blog

Okay, maybe she should've given some sort of lead-in announcement before the big one, but Tanner had been rambling and she needed him to just shut up for a second or she would've lost her nerve.

He was certainly quiet now. In fact, he looked like he was about to pass out. She'd never seen the color leave someone's face so fast. Considering Tanner was one of the most confident men she knew, that was saying something.

With a shaky hand, he reached up and gripped the newel post. His skin slowly regained some color, but his jaw clenched so tight, she worried he'd crack teeth.

Melanie didn't know what reaction she'd expected, to be honest. Right now she couldn't tell if he was shocked or angry or a healthy dose of both. The silence seemed to grow heavier, or perhaps that was just the tension that had enveloped them.

In the short time she'd known him, she'd never seen him so still, so silent. What was he thinking? Was he just as freaked out as her? Was he trying to process the full meaning of what she'd said? Had he even heard her? Because the lack of actions and words from him had her wondering if she needed to repeat herself.

Tanner's dark eyes held her in place, pinning her by the front door. Ironic, considering this is the only room of the house she'd been in. Melanie couldn't even turn and look at that large oak door without heating up again. Quite a different circumstance being here this time than just over a month ago.

"The baby is yours," she added, just in case he was about to ask that question. "I just found out this morning and I didn't think telling you when I saw you earlier was the time or the place."

Tanner blinked. "A . . . baby."

"I understand if you don't want any part of—"

"I used protection."

Melanie swallowed and folded her arms over her chest. Confrontation always terrified her. Well, not when she'd been battling cases for others. She thrived on being the voice for people who couldn't speak for themselves. But when the confrontation spun in her direction, she started to revert back to that abused housewife who'd lost her voice and her courage.

She'd worked diligently since her divorce to get over those insecurities, but she worried she might never. That woman lived deep inside her, no matter how hard she tried to eradicate her. There was always that sliver that bobbed to the surface when she least expected.

Melanie's heart kicked up, her stomach tingled, her palms dampened.

If Tanner got angry, she'd leave. If he accused her of lying or sleeping with someone else, she'd leave. She was only here to tell him the situation, and what he decided to do with that information was totally on him. But she would not take the brunt of harsh words or accusations. She was much better than that and he would have to deal with his own issues without pulling her into his fears. She had her own.

"We did use protection," she agreed with a slow nod. "Obviously it didn't work."

Tanner's eyes narrowed as he raked a hand through his hair. He muttered something under his breath before he dropped his hand and sighed. "You're sure it's mine."

Melanie gritted her teeth and counted backwards from ten . . . twice. Hadn't she already told him this baby was his? Her ex had accused her of cheating on him before. He'd made a fool out of her in front of her friends—the ones he'd approved of, of course—during a small lunch at her house. He'd humiliated her, claiming she'd been seeing one of his assistants behind his back. There was no way in hell she'd let another man accuse her of something she didn't do.

"Considering you're the only man I've slept with in the last two years, I'm pretty sure."

Tanner propped his hands on his hips. "Considering I barely know you, I had to ask."

Okay, that was a fair statement on his part. Still, she didn't want this situation to turn ugly or blow up into an argument. She'd had enough altercations to last a lifetime.

She totally got that he was shocked. Since she'd only taken the test twelve hours ago, the full reality of the pregnancy hadn't taken ahold of her, either. Other than a missed period, she had no symptoms.

Melanie stared at Tanner another minute before turning and heading into his living area. She hadn't ventured this far into his home before, and now she couldn't even appreciate the charming old house. Maybe later, once her head wasn't spinning and her stomach about to revolt.

Pregnancy or nerves, she wasn't sure, but she felt like hell right now. Maybe morning sickness was settling in? No, that didn't make sense. It was late in the day. Did morning sickness make other appearances?

There was so much she didn't know. She'd been an only child, never had a friend who'd been pregnant, hadn't been around expectant women. How in the world was she supposed to cope or even figure out what was going on when she was completely and utterly clueless?

Her world had tipped completely on its side and she was struggling to right it. But she would. At this point in her life, she knew she could bounce back from anything.

Melanie sank to the edge of the leather sofa and dropped her purse to the floor by her feet. Now that she'd told him, she could breathe a little easier . . . though the color still hadn't fully returned to his face.

The tension coiling in her lessened, now that the secret was out, but only a bit. There were still so many unknowns, like how he'd react once the shock wore off, how he'd treat her, if he even wanted to be part of the life of their child.

With everything still so new, Melanie didn't want to take what he said at face value. Once reality fully settled in, Tanner could always change his mind, and saying something and doing something were usually not one and the same. She'd found that out firsthand during her marriage.

Tanner came in and stood near the wide picture window overlooking the front yard and tree-lined street. Silence remained heavy between them, making the tension thicker by the second and doing nothing to calm her erratic nerves.

Melanie pushed her cuticles back and stared at each finger, moving from one to the next. She had to be doing something, anything other than wonder what was going through his mind. She wanted to offer some brilliant words that would ease his worry, that would ease her own anxiety. There were none.

The fact was, they'd created a human and right now she had no clue if he even wanted to be part of the baby's life when he was barely a part of hers.

Neville had only wanted children so he could use them as a publicity ploy. Everything circled back to how he could make himself look better. Having the so-called family life with the smiling wife and properly mannered kids would only boost ratings for a man running for any government office.

Much to his disappointment and rage, she'd never carried his child. He'd never remarried, instead focusing solely on moving toward his goal of the senate seat . . . all alone.

Her life with Neville had scarred her, shaped her in a way that affected each decision she'd made since living twenty-four months and eight days of pure terror. But the marriage had been over for a few years. Still, her experience was never far from her mind.

"We don't know each other well," she started, now picking at her pale pink nail polish. Jade would be irritated Melanie was ruining the manicure she'd just given her. "I acted so out of character when we were at the bar. I just . . . I let Livie and Jade talk me into going. I'd had a terrible day. Then Livie ended up leaving with Jax and Jade was dancing with some guy I'd never met. I wanted to ignore consequences and merely go with what I wanted."

She didn't need to mention her hours prior to the outing had been filled with fielding calls from her ex's assistant. His damn assistant. Apparently Neville wanted to meet with her, but Melanie wasn't about to give in to his crazy. Never again.

He'd left a veiled threat via his assistant, but Melanie had heard nonsense like that since she left him. He knew full well who held the cards now that she didn't let him control her. With her pack of photos and proof of the abuse, he'd do best to remember who had the bigger balls here.

Neville wasn't her problem right now . . . or ever again as far as she was concerned. No, Melanie needed to figure out Tanner's role in her baby's life. Did he even want a role?

"I just wanted to get out and have a good time," she went on, still keeping her eyes on her hands. She couldn't quite look him in the eyes for fear of what she'd see staring back. "Then you flirted with me, asked me to dance, and I thought, why the hell not. I didn't expect . . . well, everything that happened after."

Their chemistry had taken over, consuming them. They'd barely spoken a word, their touches and long stares spoke louder than any words could.

Melanie hadn't bothered fighting the attraction, the pull toward Tanner. She'd wanted to prove that she was in control of her world, of what happened. That was the whole reason she'd left her old life, to stand on her own two feet and call all the shots.

But a fling? One hundred percent not her style. Yet Tanner had sparked something in her from day one . . . something she'd yet to label. So what if she was human? She'd wanted him, and after two years of no sex, plus years of bad sex before, she decided it was well past time to take charge.

Still, why did she have to be pulled toward powerful men? They both worked in a world where they held so much control, both were confident, assertive, and bold. She couldn't help but compare the two, considering she hadn't dated, let alone had sex with anyone since her divorce.

But Tanner wasn't like Neville. Tanner had an ego, he had confidence, but he didn't use either of those to force his hand and take what he didn't deserve. He used his power to help others.

From the time she got into town, Melanie had heard enough about the bachelor officer to know he was well-respected and admired. Neville only had the respect of his brainwashed voters, and those people didn't know the real man behind the expensive suits and flashy smile.

Tanner still hadn't spoken and the silence became too much. They had to talk about this, or all of the uncertainty would surely drive her insane.

What happened to the guy she'd known for the past several months? What happened to the self-assured, take-charge man from the bar? The fact that he still hadn't said a word was concerning. She had no idea if he truly believed her or not, but she wished he'd say something . . . anything.

Clearly they were both not the same characters they'd been that night. Life-changing consequences would do that to a person.

"This situation isn't ideal for me, either," she added, risking a glance his way.

His dark eyes masked any emotion he might be feeling. "You seem calm."

Tanner's intense stare had her nerves swirling even more. Something dark lurked in his eyes, something she couldn't put her finger on.

"I'm not calm on the inside. I'm barely holding it together. When life constantly throws roadblocks in your path, you have to cope. Plus, I have to remind myself this isn't the worst thing that's happened to me. Getting hysterical now won't change anything and won't help me figure out what to do next."

Tanner leaned his shoulder against the wall next to the window frame and hooked a thumb through his belt loop. He stared another second before blowing out a long breath. He raked a hand down his face, the stubble along his jaw scraping against his palm.

"Damn it, I should've asked how you were feeling. Are you alright? Physically? You're healthy to carry a child to term? Have you seen the doctor?"

Healthy to carry a child to term? That was an odd question for a guy to ask, even if he was the father. But the fact that he even asked about her specifically was a true testament to the decent man he was. He might be shaken and worried, but he cared. A part of her heart melted right there, but just because a man showed concern didn't mean something was going to grow from this situation. She simply wasn't used to such acts from a guy, especially one she'd only met months ago.

Still, having a good man for a friend or an acquaintance was a far cry from having one as the father of your child.

"I haven't seen the doctor yet," she supplied. "I called my doctor back in Atlanta to try to get a referral here in town. I mean, I plan on staying here, so it just makes sense, but I didn't know who to go to."

There was just so much to consider, and she was still trying to get her feet under her in this new town. She was still living in Livie's childhood home for now. At some point she'd have to decide what to do as far as getting a place for herself and really focusing on her future, especially now that she was bringing a child into her life.

Neville had always said something was wrong with her that she hadn't gotten pregnant in their two years of marriage. What he didn't know is that she'd never stopped taking her birth control pills. There was no way she'd want to bring a baby into that loveless, abusive marriage. His political aspirations weren't her concern, and she sure as hell wasn't about to let an innocent child be used as a pawn in his game.

If he had found out what she'd done, Melanie would have surely paid the price. Taking the risk and lying was her only hope of saving an unknowing baby from growing up with that monster as a father. It had taken Melanie a long time to conjure up the courage to leave her husband. But the idea of staying and enduring more abuse, mental and physical, was worth all the risk.

She'd started running a few days a week as a way to clear her head and think. He hadn't liked that. Hadn't wanted her to better herself or lose weight and attract the attention of others. He'd gushed in public over the fact his wife had a law degree, and what a power couple they could be together. But, behind closed doors, he hadn't liked that one bit. She was too smart, too threatening to him, because what if she came across as more powerful? Neville's insecurities where she'd been concerned were absolutely preposterous.

One day something clicked for Melanie after reading an article online about loving yourself before you could love anyone else. Right then and there, she had decided if she didn't put herself first, nobody else would. Sure as hell not her husband.

And when she realized she did want to love herself first for a change, that's when she started gathering information and formulating a plan to get the hell out of that marriage. A risky move, but one she had to take if she ever wanted a new, happy life.

"I don't know what your expectations are of me." Tanner crossed the room and came to stand in front of her.

His eyes never wavered, but that muscle in his jaw ticked as if he was trying to keep his emotions in check. "But I will be part of the baby's life."

A bit of stress slipped from her. "I was hoping you'd say that."

Even though they didn't know each other really well, Melanie knew Tanner was a good guy. There was no disputing his reputation as an officer. She couldn't help but worry, though, because there was still so much about him that was kept in the dark.

She'd thought she'd known Neville pretty well when they'd married, but once they were bound together, he instantly transformed. It was almost like some switch had been flipped and he'd gotten exactly what he wanted.

Being married to such a powerful man left her questioning everything. She'd thought Neville was her way out of the poor, depressing life she'd led. She'd been young and impressionable and honestly thought he cared for her. She couldn't have been more wrong.

Melanie was a different woman than she had been. Life lessons had forced her to grow up, to face the harsh realities. The ugliness of her marriage, the behind-the-scenes in politics—she'd learned too much in such a short marriage.

Tanner was powerful in his own way. Now her one night of throwing caution to the wind and taking what she wanted had bound her to him for life. Thankfully, she wasn't leading with her heart like she had before. She was going into this with her eyes wide open. There would be no hearts and flowers and Tanner on bended knee extending a ring. The reality was, they'd created a life and now they had to come together to best decide how to proceed.

Melanie might want him to be part of their baby's life, but she wasn't about to relinquish control and jump into another relationship. Attraction was one thing, pregnancy was one thing . . . a relationship? That was an area she wanted to avoid until the right man came into her life. She knew he was out there.

Neville hadn't murdered that dream. One day, she vowed. One day she'd have a husband who loved her, and a family.

"I don't expect you to think this is some sort of relationship or that I need to be looked after." She had to make that clear. She didn't want to be cared for or handled like she was going to fall apart. "I won't exclude you from anything regarding the baby."

Tanner dropped down to sit on the edge of the coffee table. Those dark eyes pierced her, and she instantly recalled exactly the moment he'd pressed her against the door, gripping both her wrists in one hand. That entire night had been thrilling, no fear whatsoever.

And that's how she knew she had turned over a new chapter in her life. The fear of her past would remain exactly where it belonged.

Ironically, she had a new fear now. The fear of the unknown.

Melanie turned her face away and pulled in a deep breath. Just a year ago she never would've let a man handle her in such a rough yet arousing manner. But, thanks to her friends, her successful blog, and her popular social media accounts, Melanie had become more resilient than she'd ever thought possible. She was damn proud of how far she'd come.

"So you're giving me the option to see other women?"

His harsh, bold question brought her gaze back up. "I don't want you to think you're tied to me or—"

"Or what?" he spat. "Despite what you may have heard, I don't have a revolving bedroom door and I sure as hell would never turn away from my responsibilities. This baby and you are top priority from this moment on. Period. So don't put me in a category with some bastard from your past."

Okay, so she'd stepped on a nerve. Or maybe he had his own past that still haunted him. They were going to have to find some common ground and get a little personal if they planned on raising their baby without tension.

Melanie couldn't help the chatter she'd overheard about Tanner, nor could she help but compare him to Neville. She'd not been with anyone else in her life. It was impossible not to line up the two experiences in her head.

A guy like Tanner was precisely the type she'd chosen on purpose to help her get back out into the world and feel like she was in control again. New town, new life . . . and all of that.

At the time Tanner had been her safest, yet most dangerous option. Her friends all knew him, knew how great a guy he was. Yet he was only looking for a good time.

Looking back, maybe she shouldn't have been so brazen. Maybe she shouldn't have chosen someone her friends knew so well, because now there was no way they could keep that night just between them.

Melanie hadn't been able to tell her best gal pals what really happened that night they'd gone to Taps, because the last thing she needed or wanted was awkwardness to settle into their little group. She and Tanner had agreed nobody needed to know.

Clearly that was off the table now. In a few short months, her disappearing waistline would give away all her secrets.

"I plan on being with you through this entire pregnancy."

Melanie jerked back. "Excuse me?"

Those dark eyes narrowed. She realized now he didn't mean to be so ridiculously sexy with that stare, it was just naturally Tanner. Yet it was that intense gaze that had followed her down the dark, narrow hallway of the bar. It was that same heavy-lidded glare that had caused those butterflies in her belly each time he'd flashed it in the days, the weeks leading up to their intimate night.

"I wanted to see you again before I found out about the baby," he stated simply. "But now that I know you're pregnant with my child, I plan on being part of your life."

Fear grabbed hold from the inside, threatening to strangle her and rob her of the very foundation she'd worked for two years to secure. She wasn't about to have another man trying to control her. Yes, this baby was Tanner's, too, but she refused to relinquish the strong hold she'd finally gotten on her life.

Melanie rushed to her feet and stepped aside to get out of that narrow space between the sofa and the coffee table.

"No. No." She shook her head and walked to the window where Tanner had just been. "I'm not dating, I'm not . . . *anything* with you. We did one night, that's all."

The idea of getting involved with a man, of entering into a relationship or anything else that would threaten her much-needed independence terrified her even more than the idea of being a mother. Jumping into something serious with the first man since Neville would only be a rebound. No way could she trust her heart with a man she was simply physically attracted to. There had to be more to build on . . . and not just a pregnancy.

Being married with a family had always been a goal of hers. She'd not dated much before Neville. She'd always been too insecure about her weight, about getting close to a guy. She'd not lived in the best area of town or had the best education, so she was backward and shy. But Melanie's father had worked for Neville's father at their estate, doing yard work. Neville had caught sight of her one day when she stopped by with lunch for her dad. Neville had persisted until she'd finally given in to a date. He'd been charming, caring, almost too good to be true. She should've recognized that red flag.

Needless to say, Melanie's family wasn't too keen that she'd divorced a man who was so powerful and heading for bigger things. They'd wanted better for their little girl. They'd wanted her to make something of herself and move on from the depressing area they lived in.

Melanie never cared about the money or power. She cared about her sanity, her health, and getting out before something truly tragic happened.

"I'm not negotiating on this," he demanded.

Melanie gritted her teeth as she tossed a glance over her shoulder. "And I won't be controlled."

If anything, those eyes of his got darker. "I never said anything about controlling you, Mel. And stop acting like I'm your ex. That's not fair to either one of us."

She shook her head. "I can't get into this with you. I need some time to process it all."

"And you think pushing me away will help?" he asked.

Melanie turned her attention back to the window when he stood. She didn't want to keep staring at his broad shoulders, his lean hips, or those long legs as they ate up the distance between them. No matter how attractive he was, now was not the time to play the dating game. She couldn't focus on this pregnancy and worry about a relationship.

Staring out the front window toward the picturesque street, Melanie swallowed. "I don't know," she murmured.

Everything over these past few months had been so out of character for her. Perhaps she was sleep deprived from helping Livie work on the legalities of the airport and discussing the redesign and all the possibilities. Her blog and social media had skyrocketed even more since coming to Haven because Melanie had changed so much and poured every bit of her emotions out, to inspire others.

Who was she kidding? None of that was really out of character. She shouldn't have given in to her desire and slept with Tanner. Period. That's what had been so far gone from her usual comfort zone. She'd stepped out of that zone and obliterated the line.

But that voice in the back of her mind, the one that still lived there even though she'd divorced Neville, that told her nobody would ever want her . . . maybe she'd just wanted to be selfish for a bit. Now that someone like Tanner showed interest, and she was interested back, she could be in control.

She'd wanted to prove to herself that she was desirable, that she could attract a man who wanted her as much as she wanted him. Melanie had just wanted to shut up that voice of doubt even if only for one night.

"I have no idea what to do from here." Melanie smiled when a little girl ran down the sidewalk with a wand of bubbles trailing behind her. "Whatever you and I decide, this baby has to come first."

"I agree."

At least that was something. She couldn't even fathom dating him right now. Or dating anyone, for that matter. Even if she weren't pregnant, Melanie didn't think jumping back into the dating pool was the smartest idea at this point in her life.

Then again, Tanner hadn't mentioned dating. He'd said he'd be in her life . . . so what did that mean? Because all she'd heard was him saying he'd insert himself into her world and take over. Was that just the past betraying her now? Was that her mind lying to her?

She had no clue, but she did know all of this had to go

day by day. They were both shaken up, clearly dealing with the struggle in their own way.

Melanie looked back over her shoulder. "Are you close with your parents?"

"My mother just remarried a few years ago. My dad was a real bastard, but my stepdad treats her like a queen. They met at some charity event and to listen to them, it was love at first sight."

Tanner stood only a few feet away, his eyes assessing her as if he was weighing his next move or how much he wanted to share from his past.

"They travel quite a bit. My stepdad has a few vacation homes, but they'll be home for the holidays. My mom will be excited. She wanted me settled down and producing children years ago."

Oddly enough, Melanie had wanted that very same dream for herself. Yet here she was, not married or even in love, which was fine considering what marriage had presented to her.

One day, she vowed. She'd find the man who made her jittery in all the right ways, who made her want to give up her single status and return to joint everything. But that man would have to be a hell of a special guy.

"I'm not settling down again until I find a someone I want to be with forever," she told him as she searched out the window for the playful little girl. "One failed marriage was enough and now with a child in the mix, I can't afford to trust my heart so easily."

"I'm not proposing," he amended. "But you do deserve someone who's not a dick."

Melanie couldn't help but laugh as she turned back to face him. "You don't even know him."

Tanner shrugged as he took a step closer. "I've heard

enough and I see the look on your face when he's mentioned. Which is exactly why you need to quit comparing me to him. I have my reasons for wanting to stay close to you and the baby and none of them have to do with control."

Tamping down the juxtaposition of emotions, Melanie turned from the window and smoothed her hair back from her face. Neville had no place in this conversation . . . or in her life.

"If you wouldn't mind keeping this to yourself for now. I want to go to the doctor and make sure everything is okay. And if word gets back to Neville . . ."

Fear rippled through her. He would be furious. He was already mortified that his wife left him, but her overwhelming stash of blackmail had left him little choice. At least she'd been strong enough, and smart enough, to keep evidence against him.

"Hey." Tanner closed the distance between them, concern etched over his face. "This can stay between us as long as you need, but Neville won't be an issue. I'll make damn sure of that."

The intensity in Tanner's eyes, the hard set of his jaw, and the stern tone of his voice almost had Melanie believing him. But he couldn't know the type of man her ex was. Nobody did. Neville's arms reached wider than even Melanie likely knew about. He had corrupt people in his pocket in nearly every town in this state.

Tanner might think he could take on Neville, but Melanie knew nobody could take on that monster if they didn't have a good amount of ammunition.

Even though Melanie had blackmailed him—that was the only way she'd been able to leave—she still wasn't going to get too comfortable in her new life. Neville had made it clear he'd get her back. His assistant had also warned Melanie that he meant what he said. Melanie needed to be on guard . . . always.

There was no need to concern Tanner with all of her ugliness or the secrets she kept to herself. They already had enough worries between them.

"I'm hoping to get in to see the new doctor soon," she told him, needing to circle the topic away from her ex.

"I'll go with you."

"No." Melanie held out her hands, worried he'd step closer. It was difficult enough to think with him across the room, let alone right up on her. "I promise to call you and tell you everything, but if you're there, it's just too . . . I don't know."

Yes, she did. She knew exactly what it would be like. Like they were a couple and the idea of trusting another man with her heart again scared her more than the pregnancy.

"You don't want a relationship, I get it. But I'm coming with you. I'm not asking on this."

He did take a step forward and continued to do so as she stepped back. Finally, she was against the wall with him only inches from her. Nothing about this man scared her. Well, aside from her emotions and gut-clenching, toe-curling attraction. But when her ex would back her into a wall, he'd been in a fit of rage. When she looked at Tanner all she saw was concern . . . and desire.

"I know you're scared. I have no idea the hell you've endured, but I won't hurt you." Tanner reached up, sliding one fingertip along the side of her face to remove the stray strand of hair. "That's hard for you to believe, but this is my child, too. I want the very best for both of you and I intend to be there for every single step."

Melanie couldn't focus, not when she could still feel that easy slide of his fingertip, not when that simple gesture reminded her of how tender, yet passionate and reckless, he'd been. Why did she still have to want him? Why this man?

"I need space," she told him, bringing her hands up to flatten her palms against his taut chest. "I can't think when you're this close."

His eyes dipped to her lips, then back up. "It's still there."

Melanie shook her head, not even bothering to ask what he meant. "We have to ignore it."

"Why should we?"

Oh, no. "We have to," she whispered, feeling her resolve slipping away.

"Mel."

She shut her eyes. Maybe if she wasn't looking at him she wouldn't have this ache, this need inside her. But she could still smell his woodsy scent, still feel the brush of his body as he shifted closer.

She'd thought staying away from him after that night would help her move on like the strong woman she claimed to be. Unfortunately, that gap in time only made her ache for more.

"I still want you," he murmured. "Damn if I've tried not to, but knowing you're carrying my child makes me want you even more."

Panic bubbled up in her. Melanie opened her eyes and darted out from between Tanner and the wall. She made her way across the room and pulled in a deep breath. Flashes from her marriage darted through her mind, but that was all in the past. She had to keep reminding herself each time her thoughts drifted. She was safe now.

"Mel?"

With her back to him, she held up a hand to hold him away. "You can't say things like that, Tanner. No matter how attracted I am, there's nothing else for us. I can't be more than your friend."

"And the mother of my child."

Dropping her hand to her side, she nodded. "Yes."

Silence settled over the room once more before she heard the soft footfalls behind her.

"I don't know what all you endured, but I've seen some ugly shit in my day. You don't have to recover alone."

Squaring her shoulders and spinning around, she nodded. "I'm not alone and I've recovered. I revert back to that scared woman every now and then, but not as often as I used to. I'll be fine, and I really just want to focus on this baby."

He looked as if he wanted to say something else, but ultimately he gave a clipped nod. That pain still flashed through his eyes. Something had hurt him, or someone. Looks like the tough officer had his own past to deal with.

"I'll respect your wishes," he told her. "We don't have to talk about what happened before you came here, we don't have to let anyone know about the baby just yet, but the doctor's appointment isn't an option. I'll be there."

She could deal with that. "Thank you."

"But," he warned, crossing those thick arms over his broad chest. "I won't be silent in this pregnancy. You can't stop me from trying to protect you, either."

"I don't need—"

"Maybe not," he interjected, his eyes never wavering from hers. "I can't stand to see that fear in you and for my own reasons, I need to be by your side."

And here she thought she'd hidden her insecurities so well. She prided herself on being strong, on forcing herself to put one foot in front of the other, no matter the circumstances.

As much as she wanted to let Tanner console her, it

would be all too easy to fall back into the old Melanie, who worried if she stood on her own she'd fall. That woman was gone.

"I'll be fine," she assured him, confident she truly would be. "We're both just reeling from this shock and it's best if I go."

Weeks ago, she'd given in to those sultry eyes and the unspoken invitation for comfort. It had been so easy to seek solace from him that night. He'd made her forget, he'd made her feel powerful in her own right, and he'd left her longing for more.

"You're running."

Melanie threw her hands out. "Yeah, I am. Okay? I'm out of my element, Tanner, and I'm terrified. Of you and this baby. Is that what you wanted to hear?"

He didn't move, but the way his stare held her in place was just as potent as if he'd reached out and touched her. "I just want you to be honest with yourself. Don't sugarcoat things for me. You don't have to be resilient all the time."

Melanie closed her eyes and pulled in a deep breath. "But I do," she whispered. "I have to."

When she opened her eyes, she was rewarded with a soft smile and slight tilt of his head. "You're so damn remarkable."

Surprised by his reaction, Melanie stepped back and stared across the room. Compliments from a man were most definitely out of her comfort zone, so she wasn't really sure how to reply. She spotted her purse still on the floor in front of the couch where she'd dropped it when she came in.

"Will you be at the bonfire this weekend?" she asked as she crossed to retrieve her bag.

Tanner shoved his hands in his pockets and rocked back on his heels. "Yeah. I'll be there."

Hoisting her strap up onto her shoulder, Melanie turned to face him once more. Those heavy lids half shielded dark eyes. Tanner was such a potent man and could elicit a stirring of emotions inside her she'd never experienced— all from across a room.

"Stay."

Melanie stilled. That one, simple word hovered in the air between them. "Tanner—"

"Just to talk," he amended. "I just . . . damn it, I don't want things awkward, and I don't want you leaving here feeling like I should've done or said something more. And I need to know that you're okay."

His concern for her well-being could be perceived as controlling, but she wasn't getting that vibe. Whatever had him checking his emotions and keeping closed off from her, made Melanie wonder what he'd endured in his past. She wasn't naïve enough to think she was the only one with secrets.

Surely Jade or Livie would know more about Tanner's life. If they didn't, then Melanie would see if Livie could get the lowdown from Jax. That was all sneaky, but Melanie truly wanted to know what she was dealing with.

Tanner obviously wanted to fix things, if that was even the right wording here. Someone strong and resilient like Tanner used his power to help, to make everything better. But he was also in law enforcement. He was most definitely dominating and pure alpha.

Would he relinquish control where she and the baby were concerned, or would he insist he was doing everything for her benefit? Because she'd heard that lame defense before.

"I was going to light a fire out back," he added, then cursed beneath his breath. "You probably shouldn't be around smoke right now. Wait, you're going to the bonfire. I should research all of this."

He muttered the last sentence almost as if giving himself a reminder. Melanie couldn't help the clench to her heart at such sincerity. She could get used to a man who actually cared.

No. Just no. She couldn't have her heart involved right now. She needed to stick with facts and not emotions. The fact was she and Tanner were having a baby. They were no more than acquaintances, and possibly friends by default because of their group. That was fine. Friendships she could handle. She excelled at being a good friend.

Did she throw in the fact that she was attracted to him? That she actually wanted to stay because the thought of going back home and lying awake all night with worry, terrified her?

At least now that he knew, they shared that common bond of fear. That would pass, though, and she needed to keep her attraction compartmentalized so she didn't get too wrapped up in this man.

"I can't." She gripped her purse strap and offered a smile to ease the anxiety lines between his brows. "We both need to think and . . . yeah. I need to just go."

Melanie hurried to the entryway and got as far as her hand on the doorknob before she felt him behind her.

"We'll figure this out. I'm not going anywhere."

She shivered at his determined tone. Without a word, and without looking back, Melanie walked out and shut the door behind her.

Chapter Four

*Be the badass girl you were too afraid to be
yesterday.*

—Mel's Motivational Blog

"I swear if I have to look at one more layout deciding on
outlet and light switch placement, I'm going to explode."

Livie burst through the back door, the screen slamming
behind her. Melanie had already cut up all the various
cheeses she could find, had washed the grapes, and pulled
out the stemless wineglasses to go with the cheap white
she'd bought.

The newly renovated kitchen island looked like their
usual girls' night in, but this wasn't going to be like any
evening they'd shared before. Nothing after her announcement would be the same.

"So," Livie said, blowing out a sigh, "what's up?
Sounded urgent when you texted."

Jade stepped into the room from the front of the house,
still clad in her workout gear and looking like she stepped
out of some fitness magazine. Nobody should look that
stunning after working out.

The woman had even become certified in yoga and had

talked them into joining her in doing hot yoga at a studio a few towns over. Merciful sakes, that workout had been brutal.

"How can a text sound urgent?" Jade asked, taking a seat on the bar stool.

"She used the wineglass and stiletto," Livie explained. "That's SOS."

Jade drew her brows in. "I thought SOS was the wineglasses and the middle-finger emoji."

"No, that's what you wanted," Livie corrected. "We went with the stiletto."

"Regardless, you're both here." Melanie poured two glasses of wine and eased them across the bar. "Can't a girl just need a break from blogs and emails and get some time in with her friends?"

Both women stared back at Melanie, the untouched glasses on the island between them.

"What?" Melanie asked. "Don't tell me you don't like white, because that's a lie. Oh, is it the twist-off top that's giving you pause? I'm sure it's fabulous. What wine less than ten bucks wouldn't be great?"

"What's going on?" Livie asked, still ignoring her glass. "Wait. Did Neville come to town?"

"Don't even tell me that bastard is still harassing you," Jade chimed in. "I wish we could catch him doing it, but he's so damn sneaky—"

"Neville isn't here," Melanie stated, trying to calm her friends. "He's sneaky, for sure, but he uses his assistants to get in touch with me. To my knowledge, he hasn't stepped foot in Haven."

"No, he'd send his minions to do any dirty work," Jade muttered as she reached for the wine. "So what's really going on and why aren't you drinking? We always have a glass together."

Melanie reached around to the fridge and pulled out a bottle of water. "I'm trying to relax and think of new ideas for blogs, plus I'm changing out some of the ads. I was approached by a fitness trainer who'd like a guest spot once a month."

Melanie knew she was rambling and dodging the real question her friends wanted her to answer. They would find out soon enough why she wasn't drinking and what was wrong.

From the blank stares and the pursed lips from Livie and Jade, they weren't even listening to her rambling anyway.

Livie's eyes narrowed as she flashed a quick, knowing look to Jade. "She's definitely hiding something."

Jade nodded and blew out a sigh. "Alright, Melanie. What's really going on? Your nail polish looks like hell and I just put that shade on you two days ago. You look like you've been crying and you sent the SOS emojis."

She hadn't been crying, actually. Maybe she just needed a better concealer. She had been slacking on her makeup and hair lately.

"Pour her a glass of wine," Livie demanded. "She looks like she needs it more than we do."

"I can't."

Her friends stilled. Damn it. Now they were even more suspicious.

"I just mean that I really do need to keep a clear head right now," she explained. "I have a few emails to answer and I'd like to get a new blog scheduled so I don't have to worry about it Monday morning."

Because she'd be busy at the doctor.

"One glass won't hurt," Jade claimed. She slid hers across the island. "Here. Take mine."

Melanie rested her palms on the island and dropped her head between her shoulders. "I'm pregnant."

The dual gasps had Melanie cringing. She'd really wanted to keep this news to herself until she knew how to handle it better, but right now she could use all the support from her closest friends. And really, she should've found a better delivery than just dropping a verbal bomb.

"You're joking."

Melanie glanced up, meeting Jade's wide eyes. "I'm pregnant," she repeated, getting more used to the words. "I took a test this morning."

"But . . . wait." Livie reached for her glass and downed the contents in one gulp. She slammed the glass back down and reached for the bottle. "You're not even seeing anyone. How is this possible?"

Jade reached out and smacked Livie on the arm. "Don't ask stupid questions."

"I just mean, who the hell could the father be?"

Now both sets of eyes turned back to her. This was one thing she really wasn't going to expose just yet. The questions would be nonstop and she'd already asked Tanner to not say anything right now. They needed to decide together how to let their friends know.

Tears pricked her eyes. Melanie bit her quivering lip in a vain attempt to get control of herself. She really hated secrets. She'd lived with them during her marriage, she'd grown up with them. Nothing good came from keeping the truth hidden. And a baby was precious, a sign of a new beginning. Why should she feel so bad about this?

"Oh, damn it."

Jade came around the island and wrapped her arms around Melanie. She turned into her friend's embrace, needing the girl-bonding ritual.

"You deserve to cry," Jade muttered.

"I'm not crying," Melanie insisted as she sniffed.

Livie's hand settled on her back. "You're more than en-titled to a breakdown."

Maybe so, but what did getting upset solve? She eased back from Jade's hold and swiped at the moisture on her face.

"I'm okay. I'll be fine."

"You will be fine," Livie agreed. "But it's also okay to *not* be fine for a few minutes. I'd be worried if you weren't afraid."

Melanie let out a long sigh. "I know you all want an-swers about the father, and you deserve them, but I'm not ready to get into that just yet. I will, just give me some time."

Jade and Livie exchanged a look before they both finally nodded. No doubt they wanted all the answers now, and she would too if she were in their shoes.

Melanie didn't know why it was important to keep Tanner a secret right now. It wasn't like they wouldn't find out eventually. But she wasn't ready to deal with every-thing all at once. Besides, she'd asked him to keep things to himself for now. There was no way she couldn't tell her friends, though. She needed their support. But the answer to their burning question would have to wait.

Telling her friends that she and Tanner had slept together would change the dynamics of absolutely everything. Livie and Jax were marrying soon, Melanie planned on staying in Haven as well, and Jade was still up in the air. But their group had been formed, and since coming here, three guys had become part of their lives.

"We'll do whatever you want," Livie assured her. "How are you feeling?"

Melanie reached around for her bottle of water. "Tired,

mostly. I thought maybe I just needed more sleep, but then I missed my period and I knew."

Jade grabbed her wineglass and took a sip. She clutched the stemless glass to her chest and smiled. "Well, we're here and we'll do anything we can. But you've got to rest. Oh, can I take over your blog for a week? I started dating this new guy and let me tell you—"

Melanie laughed. "No. I love my followers and you'd scare them."

"Maybe not," Jade said with a defiant shake of her head and a smirk. "They may love what I have to say about motivation and bettering themselves. I can leave my new dating scene out of the picture for now. I've got a hell of a backstory."

Melanie thought for a minute. Jade did have a remarkable story about overcoming obstacles and becoming a strong, independent woman. "You know, that's not a bad idea. I could do featured posts on the three of us. That was a huge hit when I started the site. Everyone loved our meet story, so revisiting where we are now would be fun. I could mention the airport and the undertaking we're all doing. Free press down the road won't hurt."

"When you say where we are now, I assume you mean without the pregnancy announcement?" Livie asked, reaching for a piece of jalapeño Havarti.

"Yeah. I'm definitely holding out on that for a while."

Just the idea that she'd be in charge of another life was almost too much to handle. But she'd turned her own life around and she was well on her way to achieving her goal. Her blog was huge, her social media accounts boomed, and she was helping her friends turn an old airport into something grand. All in all, her life was great. Better than ever, actually.

While the shock still hadn't worn off about the baby,

Melanie wasn't sorry. How could she be? She'd always wanted a family. This might not be the way she'd envisioned her life at this point, but she would provide for this baby and be the best mother she knew how to be.

"So, do you want to talk about it, or do you want to hear about the guy who asked me out in aisle twelve and offered to take me home for frozen pizza?"

Melanie laughed. "Jade, I swear. Men flock to you."

"Not the right ones, unfortunately. But I've gone out with Brad a couple times and he seems really nice."

At least that was something. Jade never attracted the right type of man. Another thing they all had in common. Well, all they'd had in common before Livie had fallen in love with Jax. Before that union of souls, the wrong men somehow wedged themselves into the lives of Melanie, Jade, and Livie. Melanie had been the only one dumb enough to fall for false charms and marriage, though.

"What are Jax and Piper doing tonight?" Melanie asked.

Livie's smile widened as it always did when discussing her fiancé and his sweet little girl. "They're actually planning something for the wedding. They've been working on some secret project that's driving me crazy."

"That's because you don't have control," Jade chimed in. "But seriously, that's adorable. Piper is so damn cute, she's going to look precious in that pale blue dress you chose."

"I had to pick her favorite color."

Melanie groaned. "Oh, no. I'm going to have to order another size in my dress unless you two hurry up and marry soon."

Livie reached out, placing her hand on Melanie's arm. "Don't stress right now. We'll fit the wedding in before the end of the year . . . I hope. Things just keep getting pushed back because we're so focused on this airport and we want it up and running as soon as we can to start getting a return on our investments."

"Yeah, well, I'm already six weeks pregnant," Melanie complained. "What if my waist is gone by the time you all decide to seal the deal? What if I can't get my dress zipped?"

Flashes of a young girl who cried herself to sleep over ill-fitting clothes and excess weight hit her hard. Damn it. She'd pushed that girl with low self-esteem behind her, too. The body shaming, the guilt and depression, all of that had been erased.

Well, she'd thought she'd pushed that negative Nancy behind her, but occasionally she still popped up. She'd lived inside that body for so long, there was no way to completely erase her. Perhaps that was a good thing, to keep Melanie reminded of where she'd come from and how far she'd come, all on her own.

"You'll be beautiful no matter what," Jade stated. "Maybe Livie and Jax will hurry to the altar, or living room, or wherever the hell they decide on, a little sooner. This might just give Livie the motivation to move things along."

"I'm ready to marry," Livie declared. "I swear. We've just been so damn busy with all the demolition and surveys and the little things we didn't think of when taking on this vast project. I swear, if your dress doesn't fit, I'll personally buy you another one."

Melanie slid her hand over her belly, trying to imagine the life growing inside her right now. "This is insane," she whispered. "I mean, I'm excited, but if I think too much on it I get nervous."

"So is now a good time to tell the story of the guy who hit on me and wanted me to come for dinner at his house for frozen pizza? Because I promise, the story gets worse.

He also threw in reruns of *Seinfeld* like that would win me over."

Jade's question had Melanie and Livie laughing. "Now is the perfect time," Melanie said. "I may need you to also add in those nightmare blind-date stories you have, because I seriously need the distraction."

Jade blew out a breath. "Then you might want to have a seat because those blind-date-from-hell stories can go on for days."

Tanner ducked just in time to avoid a fist to the side of his face.

He let out a laugh, even though he was trying to get in a deep breath and bounce around on the balls of his feet. "You're getting slow, old man."

Tanner ducked again as he shifted out of the way of another fist. He held his gloves firmly in defensive position. Sweat trickled down the side of his face. He swiped at his forehead with the back of his arm as he eyed his opponent.

Cash laughed as he went for another jab. "Old man, my ass."

Tanner spun around, catching just the air from the punch. "Nice try."

Breathing heavily, Tanner leaned back on the ropes and pulled in some much needed air. He also took a moment to survey the weight area off in the corner. Cash had said the two guys he wanted Tanner to check up on were usually at the gym late at night.

With twenty-four-hour access to members only, that could mean any time. Any member with the access code could get in. If the two guys didn't show after a while, Tanner would get the tapes from the cameras in the parking lot and main area of the gym to get a good view of exactly who he was supposed to be looking for.

"They're not here yet." Cash came over to the ropes and draped his forearms over the top. "They're pretty regular, so they should be here within the next thirty minutes."

Tanner jerked his boxing gloves off and reached for the bottle of water in the corner of the ring. He took a hearty drink, welcoming the chill. He and Cash had gone at it for a while, which was exactly what Tanner needed.

Ever since learning he was going to be a daddy—again—he'd been a damn mess. His emotions ranged from terrified, to anxious, back to holy shit mode.

Flashes of what seemed like a lifetime ago kept scrolling through his mind. Another woman, another baby. Both gone.

Not only had Tanner never wanted to get involved long-term with someone, he sure as hell hadn't wanted to go through another pregnancy. He'd had to hold himself in check when Melanie had been at his house. The woman looked as nervous and scared as he'd felt. She'd been through her own personal hell and he damn well was going to be strong for her . . . no matter the cost to his own sanity.

That dark moment in his life years ago had never left him. He'd wondered about what might have been, or how his life would be now had his fiancée and child lived. But here he was, starting this all over again, and once again, the control was not in his possession.

Refocusing on the issue here and now, Tanner addressed his cousin. "You going to the cookout over at Jax's tomorrow?"

Cash nodded. "I'll be there. I have to train a lady at six, so it will be after that."

"You seeing her outside the gym?"

Cash snorted and stood up to pull off his own gloves. "We dated once. We're more friends than anything. She's training for a competition, so her schedule is pretty strict right now."

There were all types of people who came into Cash's gym. People who just wanted a healthier lifestyle, people who wanted to strength train, athletes who wanted to push their endurance, and those who trained for a variety of competitions. All shapes and sizes came through the doors, and Cash took pride in his place and in each and every client. This was his life, his family.

Mainly because his own family had fallen apart when Cash was younger, and Cash refused to fall into the downward spiral of his pill-addicted father. That was Cash's dirty little secret, one he didn't share because he was too proud of where he'd come after his mother's death and his father's hellish attempt to cope.

"They're here," Cash murmured.

Tanner didn't move, but his eyes started scanning the place. He took another swig of his water and noted two Caucasian men, probably no more than twenty-three. They both had black gym bags slung over their shoulders as they made their way toward the locker room. No cameras were allowed in areas where people took off their clothes, so this would have to be an area Tanner checked out personally.

Without a word, Tanner picked up his gloves and headed to the locker room. He went to the locker he'd been using and pulled out his cell, pretending to check texts as he eavesdropped.

The guys were muttering about something in the next aisle of lockers. Tanner strained to hear what they were saying, but could only make out a few words. Something about "a bag" and "ten o'clock." Tanner checked the time and noted it was just a little after nine. Looks like he wasn't leaving anytime soon.

All of this could be nothing, but it very well could be something major, and Cash deserved Tanner's undivided attention. Anyone who had a tip on drugs deserved his full focus, for that matter.

Tanner knew he couldn't possibly save everyone or stop every single illegal activity, but each time he was able to make a difference, he knew he was in the right career for the right reasons. He was damn good at his job and would stop at nothing to keep his small town and its residents safe.

A text flashed across the top of his screen. He nearly dropped his phone at the unexpected vibration.

I've been busy all day, but wanted to let you know dr appt scheduled for Monday @ 2

He pulled in a deep breath and started to reply two different times, but deleted each one. This was real. He was going to be a father and he was going to have to push aside his past and man up now, because Melanie needed him. Their baby needed him.

She might not want to admit that she needed help and support, but she did. No way in hell would he miss that appointment. He wanted to know how healthy Mel was, how the baby was doing, if there were any red flags or worries they should be concerned with at this point.

Damn it. She'd just found out about the pregnancy and he was already mentally freaking out. He had a long way to go.

The guys on the other side were still chatting. Tanner blocked out his fear and worries. He had to focus on this moment for now and reply to Mel later.

"He's nothing but a little bitch," one guy complained. "I'm not afraid of him."

They'd yet to say anything incriminating, and Tanner hadn't seen or heard their names before. So far, they were just guys working out. But Tanner wasn't about to brush aside Cash's concerns. Tanner had nothing else to do tonight, so sticking around here was just fine. He needed to work out some frustrations anyway and exorcise those demons from his past.

The woman and children he and his team were supposed to extract last night had backed out. Well, the woman had. Her kids hadn't had a choice, which only pissed Tanner off all the more. He couldn't save those who didn't want to be saved, he'd discovered that a long time ago.

But, damn it, he wanted those kids out of that house. He wanted the mother to realize that she was worth more than the shit she put up with on a daily basis.

Locker doors slammed, pulling Tanner back into the moment. He stared down at Melanie's text again. As the guys walked out, not paying him any mind, he used this moment to shoot off a quick reply.

I'll be there. See you at the cookout

The second he'd hit send, he realized how ridiculous that sounded. He'd already told her he'd be at Jax's for the cookout. Like some awkward teen with his first crush, he hadn't known what else to say. Damn if this whole situation wasn't making him a fumbling mess.

Maybe if he wasn't reliving the worst time of his life, he wouldn't be in such a panic. Oh, he was positive he'd still be scared, but having lost two people who meant so much to him, he honestly wasn't sure he could go through another loss. Which is why he needed to keep his heart out of this equation. Being physically attracted was fine, and actually he couldn't put a halt on that even if he wanted to. Everything between him and Mel had to stay superficial.

Tanner even feared getting too attached to the baby just yet. Because losing a child was a whole other level of hell he still didn't want to talk about. Cash and Jax knew what he'd been through, but even they never brought up the delicate matter.

If Tanner delved too deep, he'd go into full panic mode, but he couldn't go there. The only way to get through this was to remain ahead of his feelings and tell his past to shut the hell up.

All he could do was be there for Melanie, make sure she was safe and comfortable . . . because he couldn't take another soul-crushing loss.

Shit. Tanner raked a hand through his hair and shoved his cell back into the bag in his locker. After shutting the door harder than necessary, he headed back out into the main part of the gym.

He didn't want Melanie to ever believe he wasn't interested in what was going on with their child. He just didn't know how to compartmentalize his fears. Getting too attached at this point would be a mistake that could potentially lead to disaster. He would be there, he would be supportive and anything else Melanie needed. But he couldn't allow himself to feel.

Melanie deserved someone who would open up and love her for the amazing woman she was. For reasons he didn't want to address, the idea of her finding a man to settle down with only sent rage through him. Tanner didn't want another man to help raise his child. He tried to tell himself that was the only reason, but thinking of Melanie and how passionate yet shy she'd been with him . . . hell.

He couldn't have it both ways and he damn well knew

it. He either had to go full on with her or pretend to just be friends and support her with the baby.

Fisting his hands at his sides, Tanner set off to the free weights and refocused on the potential threat to Cash's gym. Thinking of Melanie and how damn perfect they'd been together wasn't helping. Thinking of her with another man sure as hell wasn't doing anything to calm him.

Tanner grabbed a set of weights and stepped away from the racks. He headed to the corner, hoping to work his shoulders and triceps, and hopefully overhear whatever those two guys were discussing.

With each rep and burn in his muscles, Tanner tried to hone in on the conversation about ten feet away. Never before had a woman interfered with his thought process while he was working. Technically he wasn't working, but in a sense he was.

Melanie kept shoving her way into the forefront of his mind. He replayed their intimate, heated night over and over. They'd danced around each other for months. He'd told himself taking her home would be wrong on so many levels. But when it came right down to it, he hadn't been strong enough to say no.

"He better bring the right amount this time."

Tanner nearly missed the quiet statement from one of the guys across the way. One was down on a bench while the other stood at his head spotting each press. The man standing was talking, but not loud and definitely not saying anything that would perk up most people's ears. Tanner wasn't most people.

"If he tries to cheat me again—"

"Shut up," the guy lying on the bench demanded. "He knows what will happen if he can't pay up."

Things were definitely getting more interesting. Tanner changed out his weights for heavier ones and did another set of reps. The guys didn't say much else, at least nothing of interest to him as they switched positions and started chattering about a woman on the elliptical across the way. Tanner purposely kept his side to them so he wasn't directly staring.

In the wall of mirrors, he spotted Cash talking to some redhead. Tanner did a double take. Not just any redhead. Jade. Cash crossed his arms over his chest and shook his head, then said something that had Jade propping her hands on her hips as if she were annoyed. Cash leaned closer to Jade and said something else, to which Jade turned her head as if she didn't want to hear it.

Was Cash flirting with Jade? Damn it. Their close group was getting even smaller. Though Tanner couldn't see Jade and Cash together. That woman was feisty and independent. She'd been secretive about why she wasn't in a hurry to get back to Atlanta. Rumor was she'd had a seven figure career and had walked away without even giving notice. Why wasn't she rushing back to that cushy life, and what had driven her away?

Cash might be flirting, as Cash often did with women, but Jade was his total opposite. Cash preferred his ladies falling all over him and batting false lashes his way. Besides, he rarely dated anyone from the gym.

Just as Tanner started to rack his weights, Jade hauled off and slapped Cash. The few people in the gym turned and stared. Tanner stilled, wondering what Cash would do. Obviously not hit her back; Cash had never laid a hand on a woman.

Tanner couldn't help but wonder what had transpired between them for Jade to get so angry. Those two, though, they pressed each other's buttons.

Cash simply dropped his arms at his sides. Jade did the same and they looked as if they were at some sort of standoff. Finally, Cash said something else and turned and walked away.

Tanner shook out his tired arms and crossed to the pull-up bar. He wasn't stupid enough to interject himself between Jade and Cash. They were adults and could work out whatever issues they had. He had other reasons for being here right now.

He'd gotten in ten pull-ups when a young man came in. Instinct told Tanner this was the guy the others had been waiting on. Mid-twenties, ripped muscles, glancing around as if looking for someone.

Casual as you please, Tanner made his way to the locker room. If anything was going to happen, it wasn't going to be out in the public area for everyone to see.

He wanted to already be set in the locker room so he didn't appear to be following. That room would be the key to catching any criminal activity, if there was indeed something going on. Those guys would know exactly where the cameras were located and would use that to their advantage.

Tanner grabbed a gym-issued towel on his way to the back. Swiping at his forehead and neck, he pushed through the doors and headed to his locker. He rolled the towel and draped it around his neck, then typed in his locker code. His arms and shoulders burned from the workout, but he wasn't complaining. He needed to stay strong and fit for his job.

After pulling out his duffel bag, Tanner checked his phone once again. Disappointment surged through him that Melanie hadn't responded. What would she have said, though? And why the hell was he looking for a text like some love-struck teen?

Damn it. He needed to get a grip. Melanie had done

something to him when they'd slept together. She'd gotten under his skin and he damn well didn't like it.

Why couldn't sex just be sex? There had been a time, not so long ago, that he could have sex and move on. He made no promises and women knew exactly where he stood.

Melanie had been different from the beginning, though. The steel exterior wrapped around vulnerability dug deep into his soul and gave him little choice but to be drawn to her.

He hadn't come out and asked, but she'd confirmed his suspicions when she'd said she hadn't been with anyone in the two years since her divorce.

That in itself made him want her all over again. The fact that she'd chosen him to move on with—

Commotion behind him cut off all his thoughts. Melanie had to be pushed to the back of his mind. He couldn't keep wondering about her, about the baby, not when he was working or trying to focus. Not when he was trying to hold his emotions together.

Needing to think of a quick distraction, Tanner quickly stepped on his opposite shoelace and untied it. When the group of guys came around the corner, Tanner propped his foot on the bench and proceeded to tie his shoe. Anything to delay leaving the locker room.

Unfortunately, the trio spoke too low, and when they went around the other side of the lockers, all Tanner could hear was the sound of a locker opening, a zipper on a bag, and some whispering.

Shit. There was something going on and he had no way to prove it. His instincts rarely failed him and he was convinced Cash had been given accurate information from the other gym member.

Tanner was a patient man, though. He had to be in his

line of work. It sucked at times. The waiting game was never one he enjoyed playing, but it was necessary to ensure the proper channels were all clicked off.

Not wanting to draw attention to himself, Tanner zipped his own bag and headed out the door. In the main gym area, he saw no sign of Jade or Cash. He didn't want to approach Cash right now anyway. He needed to talk to him in private and not where those guys could see.

Since videos in the locker room were out of the question, he'd have to speak with his captain about placing an undercover here in the evenings.

As soon as Tanner got into his truck, he shot off a quick text to Cash that there was something suspicious going on and he'd get back to him on the next steps to take. He didn't want Cash doing anything that could potentially scare these guys away.

Tanner drove through the main part of town, passing the quaint shops that had been around for decades. With the holidays approaching, they'd gone all out with the fodder, pumpkins, mums. Most businesses had fall wreaths on the doors. He loved protecting a town that took pride in its appearance. The buildings might be old, but the owners kept them up with fresh paint, plants, clean sidewalks in front of their doors.

Macy Monroe, third-generation owner of Knobs and Knockers Hardware, had been a good friend of his since school. She always had a great seasonal display in front of her store. They'd actually dated a couple times, but she'd always been more like a sister than anything.

Tanner headed toward the other side of town, where he lived. His eyes were drawn to the old Civil War–era home on the hill. Bella Vous. The women's only resort and spa had been the biggest thing to happen to Haven, Georgia, since the once dry town passed a liquor law ten years ago.

What had been most impressive about this women's resort was the fact that three brothers opened the place in honor of their late sister. The Monroe boys had all been hellions in their own way. They'd been just a few years older than Tanner in school, but he remembered them. The three boys and one girl had all been adopted by the Monroes. The crew hadn't been related at all and had filtered into Haven at different points in their lives.

One of the guys, Liam, was married to Macy. Liam hadn't been too keen on the friendship between Tanner and Macy at first, but Liam had quickly come around and saw that Tanner posed no threat to their relationship.

Hell, Tanner would never break up a relationship. He didn't have the time or the mental energy to date anyway.

When Melanie had mentioned him going on about his life, or whatever lingo she'd used, he'd been pissed. Did she honestly think he wasn't going to stick around for her? Did she believe he was that much of a prick that he'd get her pregnant and just move on? Like he'd just go out on dates with other women. What fool had she been married to, and why did she ever accept anything less than the best?

Maybe it was time someone showed her that she was worth so much more than the shit she'd endured. Not that he was looking to take this into a full-fledged relationship, but Tanner wasn't going anywhere . . . and neither was Melanie. She was about to discover how a real man treated a lady.

Chapter Five

Be fearless in the pursuit of what sets your soul on fire.

—Mel's Motivational Blog

The crisp fall evening couldn't be more perfect for a cookout and bonfire. There was just enough chill in the air to make the fire cozy and comfortable.

Livie sat on Jax's lap while his daughter, Piper, put another marshmallow on her roasting stick. Melanie couldn't help but wonder if she'd have a girl. Would her daughter have blond hair like hers or dark like Tanner's? Would she have those dark eyes framed by inky lashes like her father?

Or maybe she'd have a boy and he'd be strong and a protector like Tanner. Either way, Melanie's excitement grew more and more each day.

"Sorry I'm late."

Melanie glanced over her shoulder as Cash walked down the stone path in Jax's backyard.

"There's plenty of food left," Livie stated as she hopped off Jax's lap. "Let me get you something."

Cash waved a hand as he headed toward the picnic table loaded with food. "Sit. I don't expect you to serve me."

Livie played the hostess perfectly. This small-town life was quite different from the hustle and bustle of her life back in Atlanta. Being engaged, with a ready-made family, looked good on her. Melanie couldn't be happier for her friend.

"Jade," Cash murmured with a nod.

Jade flipped him the one-fingered salute and remained silent as she held her bottle of water in the other hand. Wow. It took quite a bit to get on Jade's bad side. She tended to just strike someone down with her witty banter, but Cash must've really pissed her off.

Cash let out a laugh and looked to Melanie. "You're always the nicer one," he joked.

Melanie had no idea what had happened between Cash and Jade, but who knew with those two. He seemed to always know how to push her buttons and he totally took advantage of that.

Jade was a live wire, never taking anything from anyone, and she always let people know where they stood. Apparently Cash didn't stand in a good spot with her. Melanie didn't recall any mention of a past between them. They'd grown up in Haven and had gone to school together. Maybe Cash didn't like that Jade wasn't tripping over herself to gain his attention. Poor Cash. Maybe he'd finally met his match.

"Hey," Livie complained. "I'm nice."

Cash snorted. "You're marrying Jax, so you lost points by default."

Melanie listened to her friends' chatter, but mostly tuned them out, hating how she kept glancing over her shoulder for any sign of Tanner. He'd said he'd be here, but clearly something had come up.

A niggle of disappointment settled deep. He'd been adamant he'd be around, yet she hadn't seen him for a few days. Maybe he'd changed his mind or perhaps he just decided a baby wasn't what he saw for his future.

Regardless, she wished she'd stop holding her breath at every damn noise. What happened to the "I am woman, hear me roar" mantra she'd engrained in herself during and since her divorce? Tanner had a life before her, before the baby bomb had been dropped in his life.

Melanie had no idea what he did with his evenings. The secrets he obviously kept weren't coming to light anytime soon. Flashes of Neville's infidelity kept creeping through her mind. But they'd been married. She and Tanner were . . . what exactly? Melanie didn't really feel she had a right to ask him about his disappearances. He technically owed her no explanations.

What were the boundaries when it came to personal info from your baby daddy? She'd told him she didn't expect anything from him and she hadn't been lying. He didn't have to tell her his plans or his schedule. She'd pushed him away from getting too close. Part of her wanted someone to lean on during this scary time, but she had Jade and Livie. Her gal pals had gotten her through a rough patch before. No way would they leave her now.

"Right, Melanie?"

Escaping her thoughts, Melanie turned her attention to Jade and smiled. "I'm sorry. What?"

"She said the restaurant should have a classic theme, like fifties retro with the chrome and teal and white."

Cash shook his head as if that were the most preposterous notion. "I said this is a small town, and it should be more down home and simple."

"Retro is in right now," Jade threw back. "And since when did you care so much about designs and décor?"

"Since I had a stake in this airport, too." He glared at her over his beer as he took a hearty swig before going back to making his plate of food.

"What stake is that exactly?" Jade asked, her tone sweet as honey, but her eyes shot daggers.

Melanie was rather enjoying this show, and they'd clearly forgotten they'd dragged her in for an opinion. At least watching them she wasn't stewing over the fact that one of their members was missing.

"I have a plane there, too, you know," he reminded her. "And Jax is like a brother. I want this to succeed just as much as you all do. Don't be mad at me simply because I tried to warn you away from the jerk you're dating."

"My social life is none of your concern," Jade spouted back.

"Cool it, guys," Jax interrupted. "Piper, honey, back away from the fire. You're getting too close."

Piper had been in her own little world, roasting marshmallows, and sneaking some of the chocolate bar when her dad and Olivia weren't looking. She obviously didn't mind the adults arguing, because she didn't even glance toward Cash or Jade.

"Anyone want a marshmallow?" Piper asked. "I can make them real burnt if you like them crispy."

Melanie laughed. "I actually love them that way. I'll take one, please."

Piper squealed and ran to grab her roasting stick.

"I've gotten a few design ideas." Livie wrapped her arm around Jax's shoulder and leaned her head against his. "I like too many, that's my problem. But with the higher-end clients coming through, I'm leaning toward the classic style. I want something that will not look dated in five years. I thought about asking a professional, but I'm pretty sure between all of us, we can come up with a solid plan."

"Whatever you choose will be fine," Jax stated as he patted her hip.

"I know, but then I think Haven does have so much small-town charm, I should stick to the down-home feel like Cash mentioned."

"Because I'm brilliant." He carried his plate and beer over to the vacant seat next to Melanie. "Let me know when you want me to choose paint colors."

Jade snorted. "White and off-white don't count as paint colors."

"You two act like siblings. Can we call a truce?" Livie asked. "Good grief. You're both irritating when we're all together."

"Speaking of being all together, where's Tanner?" Cash asked around a mouthful of chips.

"No idea." Jax ran his hand up and down Livie's denim-clad thigh. "He said he'd be by, but then I haven't heard from him."

Well, at least he wasn't just not communicating with her and dodging her because of the baby. Clearly he'd had more important things to do tonight. Melanie still wondered what was so important that he would just disappear. This was not the first time he'd missed a gathering without saying a word.

Jax and Cash seemed to imply this was just normal behavior. How reliable could Tanner be if he said one thing and did another? He worked for the force during the day. Did he have a second job he was ashamed about? Something took him away in the evenings, but he wasn't readily opening up about it.

"He works too hard," Cash growled. "He's been looking into something at the gym for me on top of his regular shift, and whatever the hell he does in the evenings that he refuses to clue us in on."

"You can't say bad words," Piper chanted. "Livie smacks dad's hand when he says those words in front of me."

"Well, Livie won't smack me," Cash retorted. "I'm bigger than her."

The marshmallow at the end of Piper's stick caught fire and she pulled it back, but Cash leaped out of his chair and took the stick from her, blowing out the flame.

He shook his head and extended the crispy treat. "Your dessert is done."

With a laugh, Melanie tapped the charred, gooey mess with the pad of her finger to test the temperature.

"I'm sorry." Piper frowned and glanced down at her feet. "I just wanted to get it closer to the fire to get it black for you."

"I promise, it's perfect," Melanie assured her as she took a bite. "See? My favorite, and crispy just like you promised."

Piper clapped her hands. "Do you want another?"

Melanie laughed and tried to lick the sticky mess from her fingers. "I'm good, but thank you."

"Hey, baby, I think it's time we take you in to get ready for bed."

Livie stood up and reached her hand out to Piper.

"But Uncle Cash just got here and I haven't seen Uncle Tanner yet," Piper protested.

Even though the guys were all cousins and best friends, Piper called them uncle. Melanie's heart clenched. What would her baby call Cash and Jax? The guys had no idea about the pregnancy, and Melanie didn't know if she should let Tanner tell them or if she should make an announcement. Or should they do it together?

As far as she knew, Tanner hadn't said anything about their night together, so when the announcement came about the baby and the two of them . . . Melanie didn't even want to know the reaction that would come from so many different personalities.

Melanie was just anxious to get to her appointment and make sure everything looked as it should. She'd researched online to see what to expect during the first visit. The baby's heartbeat was definitely something she wanted to hear. She hoped for an ultrasound, but apparently those weren't done this early unless there were complications or a question on when the baby was conceived.

Yeah, no question here. One night, with a condom, and boom. Granted, she'd gone off her birth control after her divorce. She'd not planned on getting involved with someone else and she didn't like putting pills in her body when it wasn't necessary. Then time moved on and she hadn't given it another thought. When Tanner had mentioned a condom, she made the naïve assumption all would be fine.

"I should get home, too." Melanie came to her feet and pushed her hair behind her ears. "I'm pretty tired."

"Are you alright?" Livie asked, her brows drawn in.

Melanie didn't want to give Cash or Jax any reason to question her leaving. "I'm fine. Just sleepy. I was up late last night reading over the next week of blog posts. Then I couldn't sleep, so I started searching . . . um, recipes."

Actually, she'd been looking at baby names. She couldn't help it. Even though this entire situation was a complete and total shock, the more she got used to the idea, the more excited she became.

The simple search for baby names rolled into nursery styles, then that turned into researching the best furniture by reviews and price. The time suck of the internet had kept her up most of the night.

Just because she was having her family in a different way than she'd always envisioned, didn't mean she couldn't have just as much fun planning. She seriously needed to catch up on the sleep, though. She'd had no idea how tiring pregnancy could be. The baby was only the size of a pea at this point, according to her newly downloaded app. How could something so tiny cause so many changes to her body?

"Do you need me to come with you?" Jade asked.

"Oh, no." Melanie waved a hand in the air. "I'm fine. Stay as long as you like. I'll likely already be in bed when you get home."

Melanie bent down to give Piper a kiss on her head. "You are my new official marshmallow maker. Deal?"

Piper nodded, her lopsided pigtails bouncing. "Deal."

Melanie said her goodbyes and headed through the backyard toward the side of the house where she'd parked. She adjusted her cardigan tighter around her as the nip in the air slid over her, replacing the warmth from the fire. Her hair around her shoulders helped, too.

She tended to keep her hair down unless she was working out. After being rigorously programmed for two long years to have it pulled back into a perfect style, she couldn't help but embrace the small semblance of rebellion by leaving it untouched.

Melanie watched where she stepped as she made her way toward the front of the house. The lights out back and the porch light around front weren't bright enough to shine into the side yard. She kept her head down to watch her steps on the little stone path leading toward the drive.

And that's when she plowed straight into something hard. No, not something, *someone*.

Melanie squealed and stumbled as strong hands wrapped around her arms.

"Easy there."

She knew that voice, knew that grip. Jerking her attention up, she landed on a soft smile. "Tanner. What are you doing here?"

He didn't release her, but his hold eased. She couldn't

see much with the lack of lighting, but she was definitely close enough to see that grin, to inhale that familiar scent that she'd come to crave.

"I said I'd be here."

"We just figured you weren't coming since it was getting late."

Damn it. That sounded like she'd been waiting on him. Hadn't she already told herself that his schedule was none of her business? Just because she was having his baby didn't give her full access to his life. Just like she didn't necessarily want him having full access to her life.

"Sorry," she quickly added. "You don't owe me an explanation."

"Don't apologize to me. Ever."

His commanding tone had her nodding. "Um . . . okay."

"You're allowed to ask me where I've been, Mel. I can't always tell you, but other than certain aspects of work, I'm an open book."

Maybe he was, but she wasn't. There were too many things in her life she wasn't proud of, too many things she'd worked damn hard to overcome . . . and she'd done just that. So, revisiting wasn't necessarily high on her list.

In all honesty, Melanie didn't want Tanner to be an open book, because someone like him would be too easy to slip into a comfortable stage with. And once she did that, he'd want to control things. Control her.

Melanie rubbed her head and stifled a yawn. "I was just heading home, but the rest of the gang is all back there. Olivia just took Piper in to put her to bed."

Tanner's brows drew in. "You look tired. Are you feeling alright?"

"Ironically, I am tired." She dropped her hand and offered a smile. "No need to worry, though. I'll just get some rest and be fine. Morning sickness hasn't settled in yet, so maybe I'll get lucky and dodge that side effect."

Tanner reached out, framed her face, and stared down into her eyes. Why didn't she back up or ease away from his touch? Why did such a simple gesture have to have such an impact on her every emotion?

"I'll take you home."

She couldn't focus on the murmured words for the fact he was still touching her as if she were the most fragile thing in the world. Those strong hands held her still and Melanie was so tired, she nearly leaned forward and just let this moment be. Part of her wanted to take the comfort he offered, but the other part still clung to the strong, independent woman she'd become.

Hadn't she prided herself on moving on? And she'd done a damn good job of it, too. Now faced with another man in her life, a man she hadn't planned on being a permanent fixture, she couldn't help but hone in on that sliver of apprehension that curled through her.

"Don't push me away," he commanded, as if he were in sync with her thoughts. "You don't have to do this alone."

Alone. She'd been alone for so long. Even when she'd been married, she hadn't had a partner. This whole concept was so foreign to her, she had no idea how to wrap her mind around trying to work as a team. This was just the beginning of their long journey together. All she could do was take this one day at a time.

Tanner dropped his hands to her shoulders and tipped his head. "This is my baby, too. I'm not going anywhere."

"What the hell?"

Melanie jerked from Tanner's hold as he muttered a curse beneath his breath. She didn't need to turn around to know Cash stood behind her. His shocked question was all the evidence she needed that he had overheard Tanner's comment.

"You two are having a baby?" he shouted.

Tanner stepped around Melanie. "Cash—"

"We are." She turned, ready to face Tanner's cousin. But when she turned around, Jax stood there, too. "Um, we didn't exactly plan on announcing the news just yet, but yeah."

The glow from the porch wasn't the best, but it was more than enough to see their dazed faces. Of course the silence added to the shocking moment.

"You two are having a baby," Jax muttered beneath his breath as if fully processing everything.

"We already established that," Tanner growled. "But we're keeping it a secret for now, so—"

"Jade and Olivia know."

Tanner jolted next to her. "They know? You said you didn't want anyone to know yet."

"We knew she was pregnant, but not who the father was," Olivia stated.

Great. Livie and Jade came into view. Their faces matched the guys', and Melanie suddenly found herself even more tired than she'd been moments ago. Guess this took the worry out of when and how to tell everyone.

"Tanner is the father?" Jade exclaimed. "Well, well, well. Things just got more interesting."

Melanie threw her arms in the air. Exhausted, exasperated, more than ready to be done with this impromptu announcement. This was definitely not how she wanted to tell her friends who the father was, and she certainly wasn't ready for Cash and Jax to know.

"I'm taking Melanie home," Tanner stated. "She's tired, but for now let's keep this between us. Okay?"

"I can take myself home."

Tanner shot a glare her way. "You can, but you look exhausted, so stop arguing."

"Maybe you should let him take you," Livie stated. "You've been so tired lately."

"I'm pregnant, you guys. I'm not dying. I can drive a car."

"But when a sexy man wants to help, you should just let him," Jade added with a grin, shooting Tanner a wink.

Cash snorted. "You're one to give advice about a man helping you out. I tried to give you valid advice and you slapped me."

Jade waved her hand to dismiss him. "I wasn't talking to you, Flex."

Melanie couldn't help but laugh. Those two definitely had some issues. Personally, Melanie found Cash charming, but she could see where Jade would find that inflated ego off-putting.

But she had her own issues to deal with, and it wasn't the dynamics of whatever the hell was going on with Cash and Jade.

"I think I need another beer," Jax said, wrapping an arm around Livie's waist. "Is Piper asleep?"

"She is." Livie leaned her head against Jax's shoulder. "Maybe we should go back to the fire and leave Melanie and Tanner alone."

She didn't want to be alone with Tanner. Well, her body did. Her mind was telling her to get in her car and get home. The more she was around him, the stronger her attraction became, and she was starting to wonder if that was just baby hormones talking.

"I could use another beer, too." Cash stepped toward Melanie and wrapped an arm around her shoulders. "We're all here for you. I think I speak for everyone when I say we're shocked, but we're a damn loyal bunch. Except ol' Red over there."

Jade narrowed her eyes at the back of Cash's head. "Be more original than calling me Red, asshole."

Returning Cash's half hug, Melanie slid her arm around his waist and patted his back. "I appreciate the support. I'm a bit nervous, but I just need to get used to my new normal."

"And you need to rest," Tanner interjected. "Cash, get your hands off her."

Cash didn't release her as he leaned down and kissed her cheek. "He's territorial when it comes to what's his," Cash whispered in her ear.

Territorial? *His?*

Melanie didn't want to be anyone's property. She'd been down that road and it had nearly ruined her. She still carried the scars.

Part of her mind knew Cash was just using a figure of speech, but the other part fully feared she could slip back into that role of a secondary character in her own life story. She had to remain in the lead, damn it.

Being pregnant put her completely out of her realm of knowledge. How did she keep Tanner in the baby's life, but at a safe distance from her own?

"Don't be stubborn," Jade chimed in. "Just let Tanner take you home. I'll hang here for a bit longer so you two can talk."

"But—"

"We'll make arrangements to get your car home," Cash supplied. "I think Red and I can get along enough for that."

Melanie wasn't so sure, but she was so ready to get home, and if Jade thought she needed rest and to trust Tanner, then she'd go. Why was her mind such a jumbled mess lately? Why had everything she'd worked so hard to become suddenly morphed into the woman she used to be? Second-guessing every decision was the old Melanie—and apparently the pregnant Melanie.

"Let's go," she conceded. "I smell like smoke and I'm in desperate need of a shower and clean clothes."

She said her goodbyes to her friends and headed toward Tanner's truck. She wanted to protest when he got the door for her and assisted her up, but she knew picking on every single thing would just be petty. He was trying to help, he was trying to do the right thing and be there, but Melanie couldn't help but wonder how long that would last. When she got fat, would he still be there? When she was in labor, would he hold her hand? Would he take care of their baby so she could rest when she'd been up all night?

At what point would Tanner be done with her?

Chapter Six

I'm working on myself for myself by myself.
                                                   —Mel's Motivational Blog

She was going to make him fight this relationship—or whatever the hell they had going on—every step of the way.

Tanner waited while Melanie took a shower to rinse off the smoke. He told her he wanted to talk, but hell if he knew what he wanted to talk about. All he knew was that he didn't want to just leave her. He'd had a hell of a night trying to get a twenty-five-year-old mother of two and her children to safety. She'd been hesitant, especially when the kids started crying and were confused as to why there was a stranger trying to get them to leave.

Such a dramatic change in their lives, but necessary if they wanted security and safety. Tanner had held the weeping toddler in his arms while his partner had talked with the mother.

He'd taken longer than he'd originally thought, but as much as he'd wanted to get to the cookout and see his friends, see Melanie, that family had to come first. Then he'd felt guilty because he'd created his own family and they would have to come before the job.

So now he was waiting for Melanie to finish up because he hadn't seen her for a couple of days, and damn it, he just wanted to. He didn't want her to believe he'd just ditched her or their friends tonight. At some point he'd have to let her know a portion of what he was doing. Melanie deserved to know she wasn't coming in second.

For years, he'd been married to his job, but all of that would have to change and his priorities had to shift. Somehow, he'd figure everything out. Too many people needed him—whether they admitted it or not—and he wouldn't let them down.

Tanner had no idea what was going on between Melanie and him. The passion they'd shared hadn't stopped, at least not on his part. He still desired her just as much—no, more—than before the pregnancy announcement.

Speaking of announcement, he'd have some explaining to do to Jax and Cash when he saw them again. Knowing his nosy cousins, they'd show up at his house tonight or first thing in the morning.

No doubt they'd want to discuss his feelings and rehash the past. There was no need to state the obvious parallel circumstances. He knew this was going to be hell on his nerves for a while, but perhaps the doctor visit on Monday would help alleviate his fears somewhat.

Tanner took a seat on the new leather sofa. This house was Livie's childhood home, and she'd done some sprucing up when she'd originally intended to sell the place.

Livie, along with Jade and Melanie, had come into town when Livie's father had passed. He'd willed his old airport to her and Jax. Of course, those two hadn't seen eye to eye on anything, and Livie had been hell-bent on getting in and out of Haven, keeping her emotions out of the equation.

That had gone straight to hell when she and Jax fell in

love and Livie started playing mommy to Piper. Now they were all gearing up to renovate the run-down airport, making it into something grand and luxurious for higher-end clientele.

At first Tanner wasn't sold on the idea. High-end clients in Haven? But the film industry was booming in Georgia and more and more people were coming in to the small towns in the state. Why not offer them a quaint place that would cater to their needs and be more personable?

Actors, directors, producers, they were flocking in, and Livie had come up with a plan to accommodate this type of business.

So here they all were with a hand in the operation. Tanner didn't have quite a heavy hand other than voicing his opinion occasionally and renting a space for the Cessna Skycatcher he and Cash shared.

The water stopped running. Tanner glanced overhead, imagining Melanie stepping from the shower and toweling off. In their rush of frantic sex over a month ago, they hadn't taken all of their clothes off . . . something he regretted now. Tanner hadn't gotten to take his time and truly appreciate her.

That still irritated the hell out of him. She'd obviously had a hellish marriage and past before coming to town, and he'd treated her like a one-night stand.

Technically she had been just that, but it wasn't until after their night together that Tanner started kicking himself for not being a bit more of a gentleman. Apparently his bedroom manners had vanished about as quickly as a portion of their clothes.

Raking a hand down his face, Tanner pulled out his cell. He needed sleep in the worst way. Burning both ends of the candle was exhausting, but he wasn't leaving.

He focused on looking up random pregnancy facts instead of thinking of the naked woman so close, yet so far.

There were so many things he'd blocked out from before. Every pregnancy was different, every woman's body was different. He had to be mentally prepared this time. Maybe if he thrust himself into research and educating himself, he'd have a better grasp on how to handle all of this.

One site Tanner hit on had images he really hadn't readied himself for. Backing out of that one, he chose one that sounded less terrifying. Statistics of things that could go wrong was sure as hell not an area he wanted to read about. He knew full well what could go wrong.

He had no idea what he was looking for, though. Something to reassure him that everything would be fine. Some type of crystal ball into the future would be nice about now. He wanted to know what was going to go on with Melanie, with doctor's appointments—hell, with everything.

His first time going through this he'd been shut out. His fiancée had told him he was worrying too much and his worry made her nervous. He hadn't attended the appointments, except for the one where they learned they were having a boy.

A swell of emotions balled up in his throat and he gritted his teeth and shut his eyes, willing the past to stay where it belonged.

Tanner prided himself on always being prepared, but nothing could get you ready for losing everything. When he'd been in the air force, he'd educated himself on anything that would further his love of the skies. Then when he'd gotten out, he'd joined Haven's PD and always had a backup plan for any situation. He'd always had a sense of security, even during dangerous situations.

Right now, though, he was freefalling with no end in sight and no cushion.

He continued to scroll, reading about the different ultrasounds, the size of the baby at different weeks, how their little bodies developed at different stages. Fascinating and terrifying all at the same time.

When he scrolled by the term *preeclampsia* he'd had to keep going. There was no room for fear. Not with Melanie.

"Find something interesting?"

Tanner's gaze drifted to the doorway where Melanie stood smiling. "What? Oh, just reading."

"It must've been some article. I stood there for a good three minutes and you didn't even budge."

Had he been reading that long? How had he not noticed her there? So much for those cop instincts.

Melanie crossed the room and came to stand beside him. She tilted her head and glanced down to his phone. He watched as her brows shot up, her gaze darting to his.

"Reading up on all the things to come?"

Tanner set his phone on the antique coffee table in front of him and leaned back against the cushion. He wasn't ready to tell her he'd been down this path before. She'd want to know what happened, and informing her of how things ended wouldn't be the best. No need to incite fear in her when it wasn't necessary.

Melanie was different. This pregnancy was different. It had to be, and no matter how many times he had to repeat this mantra to himself, he would until he believed every single word.

Tanner raked his eyes over her, which was impossible not to do when she looked so damn good. Melanie had changed into a little pair of cotton shorts and a tank that molded to her curves. Was she trying to torment him? Her wet hair was twisted up on top of her head, and whatever soap or lotion she'd used was driving him out of his ever-loving mind.

Knowing Melanie, she had no clue about the power

she held. She was going for comfort and relaxing, but her innocent look had his imagination working overtime.

"Just trying to wrap my head around everything."

Melanie blew out a sigh and turned away. She crossed to the oversized leather chair with an ottoman in the corner. Tanner kept his focus on her as she curled up in the chair and stared back.

How could this awkwardness settle so easily between them when they'd been so hot for each other? Hell, he was still hot for her. She felt the same. He hadn't missed the way her breath caught when he'd held her earlier, he hadn't missed when her eyes widened a split second before darting down to his lips. Melanie was just as attracted . . . she just didn't want to be.

When she tried to stifle a yawn, Tanner felt guilty for hovering. That was something he'd have to work on so as not to freak her out, but it was damn hard not to want to be near her, to make sure she truly was okay.

"We can talk tomorrow," he told her. "I don't have to hang around."

Melanie shook her head. "You're fine. I mean, I'm tired, but the shower helped and I couldn't fall asleep if I went to bed now. Too much on my mind."

As busy as he was with work and the undercover evenings, Tanner had to remember she was the pregnant one and just as busy. In addition to her blog site, the social media accounts, most likely her emails exploding because of her popularity, she was also working the legal side of the airport renovations.

"How are the airport plans coming?" he asked.

Getting back on common ground and away from the attraction, the pregnancy, perhaps they could eradicate this damn uncomfortable tension.

She tipped her head and narrowed her eyes. "Not what I thought you were sticking around to talk about."

Tanner smiled. "I pride myself on keeping people on their toes."

Melanie gave a slight shrug and rested her cheek on the cushion. "They're actually coming along pretty well. All of the permits are a go. Zach is talking with the architect to finalize the design."

Speaking of busy, Zach Monroe was one hell of a construction worker, and in high demand. He and his brothers had opened a women's only resort and spa only two years ago. So many around the town had laughed at the concept of three manly men opening something so feminine. But then everyone learned they were fulfilling their late sister's dream.

Once word had gotten out, the place had exploded onto the map. Day-trippers from Savannah flocked in, ladies flew in for long weekends. Bella Vous was quite a sight. They'd branched out and had a small café run by Liam, the chef of the brothers.

Now Zach was putting some of his jobs aside to assist with the airport renovations and there wasn't a better man for that job.

"I need to get in another flight soon," Tanner commented. "I haven't been in too long."

"You're too busy with work."

He'd never thought being busy with work was a problem, but now that he had just added more to his life, he might need to reevaluate his schedule.

No, he hadn't just added to his life. He'd made a family. A family that needed him to provide security and stability. Melanie still worried about her ex. She'd hinted before, but Tanner wasn't going to let anything or anyone threaten his family.

"What is it you really wanted to talk about?" Melanie asked, unfolding her legs and stretching them out on the ottoman.

Damn. Those shapely legs and bare feet held his attention longer than they should've. Seeing her so relaxed, with a touch of heavy lids that reminded him of her face when he'd had her pinned against the door . . .

Tanner shifted his focus and leaned forward, resting his elbows on his knees. "I don't know, Mel. All I know is that I wanted to see you."

When she didn't say anything, he risked glancing her way again. She worried her bottom lip with her teeth for just a moment.

"You want honesty, that's it," he added.

"We agreed to one night," she murmured.

Tanner held back his laughter. "We didn't agree to any such thing. We were too busy breaking speed records getting back to my place and tearing each other's clothes off."

Her eyes widened. "I don't think we should talk about that night."

Irritated and more than turned on, Tanner came to his feet and made his way across the room. He sat on the edge of the ottoman right next to her feet.

"And why shouldn't we discuss it?"

He had to give her credit, she kept her eyes on his, even though he silently challenged her by staring right back. He wanted to know what she was thinking, what she was feeling. Damn it. He wanted her, and he knew full well she was just as attracted.

"Because of the way you're looking at me," she whispered.

Tanner couldn't suppress the smile. "And how is that?"

"Like you want me."

"Because I do."

Melanie stared at him a moment longer before she reached up and pulled the holder from her hair. Wet sections hung like thick ropes over her shoulder. She slid her fingers through the strands as she continued to hold his eyes.

"You can't say things like that. We have other issues than sexual attraction."

"My attraction isn't an issue," he countered, settling a hand on her ankle. She jerked beneath his touch, but didn't move. "Let me take you to dinner."

"It's late."

He slid his hand up to her calf. "I didn't mean now. Tomorrow."

"You think dating is going to solve things?"

"We both have to eat dinner." His hand slid an inch higher. "We should probably get to know each other even better, since we're bound for life now."

The second she tensed beneath his touch, Tanner knew he'd said the wrong words. When she tried to slide her leg from beneath his hand, he kept a firm hold.

"Don't," he warned. "Don't put me in some category when you have no idea where I truly belong. Get to know me, the real me."

Melanie tipped her head just enough to showcase her defiance. "I recognize power and control."

Tanner leaned forward just a bit. He didn't want her to be afraid of him, not ever. He'd seen the hell his mother had lived through at the harsh words of his father. He'd seen the eyes of the women he'd helped over the last year. Those who had been broken, beaten down, nearly destroyed, and were just trying to reclaim their lives.

Melanie had that. Every now and again he'd catch a flash in her eyes. If he hadn't worked so closely around evil, he might not have noticed. Then again, he noticed everything about Melanie.

"Power and control come in many different layers, Mel." He softened his tone, his touch on her leg. "You've only been exposed to the ugly side."

Those bright eyes narrowed. "You have no clue what I've been exposed to."

Dirty politician, jerk of a husband, a man who didn't appreciate the woman he had. Tanner had a pretty good idea.

"Then tell me." He removed his hand and shifted so he wasn't touching her at all. "Explain to me so I understand. Let me take you out."

She swung her legs to the side and came to her feet. As she started to pass him, Tanner reached out and held on to her hand until she turned her attention down to him.

"Why won't you let me in?"

Her thumb feathered over his knuckles a second before she removed her hand from his. "Because I can't afford to."

He'd never heard her so conflicted, but he didn't get a chance to question her parting shot. One moment she was looking at him with pain in her eyes and the next she was gone. He heard her mounting the steps and Tanner knew he'd pushed too hard, too fast. He'd made the mistake of assuming they could move forward based on their chemistry.

What now, though? As much as he wanted her physically, he wanted her to see him as non-threatening. She obviously hadn't been afraid of him before or she never would've slept with him.

Clearly this pregnancy had her more scared than he'd thought. Well, that made two of them. Even if he weren't so worried about the baby, about her, he'd still want her.

There was no denying that he'd been interested in her from the moment he'd pulled her over and given her a ticket her first day in Haven.

She had rolled that window down on her Beemer and glared at him over the tops of her gold sunglasses. She'd been irritated and so damn sexy.

The front door opened and closed and Tanner jumped to his feet.

"My eyes are closed," Jade announced. "Don't mind me."

Tanner couldn't help but laugh. "It's all clear," he called back.

Jade poked her head into the living room, her eyes darting all around until she finally zeroed in on Tanner. "Where's Melanie?"

Looping his thumbs through his belt loops, Tanner stepped forward. "She just went up to bed."

Jade stared at him a minute longer before crossing her arms over her chest. "I'm still processing all of this."

"I'd say that's the theme for all of us."

Pursing her lips, she continued to eye him. "Look, I know you're a great guy, but—"

"Really, Jade?" Tanner shook his head and offered his childhood friend a smile. "We've known each other for years. Are you really going to pull out the clichéd warning about hurting your friend?"

Jade blew out a sigh and dropped her hands. "Hell, Tanner, I was. I don't even know what to say to you or Melanie. You both have been through so much."

Tanner figured Jade knew everything about Melanie's marriage, and as much as he wanted to know, he respected Melanie enough to wait. She needed to be the one to tell him.

"I have a feeling she's been through far worse than I have," he replied.

"That would be a matter of opinion. You lost a great deal once." Jade smoothed her hair back from her face and offered him a smile. "Just give her time. She may seem tough and independent, but she's still healing."

"I can see that. I just wish she didn't lump me in with that asshole she was married to."

Jade reached out and patted his cheek. "Honestly, I don't think she knows any different. She's a strong woman, but even strong women have a weak spot. Her dad wasn't the best, so she's never had a good man in her life."

Tanner gritted his teeth. He wanted to hunt down the jerk dad and bastard of an ex and . . . hell, he didn't know. Every scenario that ran through his mind involved something that would strip him of his badge. Someone like Melanie's former husband would use his power to get what he wanted. Tanner couldn't even imagine what she'd endured.

How could anyone treat Melanie, or any woman for that matter, without their due respect?

"I know she's strong," he stated. "She wouldn't be here if she wasn't. I'm a patient man."

Jade took a step back and smiled. "I know you are, and you're exactly what she needs. Maybe you two can heal each other."

"That's pretty deep for you, Jade."

With a slight nod, a flash of a sad smile came and went. "Yeah, well, sometimes I can be sensitive, especially where my friends are concerned. Melanie is special. If you two knew the full backstory about each other, I think you'd understand each other so much more."

Something curled low in his gut. Trepidation? Maybe. He wasn't sure where he wanted the personal relationship to go with Mel. He knew he didn't want her to worry, he knew he was attracted, and he knew he'd never leave her alone to deal with a pregnancy and raising a child. *His* child.

"I need to get home."

Jade scrunched her nose, drawing her brows in. "You look like hell. You feeling okay?"

Leave it to Jade to be brutally honest after seconds ago being so sweet and caring. "Just working my ass off. Nothing a good night's sleep won't cure."

That is if he could sleep. Lately he'd been experiencing more and more anxiety. He didn't have time for that, and he sure as hell couldn't have anybody picking his brain and telling him to calm down or stop worrying.

He worried about each case he took on undercover. He worried about the kids and the impact on their young lives, he worried about the women who thought they had no choice sometimes but to return to the abuse they'd endured for far too long.

Maybe all of that made him a soft cop, but he couldn't change who he was. He'd been one of those young kids, he'd seen the damage hurtful words could cause. While he never witnessed his father raise a hand to his mother, he saw how day after day his mom had lost pieces of herself until she was a product of what his father wanted her to be.

"Hey. You alright?"

Tanner blinked Jade back into focus. "Yeah. I'm fine. I'll see myself out."

He shot her a slight grin when she continued to stare with those worried brows and frown.

"I'll see ya."

With a friendly kiss on her cheek, Tanner let himself out of the house. The cool fall night sent a chill through him as he made his way to his truck. Once he settled in behind the wheel, he glanced up to the second story of the old home and wondered which room Melanie used while she was here.

Then another thought hit him. Was she planning on staying in Haven? She'd never said one way or another. He knew she was here working on the legal side of the airport renovation, and with her blog site that she'd claimed was successful, she could work from anywhere, but had she decided to settle down in Haven?

Tanner thought of his simple one-story bungalow and couldn't help but wonder if Melanie would want a place like that for their child.

Melanie had been married to a wealthy politician; no doubt she'd had a fancier home and lavish lifestyle. Tanner only had a cop's salary. Not that he was poor. He didn't really spend his money, so he had a hefty nest egg.

Still, what could he offer her long-term?

Raking a hand over his face, he started his engine. Not only were his emotions all over the place thinking where they'd be years from now, Tanner also had to consider the fact that she might not even want to be part of this town once her involvement in the airport was done.

As he drove home, he blinked against the burn in his eyes and vowed to make this all okay. He needed Melanie and the baby to feel secure and safe. Anything else would be failing on his part.

Chapter Seven

*I love when the coffee kicks in and I realize what
an adorable badass I'm going to be today.*

—Mel's Motivational Blog

"Officer Lansing will be by around seven." Tanner held
his cell and let his gaze travel around the doctor's office
parking lot. "He is new to the department and not from the
area. He's perfect to put in place."

"And then what?" Cash asked.

Tanner kept his eye on his rearview mirrors, waiting for
Melanie's car. He was early, but he didn't want to miss this
first appointment. He'd rather wait for her. At least if she
saw him when she arrived, she might just take a small step
toward trusting him. Anything he could do to ease her
worries, he would.

"We're just setting someone in place to listen for chatter. Lansing is a young guy who lifts heavy. He'll fit right
in. You'll want to be there to sign him up and make sure
the appearances are all legit and real. The department is
paying the gym fees, by the way."

"I don't care about the money," Cash growled. "I want

those guys out of my gym. The thought of drugs going through my business—"

"We'll get them," Tanner assured his cousin. No doubt Cash's mind went immediately to his father, who had been in and out of rehab over the years. "But you'll have to learn patience."

Cash snorted. "You know that's not my strong suit. My patience ran out the second time I caught my wife cheating on me."

Tanner couldn't believe Cash had stuck around long enough for there to be a second time, but that had been his business. Between Cash, Jax, and Tanner, the three of them had endured their own personal hell when it came to women. They just rarely spoke of that time in their lives. Tanner knew Cash was a hell of a loyal man and no doubt he'd wanted his marriage to work. Clearly his ex had had other plans.

A flash of an older model black car caught his eye as Melanie pulled in a few spots away. "Listen, man, I have to go. I'll touch base later."

"You sure as hell will," Cash retorted. "I still haven't heard how the hell you and Melanie . . . well, how you two are suddenly going to be parents. What were you thinking?"

"At the time, I was thinking of one thing. Isn't that how this happens to everyone?"

"Smart-ass. You know what I meant. I'll be at Taps later if you want to meet up," Cash added. "First round is on me."

Tanner shut off his truck and stepped out, pocketing his keys. "Just make sure you're at the gym at seven to get things going for Lansing. I'll text you about a beer later."

As he disconnected the call and pocketed his phone, Tanner rounded his truck and met up with Melanie on the sidewalk.

She jerked around, clearly startled. "Oh, you're here."

"Did you think I wouldn't be?"

"Honestly, I wasn't sure." A smile spread across her face and hit him square in the chest. "I'm glad you made it. I mean, this is awkward, but I want this baby to know both parents, and if you plan on supporting me along the way . . ."

"I do." Tanner clenched his fists at his sides to prevent himself from doing something absurd like reaching for her. She was still learning to trust him and he had to remember that. "I told you I'm not going anywhere and I meant it."

"Well." She glanced toward the entrance to the doctor's office. "Let's go see what they have to say."

Tanner held the door open for her and waited while she filled out all the paperwork. The waiting room was full of pregnant women, some accompanied by toddlers and men who he assumed were potential new fathers. The pictures on the walls were of silhouettes of women in various states of pregnancy. Magazines had bare bellies on the front or women holding newborns. Every single place he looked he was assaulted with the images of what his life was about to spiral into.

He couldn't stop the assault on his mind of how excited he'd been once before. How the baby's name had been chosen, the crib had been purchased.

Tanner closed his eyes for a moment and attempted to get his breathing under control. He just needed to relax. There was nothing to worry about. They didn't have anything to go on in regards to problems. Melanie felt fine and no doubt the doctor would tell them shortly how healthy the baby was.

Melanie had turned in her paperwork and just sat back

down when his cell vibrated in his pocket. Even though he was off duty, he couldn't ignore calls or texts.

Tanner pulled out his phone, angling it away to check the caller. Disregarding the call, he slid the phone back in his pocket.

"You can get that," she told him.

"It can wait."

Melanie smoothed a hand down her little red sundress and crossed her legs. Even here in a waiting room where he knew her nerves were on high alert, she was all class and poised.

The damn thing vibrated again in his pocket. Tanner let out a sigh and pulled the phone back out. Different number, but still work related.

He shot off two quick texts stating that he would get with them in an hour or so, but if there was an emergency to let him know. He couldn't take off completely, but there were definitely things that could wait. From here on out, Melanie and the baby had to come first.

"I don't expect you to drop your life for me."

Tanner clutched his phone and turned at Melanie. "You should expect exactly that. This baby is more important than any job . . . and so are you."

Her eyes widened a fraction and he knew she hadn't expected him to put this appointment, this child, or her, first in his life. One day she'd come to see that he wasn't an enemy, that he wasn't out to control her or take charge. Tanner actually admired the hell out of her for her strength and independence. She'd truly made a life for herself after coming out of the shadows of her ex.

He had no idea what she thought about him being the father, but he sure as hell wouldn't use this child as a way to keep her in his clutches. Whatever battle she waged with herself, he wished like hell she wouldn't drag him along for the ride. Time would be his greatest asset, because he could tell her over and over that he'd be there and wouldn't let her down, but she would have to see for herself.

The waiting room of the doctor's office wasn't the time or the place to get into the whole host of topics they needed to cover.

Melanie turned to face him. "Tanner—"

"Melanie Ramsey," the nurse called from the doorway.

Those bright, wide eyes held his for a second. Whatever she'd been about to say would have to wait.

Melanie stared at the curser on the screen.

Blink. Blink. Blink.

The damn thing mocked her. She'd had a brilliant blog post, but each time she'd started compiling the words, they fell flat. Maybe she needed more creamer in her coffee to perk her up.

This had never happened since she'd started her blog as a way to hold herself accountable in moving on. She'd not ventured into this as a way to bash her old life or drag her ex through the mud. He was too powerful and knew too many people who could make her life hell.

No, Melanie had turned over a brand-new page once she decided to leave Neville. She'd finally put herself first. Her eating habits changed, her attitude changed, her outlook on life changed. All because of one online article she'd read about loving yourself before you could ever begin to love anyone else. The moment she'd read that piece, she knew she wanted a change. But not only did she want a change, she also wanted to inspire others. She wanted other women to know they weren't alone in their struggles, no matter what they may be.

Something in her posts and social media accounts resonated, and within the past two years she had absolutely exploded online. She had sponsored ads, and various businesses and entrepreneurs contacted her wanting a featured spot on her blog.

The little girl who'd grown up with nothing, then married into more money than she knew what to do with, had finally settled into a life she loved.

Right now, though, all she could think of was the doctor visit and how awkward she'd felt upon seeing Tanner in the parking lot. Then something had shifted and she found that she actually wanted him there. The fact that he'd taken off work for her shouldn't surprise her. She knew he was a loyal friend, but this was totally different. This baby had changed their lives forever.

Melanie reached for her peanut butter and banana protein shake and took a drink. She still couldn't get over how definite Tanner had sounded when he'd told her she should expect him to put his life aside. Like it was absolutely absurd for her to think otherwise.

She wasn't foolish enough to believe he was there strictly for her. He wanted to know what was going on with his child. Tanner might find her attractive, he might still want her, but that didn't mean a relationship. That was the dead last thing she wanted anyway.

However, she wasn't about to deny that when he'd been in that exam room and asked questions about the due date, the delivery, if there were classes they should take, sites they should explore, Melanie had melted. She never would've dreamed someone like Tanner, all big and buff and authoritative, would be so inquisitive.

He'd also asked more in-depth questions, things she

never would've thought of, that made her wonder just how much research he'd done beforehand.

Maybe there were layers to him that she hadn't fully uncovered because she'd found his actions, especially over the past couple days, more than attractive.

On a groan, Melanie put her shaker bottle back on her desk and tried to shift her focus back to the blog. She had a few blogs in reserve for emergencies, but daydreaming about the hunky officer who had given her the best night of her life, probably didn't constitute as an emergency.

Melanie shoved her hand through her hair and rested her elbow on the desk as she continued to stare at the blank screen just waiting for something to magically appear. She'd prescheduled the guest blogs for Wednesday and Saturday, so she wasn't shifting them. Today was all her— which had never been an issue before.

When her cell chimed and vibrated across the desk, Melanie jumped. She really needed to turn on some music to calm her nerves.

She glanced at the flash of text, but didn't get a good look before the screen went black. Eager for a distraction, she reached for her phone and brought it to life. Immediately she regretted that decision.

Call Me

Her heart clenched as she dropped the phone back onto the desk. Most people would see that message and never think of it as a threat. Those people hadn't been involved in her two-year marriage. Two years of pure hell and never knowing what the next day would bring.

Neville was always so careful with his texts. He'd never do anything she could use against him. She had enough blackmail material on him if she chose to go public.

But he'd granted her the divorce in exchange for her promised silence on what had really happened behind their closed doors.

During the course of their marriage, anytime she'd receive a text or call from him, fear would instantly settle in deep. Now when she saw his number pop up—she'd deleted his name—she didn't feel anything but rage. She'd changed her number four times since leaving. She finally gave up once she realized he would get her new number no matter what.

How dare he contact her, like she was going to respond? Did he truly believe she'd call? His assistants had often called or messaged, and Melanie chose not to talk to any of them, either. There had been one assistant Melanie had gotten somewhat close with. Of course Neville never knew or he'd have put a stop to that. He'd claimed she didn't need anybody but him. Friendships were off-limits because Melanie might actually confide in someone about the goings-on in the Prescott house.

Turning her phone over, Melanie turned back to the screen. Nothing motivated her like that reminder of what she'd come from and who she was now.

The cell chimed and vibrated again, but she ignored it. Her fingers flew over the keys as she started in with the topic of Making Your Own Happy. It had taken a long, long time, but Melanie could finally say she was happy. Thrown off by the unplanned pregnancy, yes, but she was happier than she'd been in, well, forever.

Removing herself from the clutches of Neville and knowing she held something over him had given her the courage and the power to leave. So why was he continuing to reach out to her?

At first he'd been all apologetic, but she'd heard that

before and didn't believe a word out of his lying lips. Then he'd slacked off a bit and now he was back full force.

Melanie opened up the music on her laptop and cranked her favorite song. Anything was better than the silence and thinking of her ex's next move. Jade had gone with Olivia to look at some restaurant booths and tables. Not that they were anywhere close to needing that stuff yet, but Sophie Monroe had given them a tip about a nice restaurant closing only a couple towns over.

Sophie had married Zach Monroe. The couple was quite dynamic, with Zach and his construction business and Sophie with her real estate office. They knew all the ins and outs in and around Haven. Anything to help save a dollar was going to add up in the long run. Melanie couldn't wait to see the end result of this airport. The vision and dreams they'd all discussed, the hard work and determination to pull this off, it would take time but be so worth it.

As Melanie continued to type, she started singing. She searched for images to slide in various points in her post.

"What the hell, Melanie?"

Melanie nearly fell back in her seat as her singing came to a halt and she jerked around to see Tanner in the doorway.

With a hand to her heart, she attempted to restore her breathing. "What on earth are you doing here?"

Tanner swiped a hand down his face, his chest heaving as he pulled in a deep breath. "I thought something was wrong. I called, but you didn't answer. I texted, no answer. Then I think I broke laws getting here. I rang your doorbell when I saw your car and bike outside, but . . . Damn it, can you turn that music down?"

Melanie reached back and tapped on the keyboard.

Pushing her seat back, she came to her feet and rested her hip on her desk. "What are you doing here, Tanner?"

"Right now I'm getting over the slight heart attack I had thinking something was wrong with you." He pulled in a deep breath and raked a hand over his jawline. "I took the day off work and I wanted to surprise you with something."

Shocked, Melanie crossed her arms over her chest. The second day off in a week? Maybe he truly was reprioritizing his life.

"You took time off to surprise me?"

Tanner shrugged. "I had an idea I thought you might enjoy. I never take time to myself. Trust me when I say the captain was more than eager to sign off on this."

Melanie heard the words, but things still weren't processing. Being cautious at every step was the only way she could move forward.

"Okay, so you never take vacation days and now you've done it twice just this week. You're sure you want to spend it with me?"

"Pretty sure we've already established that."

Yeah, they had, but that didn't mean she understood his reasoning any better. Neville had never surprised her with anything, let alone taken an entire day off. Melanie couldn't help but compare the two men because, honestly, she hadn't had many serious relationships.

Not that Tanner was a serious relationship, but they were certainly more than casual. Weren't they?

Not really. They were still getting to know each other as friends, they were barely above strangers trying to make this unexpected situation not so tense.

"I see the wheels turning in your mind." Tanner offered her one of those signature grins that had the corners of his eyes creasing in that sexy way only men could get away with. "If you're busy working, then that's fine. But if you're wondering why I'm asking or what this means between us, stop thinking. Let's just have a fun day without over-analyzing."

Something shifted inside her. He'd taken a day off work. The man who would sometimes just not show up to friends' events or have to leave in the middle of one because of his work demands, was here asking her out for fun. Maybe he needed this break just as much as she did.

"Can you give me five minutes?" she asked. "I've almost got this blog post ready to go live. I just need to tweak a few more things. Oh, then I'll need to change."

"You look fine."

Melanie stared down at her jeans and off-the-shoulder tee. "I'm a slob, Tanner."

"Throw on a pair of shoes and you'll be fine for what I have in mind."

Melanie eyed him, but he only quirked a brow as if daring her to argue. Not too long ago she'd never be caught outside without a properly fitted dress and stilettos, with her hair in a perfectly coiffed updo and her makeup on point.

To say coming to Haven had given her a new sense of freedom was a vast understatement. She hadn't even packed the items that the old Melanie would be seen with. Her new wardrobe consisted of comfort, her hair products were shampoo and a few rubber bands, and her makeup was lip gloss and some concealer.

Tanner continued to stare, waiting for her to answer him. She'd have to give a little, to learn to trust at some point. Why not start with the man who had fathered her child?

When was the last time she'd fully trusted a man? She had barely trusted her father, she'd never trusted Neville.

Melanie supposed she could add Jax to the short list of men she could rely on, because he'd been so loyal and faithful to Livie. Plus, he was an amazing father. The man hadn't thought twice about giving up his career in the air force and coming home for good when his wife left him just after Piper was born.

But putting all her trust in Tanner . . . she wasn't so sure that would ever happen. Oh, she'd trusted him briefly one night. If she hadn't been confident he wouldn't hurt her, she never would've slept with him. There were different levels of hurt, though. Melanie was pretty confident Tanner would never lay a hand on her.

Melanie turned from him and sank back into her chair. She couldn't start reliving that night. Not while he was in the same room as her, not while they were unchaperoned and her hormones were bouncing all over the place.

The planner in her wanted to put a label on whatever was happening. She wanted to look into the future and see exactly how this was all going to play out. There was no other way to keep her heart secured and her piece of mind in place.

After some minor adjusting, Melanie published her blog and shut down her laptop. Once Livie had moved out, Melanie set up a little makeshift office in the extra bedroom. With the desk tucked into the curved wall and looking out the windows, she often found herself sitting here daydreaming.

"Grab those shoes and let's go."

Melanie headed out of the room and into the bedroom she'd been using. She'd taken the smallest one at the end of the hall. Now that she was in here and Tanner stood in the doorway, the room seemed even tinier than ever.

"We're not going for a run or anything, are we?"

Tanner shook his head and pointed to her flats in the corner. "Throw those on."

Melanie glanced from the striped shoes back to him. "Those don't go with this at all. I need something more casual."

"We're not going where anyone will see you. Your shoes don't matter."

They mattered to her. That was one thing that hadn't been exorcised from her old life. She still wanted to look nice, but now she wanted to look nice for herself and no one else.

She pulled out a pair of red Converse and put them on. Her super casual look would have to do.

"I'm ready," she told him as she came to her feet and adjusted her tee. "So, can you tell me where we're going?"

"I could, but I'm not going to."

Melanie started for the doorway, but Tanner didn't budge. She wasn't backing down or shying away. She met his dark eyes.

"So you're taking me somewhere that we'll be alone and you won't tell me." Melanie tipped her head and pursed her lips. "Sounds suspicious."

Tanner reached out and tucked her hair behind her ear. "I assure you, you'll be safe with me. Always, Mel."

Chills raced over her skin at his declaration. She wanted to believe him. There was nothing more in this world she wanted than to believe that she'd find a worthy man to trust.

"I reserve the right to come home if I don't like this surprise," she told him.

Tanner laughed and slid his hand over hers before leading her from the room. She wasn't so sure how she felt about that. The simple touch shouldn't throw her off, but it did. They'd never held hands. They'd gone from awkward banter to sexual tension to sex in a foyer, but never once had they shared such a sweet moment.

Melanie decided she could let her guard down long enough to allow this. How else was she going to discover more about the father of her baby?

Chapter Eight

People in your life either inspire you or they drain you—pick them wisely.

—Mel's Motivational Blog

Tanner didn't know if this was the most absurd idea he'd had or if this was a stroke of brilliance. But, as he pulled into the airport and risked a glance at his passenger, he knew instantly he'd made an excellent decision. A breath he hadn't realized he'd been holding eased away some of his tension.

"Tell me we're going for a flight."

Smiling, he drove down the narrow gravel road toward the very last hangar where he and Cash kept their Cessna. "We are."

Melanie let out a little squeal. "I've wanted to go up in one of these planes, but I hated asking Jax since he's been so busy."

"You could've asked me anytime."

Tanner actually wished he'd thought to ask her months ago. He'd been attracted to her, but they'd rubbed each other wrong and he wasn't so sure asking her would've been wise.

Then again, maybe a plane ride would've been the better route to take as opposed to grinding on the dance floor and taking her home for a quickie. Yeah, he definitely needed some help with his gentlemanly manners, because where Melanie was concerned, his hormones seemed to override everything else.

"So, where are we going?" she asked, unbuckling her belt as he pulled into the parking space.

"Where do you want to go? I still have to go over the flight plan. I didn't choose a final destination because I wanted you to decide. We can go to lunch somewhere or we can just fly for a while and come back. It's your call."

He hadn't thought too far ahead in regards to plans. Tanner just missed the skies, and had double-checked with Cash to make sure he wasn't going to be using the plane today. But whenever possible, he wanted Melanie to have control. No matter how minor, no matter how silly it might seem, he wanted her to feel like she was in the driver's seat.

"Oh, no. I'm just along for the ride." She turned in her seat and flashed him a smile that cut straight to his gut. "I'm at your mercy."

Tanner's gaze dropped to her lips. Her pink tongue darted out and her eyes widened as if she realized the impact those words had in this enclosed space.

"I just meant—"

Tanner reached across and gripped her hand. "I know what you meant, Mel."

"Then why are you looking at me like that?"

"Like what?" he asked.

She blinked. "Like you want to kiss me."

"I've wanted to kiss you since you left my house that night. I can respect you enough to control myself, though."

Melanie's brows drew in. She closed her eyes and

shook her head before focusing back on him. "I don't understand you."

"I'm a pretty simple guy." With a past he wasn't ready to share and a job he couldn't. "You know I'm attracted to you. But for now, we're going to get to know each other."

"I'm not doing a relationship."

Tanner lifted her hand to his lips and kissed her knuckles. "I'm not, either. At least not today."

Melanie tipped her head and narrowed her eyes. "Tanner, I can't. This baby has to be our focus. Not the attraction."

Unable to help himself, Tanner closed the distance between them and nipped at her lips. "The attraction is only going to get stronger, so fighting it is a waste of energy."

Silence enveloped them and Tanner wanted to know what she was thinking. The fact she hadn't eased back or pulled her hand from his was a good sign. He wasn't quite sure himself what he wanted with her, but he needed to start somewhere. Chemistry was a hell of a place.

"I promise not to kiss or touch you in the plane." He sat back and watched as her lids fluttered open. "You'll be completely safe."

The side of Melanie's mouth kicked up. "I wouldn't go that far. Being in a confined space with you . . ."

"Care to finish that sentence?"

Melanie curled her lips in and shook her head. "I better not. Let's go for that flight. Take me anywhere for lunch. My treat."

Like hell. "When I take a woman on a date, I pay for the damn meal."

She tugged on her door handle. "This isn't a date."

Tanner reached across and took her hand once more. The movement brought him right back within an inch of her mouth. He covered her lips with his, swallowing her gasp. He ended the kiss just as abruptly as it started.

"This is a date, Mel."

He hopped out of the truck before she could disagree or give him another excuse to put her mouth to better use.

As he rounded the hood, Melanie hopped out and slammed the door. Of course she wouldn't wait on him to get the door for her.

"Uncle Tanner."

Tanner turned to see Piper racing across the gravel and grassy lot. Lopsided pigtails bounced with each step. The energetic girl never failed to put a smile on his face. Jax had done an incredible job raising her on his own. Tanner couldn't even imagine how scared Jax had been when his ex had decided to skip out on them. Tanner was terrified, and he had Melanie.

That last thought put an image in his head he wasn't quite ready to explore. He and Melanie weren't some happy little family. They were somewhere between strangers and friends with a baby in the middle. He'd done the family thing before. Well, he'd been on his way to the family life, but fate had stolen everything from him in a split second.

"Hi, Mel." Piper ran up and hugged Melanie around her legs. "Can I call you Mel? I've heard Uncle Tanner say that."

Melanie smiled and tugged on one pigtail. "I'd love for you to call me Mel. Is there a special name you want me to call you?"

Piper pursed her lips and scrunched her nose. "Hmm . . . I like Badass, but I don't think Dad will say yes to that one."

Tanner laughed. "Yeah. Your dad isn't going to go for that. You need a call sign."

"Yes!" she exclaimed, then drew her brows together. "But nothing will sound cool like you guys."

Tanner, Cash, and Jax all had call signs. Anyone in the air force had one, usually not one they preferred, but it definitely stuck, no matter what. Tanner had quickly learned that if you complained about your given nickname, another more offensive one would be given to you.

"I've got the perfect one," Tanner stated. "Pip."

Piper wrinkled her nose. "Pip? That doesn't sound fierce or brave."

Reaching out to tug on one of her curly pigtails, he shook his head. "Pip is just the nickname. You're brave and fierce, so you'll make the name way cool. How's that sound?"

She took about a second to process before her face lit up. "I love it! I'm the bravest girl here. Right, Uncle Tanner?"

"Absolutely."

Piper nodded as if affirming her new title. "Okay, Mel. You can call me Pip. Is that okay?"

Melanie took Piper's hand. "That's perfect. Tanner and I are going up in his plane. Do you want to come? If your dad says it's okay."

Tanner had no problem taking Piper, but at the same time, he'd wanted some one-on-one with Melanie. Which is precisely why he figured she invited the young chaperone.

"Daddy gave me chores." Piper pouted as she tugged on Melanie's hand and led her toward the offices. "Maybe if you come in and ask him."

"Hold up, Pip." Melanie stopped just outside the side entrance. "If your daddy needs you, I'm sure Tanner and I could take you another time."

Tanner didn't bother hiding his smile or flashing

Melanie a glance. Her implication that there would be another time thrilled him. Knowing she was eager to fly was definitely an added bonus to their attraction, the pull they had going on, whether she wanted to admit such a thing or not.

The baby would obviously bind them together, but Tanner wanted to get to know Melanie. He wanted to see where they went together, because he was absolutely on board with spending more time with her, in the bedroom and out.

"Piper!"

Jax's yell had Piper cringing. "Oops, gotta go."

She took off running back toward the office. Once she disappeared behind the rusty office door, Tanner reached for Melanie's hand. She turned and attempted to pull back, but he gave her a gentle squeeze.

"Don't do that."

Adjusting his shades, he asked, "Do what?"

"That smiling thing when you think you're getting away with something."

He hadn't even realized he was smiling, but now he couldn't stop himself. "I'm holding your hand, Melanie. I've gotten away with far more."

Her eyes widened a fraction before she tipped up that defiant chin in her signature move. Damn if he didn't find that attractive, too. A woman who challenged him, who made him smile more than he had in a while, how the hell could he pretend he didn't want her?

"Let's go," he stated, tugging her hand and leading her toward the far hangar. "If you're a good girl, I might even let you fly the plane."

"What? I've never flown a plane."

"Relax. You can take the controls once we're airborne

and I promise to talk you through everything. You think I'd let something happen?"

"I'm a little cautious when it comes to trust."

"No kidding. I hadn't noticed."

She glanced his way with a half grin. "You're a smart-ass."

Tanner shrugged. "I've been called worse."

He released her hand and slid the large hangar door open. Melanie squealed and ran inside to the Cessna. Just as he was about to follow, his cell vibrated in his pocket.

Please, please, don't let this be work.

He loved his job, loved helping where he could, but today he wanted to be completely selfish. After all the years he'd worked and put his personal life on hold, he deserved to take these stolen moments with Melanie.

When Tanner pulled his phone out, relief settled as he swiped across the screen to answer. "Hey, Mom."

"Hey, sweetheart. Is this a bad time?"

Tanner kept his eyes on Melanie as she slowly circled the plane. When she reached up and stroked her fingertips along the edge of the wing, he had to shut his eyes and focus on the fact that he was on the phone with his mother.

"No," he replied, turning away from Melanie and her tempting fingers. "What's up?"

"Thanksgiving."

That one word had him holding back a groan. Holidays were always a bone of contention. He worked and let someone else stay home with their family. Why should he take those days off when he didn't have a wife or children to spend time with?

This time next year would be a whole different scenario, though . . . and his mother still had no idea about the baby. Perhaps Thanksgiving would be the time to tell her she was getting a grandchild. Of course, he'd have to discuss that with Melanie and he wasn't so sure how she'd handle the whole "meet the mom" scene.

Raking a hand through his hair, Tanner sighed. "I'll be there."

Silence.

"Mom?"

"I'm here, I'm just not sure I heard you correctly. You mean you'll be here for dinner on actual Thanksgiving, or a week later when you can squeeze in family time?"

He focused his attention back to Melanie, who stood next to the plane, her eyes on his from across the hangar. Family time was about to take on a whole new meaning and priority in his world.

"I'll be there on Thursday," he assured her. "Just tell me the time."

"Oh," his mother gasped, then sniffed.

"Don't cry," he begged. Tears never did anything but make him feel awkward because he had no clue how to console. "It's just dinner, Mom."

"It's Thanksgiving," she said in her tear-clogged tone. "This is going to be the best year ever. I won't even ask about Christmas."

Tanner laughed. "We'll discuss that next month."

He weighed his decision for about a nanosecond before he decided to jump face-first into this next conversation.

"I'll be bringing someone, if you don't mind."

"Cash, or Jax and Piper?"

He had brought his cousins in the past, and his mother doted on them. Family was so important, and considering she was the sister of their late mothers, she adored the guys.

"Actually her name is Melanie."

Silence once again, followed by another sniffle.

"A holiday and a woman," she squealed, and Tanner

had to pull the phone away from his ear for a moment to save his eardrum. "I'm going to have to go back to the store and get ingredients for something special to make. Does she prefer chocolate or pumpkin for desserts? Or maybe I should pull out the recipe for my mother's cinnamon cake with that glazed icing."

Tanner started toward Melanie, her eyes locked on his, and he flashed a smile . . . the kind he knew she didn't want to see again. Too bad.

"I'll ask her." He covered the phone with his hand and whispered to Mel, "What's your favorite dessert?"

"Um . . . I have no idea. I don't recall the last time I had dessert." Her eyes narrowed as she darted a glance toward his phone. "Why? And who is on the phone?"

Tanner removed his hand. "She said to surprise her. See you Thursday. Love you."

He disconnected the call and slid the phone back into his pocket. Melanie's bright eyes were still in dramatic slits, completely focused on him.

"Who wanted to know about my likes and who do you love?"

Tanner leaned his shoulder against the side of his Cessna. "Is that jealousy I hear?"

"Of course it's not jealousy." Melanie rolled her eyes and crossed her arms over her chest. "But it's rude, considering the mother of your child is standing right here and you're on the phone telling someone you love them and—"

"My mother."

Melanie's mouth instantly snapped shut. "Oh. Well, then. Why was she asking about desserts?"

"Because you're coming to Thanksgiving dinner with me."

Tanner spun away, knowing full well she was about to

explode, and he didn't want to be standing too close. He wasn't completely stupid . . . only when it came to bringing her home to meet his mother without asking.

He started to circle the plane, doing his exterior pre-flight check, when a hand clamped around his arm.

"What the hell, Tanner?"

Spinning back around—yup, there was that anger if her pink-tinged cheeks were any indicator—Tanner removed his shades and hooked them on the V in his shirt.

"My mother called about Thanksgiving and I figured it was the perfect time for you two to meet, and we can tell her about the baby. She has to learn sometime. Why not then?"

Lips thinned, eyes widened, fists clenched at her sides. Maybe he was an idiot where she was concerned.

In his defense, he had no idea how the hell to deal with taking a woman home to meet his mother. He'd done so once with his fiancée, and his mom had gotten all excited about the upcoming wedding and the grandchild.

Damn it. He was indeed a complete and total moron.

Tanner spun around and paced to the open end of the hangar. He hadn't thought through the implications of taking another woman home, a *pregnant* woman, to meet his mother. Would she even be ready to jump on this roller coaster again? Because Tanner wasn't so sure he was ready, either, but he damn well wasn't going to allow himself the vulnerability of doubt. He had to be strong for Melanie, for the baby, for his own mother, who would no doubt be thrilled at the news.

"Tanner?"

At Melanie's questioning tone, he shifted back around to face her. She'd followed him, but stood a few feet away.

No longer was she staring at him with anger and disdain, but with concern and confusion.

"What's wrong?"

When was the right time to tell her about his past life? The life he hadn't planned, but had been ready to grab hold of and live to the fullest. When did he tell her he was terrified, if he was being brutally honest?

Never was the answer to that last question. He'd never admit that he was scared or worried. The last thing he needed was to cause Melanie any type of stress.

As for the question of when to tell her about his former family . . . now wasn't the time.

"I should've asked you first." There. He'd play it off like he was apologetic with regards to the holiday and his mother. "When she called she was so excited I was actually coming for dinner, I just asked if she cared about a guest."

Melanie pulled in a deep breath and licked her lips. She swiped her hand over the top of her hair and smoothed her fingers through her ponytail.

"I'm not sure how to do the whole family thing," she stated. "My father worked for my in-laws, so I always knew them in some way. I guess I never thought about your family or having to play the role of . . . I don't even know what to play here."

Tanner quickly realized Melanie was trying to figure out how to fit in. Had this been an issue in her previous life in Atlanta? Clearly, and that filled Tanner with rage when he thought of that asshole Melanie had been married to.

"Listen," Tanner stated, closing the gap between them. "My mother won't care if you burp at dinner or know which fork to use and have your napkin in your lap. There's no right or wrong."

Melanie stared back, unblinking. "There's always right and wrong. But don't worry, I know how to handle mothers."

"You're not listening." He reached for her hand, but she held them both up.

"I'm listening," she assured him. "I'm meeting your mother and we're telling her about the baby all while having Thanksgiving dinner. It sounds a hell of a lot more serious than I was ready for."

Tanner swallowed and shot a grin. "And here you just thought you needed to find some other term for today other than *date*."

Melanie laughed, which was exactly the response he wanted to pull from her. "This still isn't a date. Now, are you taking me up in this plane or not? I believe I was promised a flying lesson."

Tanner gestured back toward the plane. "Lead the way."

"You know, you are really good with Piper," Melanie said as she reached the side of the Cessna. "You guys are her family, aren't you?"

Tanner nodded as he reached into the cockpit and pulled out the pre-flight checklist. No matter how seasoned a pilot was, the checklist was of the utmost importance.

"Jax gave up everything for her when his ex skipped out," Tanner explained. "There's nothing Cash or I wouldn't do for them."

"She's one lucky little girl."

"Now that Livie is staying here, I'd say Piper hit the mother jackpot."

Melanie let out a laugh. "A year ago I never could've imagined Olivia in that role, but she's perfect here. Playing hostess and mommy. She smiles more than I've ever seen. Her job back in Atlanta was sucking the life out of her."

Tanner propped one arm along the wing and met Melanie's eyes. "And what about you? Was Atlanta sucking the life out of you?"

"I'm not sure I had much life left there," she murmured. "But today isn't about that, right? Let's go for a flight and leave our problems down here."

Tanner wanted to press her for more. He wanted to know everything she came from, everything that still haunted her. He wanted to slay every damn one of her dragons and make the rest of her world puppy dogs and rainbows.

Since when had he turned into such a sentimental guy? He was always quick to ride to the rescue, but after that he moved on to the next job.

Melanie wasn't a job, though. She was the mother of his child and the woman in his life whom he vowed to protect at all costs. Soon he would find out about her ex and what she was still dealing with there.

"Leaving our problems down here sounds like the perfect day," he agreed. "Now why don't we start your first lesson with the standard pre-flight check?"

Chapter Nine

Be somebody nobody thought you could be.
                    —Mel's Motivational Blog

Tanner eyed his Harley Fat Boy in the corner of his garage. Perhaps he should sell the thing. He hadn't found time to ride in too long, and with a baby coming he should probably start putting funds back for . . . hell, he didn't know. But getting a nest egg started sounded like the smart move to make.

He wasn't struggling for cash, but he was realistic enough to know that children weren't cheap and he didn't want Melanie to have to worry about anything. He had no clue what her financial status was, but he did know that when she was married she'd obviously had money . . . if Neville let her spend any.

That was just another aspect Tanner had no clue about.

Regardless, he would provide for Melanie and their child. He never wanted her to have to worry about anything like that.

After a hellish day at work, Tanner needed an outlet. He'd tried the punching bag in the basement, but he was still restless.

Being on the force meant no day was the same. Today wasn't anything too crazy, just one fender bender after another, and then some teen thought he could hold up the local bank with a water pistol in his jacket.

Tanner wasn't in the mood to head to Cash's gym and see all the people. Besides, his inside guy was working tonight and so far had come up with some tips that indeed drugs were being pushed through the gym.

Tanner wasn't going to Cash quite yet. Knowing Cash, he'd beat the shit out of the guys and then the system couldn't process the criminals. And Tanner really didn't want to arrest his own cousin for assault.

With his own little makeshift gym in the back of his garage, Tanner did several dead lifts, some pull-ups with the bar, and his free weights. With his shoulders and back burning, especially after he'd done the punching bag, Tanner took a hearty swig of water and dumped the rest of the bottle over his head to cool off.

The second he turned around, he spotted another item in the corner he hadn't touched in years. The rocking chair. After his fiancée and baby died, he'd covered the damn thing with a sheet.

This old wooden rocker had been the one his mother had used when he'd been a child and she'd passed it to him. It needed to be repaired and painted, but once he'd lost everything, he hadn't seen the point.

He also hadn't been able to bring himself to get rid of the silly thing. It wasn't like it was some heirloom passed down through generations. His mother simply thought he might like to have it.

Swiping the sweat from his forehead with the back of his arm, Tanner crossed to the rocker. With a swift jerk, he sent the dusty white sheet silently to the concrete floor. The rocker shifted, swaying back and forth from the sudden movement after years of being still.

He ran his hand along the rough edges of the arm. Maybe he could start working on this for Melanie. Did she have a vision of what she wanted in the nursery? Hell, where would the nursery even be? If he had his way, he'd put Mel in his home so he could keep an eye on her and the baby, but he hadn't been able to keep his own fiancée safe, and he knew Mel well enough to know she wouldn't just come because he asked. She would see him as over-bearing . . . which, when it came to this, he was.

For good reason, Melanie wanted to stand on her own right now. After years of hell, she wasn't going to take commands from him and he didn't expect her to. He respected the hell out of her and it was past time she understood that she should expect such admiration from a man. She deserved no less.

From the workbench across the garage, his cell chimed. Tanner turned from the rocking chair and crossed the space, circling his truck and reaching for his phone.

"Hey, Jax."

"Dude, are you busy?"

"Not at all." Living with his memories and struggling to compartmentalize them so he didn't screw up his future wasn't busy at all. "What's up?"

"How soon can you get over here?"

Already moving toward his truck, he hopped in and hit the garage door opener. "Less than ten. What's wrong?"

"Nothing major, I just need another set of hands."

Relief settled over him. "Damn it, man, I thought something was happening."

"Relax, copper. Piper flushed something down the toilet and I need help getting it out and cleaning up this mess."

"Shit."

"Exactly." Jax laughed.

Tanner turned off his street and headed toward Jax's house. "I'm suddenly busy."

Jax's laughter grew louder. "See you in a few."

He disconnected the call, leaving Tanner muttering another curse and setting his phone into his cup holder. Did five-year-olds flush things down toilets? Obviously, but Tanner would've thought Piper was beyond that stage. Not that Tanner knew much about stages of childhood.

Damn, how the hell was he going to parent? The entire process was scary as hell, and that was once the baby actually arrived. Tanner's anxiety had soared since finding out Melanie was expecting his child.

His heart beat faster in his chest as he gripped the wheel tighter with one hand and cranked the radio up with the other. He needed to relax and think in this moment. Not the past, not the unknowns of the future.

Tanner pulled into Jax's drive moments later and had calmed himself. As soon as he stepped from his truck, Livie stepped outside. Regal and poised as always, she had her blond hair pulled back and a nervous smile on her face.

"Anything else and I would've helped," she stated as Tanner made his way up the sidewalk. "But toilets are a hard no for me. I'll buy you any amount of beer, bourbon, steak, whatever. Just unclog the toilet in the master bath and leave me out of it."

Tanner placed a hand on her shoulder. "Relax, Livie. It's a toilet, not a bomb. What did Piper put down there, anyway?"

"I bought her a little bath set and she didn't want the shower gel so she said she tried to get rid of it, but didn't want me to see it in the trash."

"So she flushed a plastic bottle?" Tanner asked on a sigh and stepped around Livie. "Don't be too hard on her. At least she was trying to spare your feelings."

"I guess so, but Jax is pretty pissed and now Piper is crying in her room."

Ah, family life. He couldn't wait. Drama and tears, clogged toilets. Days of unknowns awaited him.

Of course he wasn't marrying Melanie and they weren't living together, so this wasn't exactly the same situation he'd have. But even with all the craziness in the Morgan household tonight, Tanner felt a pang of jealousy. Maybe he did want all of this—the crazy and the unexpected.

Tanner headed inside and up the stairs to the second floor. The second he stepped into the bathroom, he lost it and doubled over with laughter.

"Shut up," Jax said through gritted teeth. "Keep laughing and I'll give you a swirly as soon as this toilet is back up and running."

"Threaten me and I leave." Tanner squatted down beside the commode. "I assume you tried the plunger."

Jax's dry look answered the stupid question.

"Fine, so what's the plan?"

"We're taking the toilet off," Jax stated. "I'm going to go turn off the water valve and then we'll lift the toilet off and hopefully find the bottle of whatever the hell she put in here."

"Sounds like a fun night."

Jax rolled his eyes. "Were you spending it with Melanie?"

"No." Not that he wouldn't have in a heartbeat. "She's coming to Thanksgiving at Mom's, though."

Jax stilled for a split second before a shitty grin spread across his face. "Meeting the family. Sounds perfect for you two."

Tanner sank onto his butt and raked a hand over his face. "Can we just do this so I can get home?"

"Don't want to talk about family life?" Jax questioned. "It sneaks up on you, man. Nothing you can do but hang on for the ride."

"Yeah, I've discovered that. Twice."

Jax grabbed the wrench and tapped it against his palm. "You told Melanie about—"

"No. Not yet."

Coming to his feet, Jax blew out a sigh. "You don't have to take my advice, but if you want a future with her, not just the baby, but with Melanie, then you need to be completely honest."

Tanner nodded. "I don't want to have this conversation with you over your shitter."

Jax smiled. "You wouldn't want my advice no matter what. Figured now was as good a time as any."

Flipping Jax his middle finger, Tanner stood up. "Let's get this over with. I left your wife near tears, and apparently Piper is in her room crying, too."

"Yeah. Dealing with a clogged commode is nothing compared to two crying women."

"Ask your doctor about marathons."

Melanie chopped the cauliflower and eyed Jade across the island. "I'm not so sure about a big belly crossing the finish line."

"It's only two months out," Jade explained. "You won't be huge by that point."

"Who knows with me."

Jade set her phone on the island and braced her hands on the granite. "Listen, I'm sure you're concerned with the weight, but you're a different person now. You're supposed to gain when you're growing a person."

Melanie attempted a smile, but the burn in her throat

indicated tears were a definite threat. "It's still scary, Jade. I mean, I worked so hard to better myself and what if I lose sight of that person, that vision?"

"Or what if you are in the best shape of your life and inspire other women who are expecting?"

Melanie refocused her attention on the cauliflower. She was hoping to try a new recipe and take some pictures for her blog. The last recipe she'd posted two weeks ago had been a huge hit and had gotten her the attention of a few personal chefs. She was in contact with them now about guest appearing on her site. Bringing in people from various fields, like chefs and trainers and motivational speakers, was only one of the ways she'd expanded so quickly in such a short time.

"When are you announcing your pregnancy on your site?" Jade asked.

"I was thinking in the next couple weeks, but apparently I'm announcing it at Tanner's mother's house first."

"What?" Jade gasped.

Melanie met her friend's shocked gaze. "On Thanksgiving."

Jade let out a whistle. "Damn, girl. When you go for the family thing, you go all-in."

Using the edge of her knife, Melanie slid the chopped veggies to the side and pulled out another freshly washed chunk of cauliflower.

"This certainly wasn't my idea."

Jade shifted on her stool and crossed her arms on the island top. "But you're going along with it."

"Might as well, right? I mean, it's not like I can hide from his mother forever. She is going to be the grandmother to my child. I just hope she's not an ogre and overbearing."

Her ex-mother-in-law flashed through her mind. The

woman epitomized the MIL from hell. It was no wonder Neville was so damn controlling and abusive. His mom definitely wore the pants in the family and his father bowed to her every command.

Melanie couldn't even imagine what her life would've been had she gotten pregnant by Neville. A whole new level of hell she was thankful to have escaped.

"Tanner's mom is a sweet woman," Jade stated. "Trust me. In fact, you two may have something in common. Tanner's father was a complete asshole."

Melanie studied the notes on her phone to see what steps she needed to do next. Her recipes were completely original, but she always jotted down her ideas when they came to her.

"Tanner mentioned his mom remarried and his stepdad is nice."

Jade reached over and grabbed a piece of the sliced red pepper. "I've never met the stepdad, but that woman deserves all the happiness after what she endured. Same with you. I want to see you happy and I think Tanner is perfect for you."

Melanie set the knife down and glanced up from her phone. "Tanner and I aren't . . . we aren't . . . well, shit. I don't even know how to finish that."

"Exactly." Jade laughed. "This may have all started with physical, but you feel something for him."

"Of course I do," Melanie argued. "I'm having his child."

Jade leaned across the island, holding her gaze steady. "You know that's not what I meant. You feel something for him. Had you not gotten pregnant, would you have seen him again?"

Melanie wanted to deny it, but in all honesty, she wasn't sure she could've stayed away. Tanner tugged at something deep inside her. The strong, powerful man was sexy and intriguing and he continued to prove to her that he wasn't like her ex, that he respected her and he wanted to show her how she should be treated.

Everything about him had her wanting to discover more.

"You don't need to answer." Jade took a crunchy bite of the pepper. "I'll let that subject drop for now."

"I'm sure we'll revisit it before the night is over," Melanie muttered.

"Maybe, but let's discuss what you're making, because my stomach is growling."

Melanie smiled and shifted her phone around for Jade to see. "I thought this up the other night when I couldn't sleep. Tell me what you think."

Jade read over the notes before sliding the phone back across the island. "I think I want the first bite the second it comes out of the oven."

Melanie went to pull a baking sheet from the cabinet. "I love how you and Olivia always want to be my test dummies."

"And I love how she's gone now so it's all mine."

Melanie put everything together and slid the pan into the oven. After wiping her hands on a dish towel, she pulled a glass from the cabinet. She smiled at the outline of a plane and the words *Pilots: Looking down on people since 1903.*

When Olivia had come back home after her father passed, she'd made several changes in an attempt to sell the house and push her past behind her. But she'd kept most of her father's things, including the humorous dishes and several T-shirts with snarky pilot humor.

Melanie filled her glass with a smoothie concoction she'd made earlier.

"Care for some?" she asked, holding up the pitcher.

Jade shook her head. "I'm saving room for what you just put in the oven."

"Want to talk about Atlanta?"

With a slight jerk, Jade tipped her head and narrowed her eyes. "My issue with Atlanta or yours?"

"Yours."

"Not really." Jade blew out a long sigh, tapped her fingers on the counter, then shook her head with a humorless laugh. "What have you heard?"

"I didn't hear anything," Melanie stated. "But you've acted a little strange the past few days."

"How can you say that when you've barely seen me? I've been out with Brad nearly every night."

Melanie took a drink of her fruit smoothie. "That's my point. You hide from other people, but you've never steered clear of me or Livie."

"It's nothing major. I was offered my job back with a hefty bonus, but after the humiliation I endured and then to have my loyalty and reputation smeared, I think I'll find another route to take."

Jade had gone through too much emotional turmoil in her career over the last year and a half. She'd been a victim of sexual harassment by one of the partners in the firm, and then when she attempted to come forward, he'd denied all claims, stating it was Jade who had harassed him.

Once the truth finally came out, the other partner tripped all over himself trying to get Jade back.

"No amount of money could make you go back?" Melanie asked.

"None. I've saved enough over the years, but I'd rather downsize everything and live simply than go back there. Maybe I'll even build one of those tiny houses. I don't need anything major in my life."

"Good for you." Melanie peeked into the oven. "Just a few more minutes."

Jade's brow quirked. "Enough time that I want to hear more about you and Tanner."

Rolling her eyes, Melanie let out a groan and set her cup on the counter. "He's hot, okay? Is that what you want to know?"

"Obviously you're attracted or you wouldn't have slept with him. I want to know how you really feel."

"I wish I knew the answer to that as well. I mean, I go back and forth between wanting to get to know him more and then pulling back because I feel like I'm trapped. That's a terrible thing to say, but I'm being honest."

Jade came to her feet and circled the island. "Trapped because of the baby?"

Melanie nodded. "Not that the baby is trapping me, but I'm going to be part of Tanner's life forever, no matter what."

"Tanner isn't Neville."

A fact Melanie had reminded herself of, over and over. "I'm learning that. Just because I'm pregnant doesn't make Tanner and me some perfect couple. We had sex once and it's been awkward since."

"Awkward from sexual tension," Jade stated with a wry grin. "I've seen how that man looks at you and it's no wonder you couldn't hold out from sleeping with him. I don't know how he feels about you, but it's damn obvious he wants you. Bad."

Well, at least their physical attraction was on the same page. It was everything else that remained fuzzy.

"Why don't you just go to his house and have your wicked way with him?"

A bubble of laughter escaped her. "Jade, I was ballsy

one night and ended up pregnant. You know that's not usually me."

Jade shrugged. "You can't get pregnant again and there's no way he'd turn you down. Why don't you just go?"

Nerves spiraled through her. She wouldn't go because . . . well, just because. Sex and attraction was one thing, but shouldn't she be more controlled, focusing on her baby? Melanie's sex life wasn't top priority, which was a shame because Tanner was the second man she'd been with in her life and she was still reliving their passionate night together.

"I do like that gleam in your eye," Jade murmured. "But if you could fantasize later and get that dish out of the oven, I'd be grateful."

Melanie jerked from her thoughts and spun toward the counter for a pot holder. "Damn it. I almost forgot."

"Which is precisely why you need to go claim your man."

Her man? Was Tanner hers? Did she *want* him to be hers?

Melanie swirled one question after another around in her mind as she served Jade the new dish.

One thing was for certain, she wasn't so sure she could just march over to Tanner's and "claim" him. She may have gotten stronger and more courageous since her divorce, but she was still a woman longing for a man, and the fear of rejection of any kind kept her from what she wanted.

Chapter Ten

Cupcakes are muffins that believed in miracles.

—Mel's Motivational Blog

"Tell me again why I can't just beat the hell out of them?"

"Because Tanner doesn't want to arrest you," Jax told Cash.

Tanner propped his feet up on the edge of Jax's desk in his small office. They'd met up earlier in the day to get some demolition done. By doing some things themselves, they were saving money on these renovations.

"If these guys are peddling their drugs through my gym, I'm pretty sure I have a right to kick their asses."

Tanner laced his fingers over his abdomen. "You can do whatever you want, but don't bitch at me when I have to arrest you."

"Arrest them," Cash demanded.

"We will," Tanner assured him. "Following the law and letting the justice system work takes a little time. But I'd say we'll have them behind bars within the week. My guy on the inside is waiting to get the name of the supplier these guys are buying from. We want the top dog, too."

"Well, I want them out of my gym."

"He's got it covered," Jax chimed in. "Just let him do his job."

Cash took the final drink of water from his bottle and tossed the bottle into the trash in the corner. "Fine."

"When is Zach coming by?" Tanner asked, needing to shift the focus away from Cash's frustrations.

"He and his crew will be here Monday. I told him with the holiday coming up that he didn't need to stop and start."

The holiday. The one where he was taking Melanie to meet his mother and tell her about the baby. Just the first of many holidays that would be completely different now that Mel was in his life forever.

What would this time next year look like? Would they be sharing their time with the baby or would they live together? Would there ever come a time when she wanted to try to make this work like a legit family all under one roof?

"Livie is going to make dinner tomorrow if you guys are free and want to come," Jax invited.

"I'll never turn down a free meal." Cash stretched his legs out in front of him and crossed his ankles. "Tell me you're going to smoke the turkey."

"Is there any other way to have it?" Jax asked.

"I'm going to my mom's house," Tanner stated. "I never make it on the actual holiday, so there's no way I'll miss this year."

"You're taking quite a bit of time off lately," Jax commented, then shrugged. "Not that I'm judging. You need the breaks. Melanie is good for you."

That last statement stirred something deep inside him. At this point Melanie was the mother of his child, a one-night stand, and a friend. She was cautious, but he was persistent.

"Everything go well at the doctor visit?" Cash asked.

Tanner nodded. "So far everything with Melanie and the baby looks fine."

"You're still terrified."

Tanner eyed Cash and simply nodded. His cousins knew full well what he'd gone through before. They knew the pain he carried and the guilt that had never vanished.

"Hard not to be," he admitted. "She's hesitant to let me get too close and if I had it my way, I'd move her in with me so I could keep an eye on her."

Jax eased forward in his squeaky office chair and rested his forearms on the old metal desktop. "You can't save everyone, and Melanie will be fine."

Tanner nodded and pulled in a deep breath. "I keep telling myself that."

"Maybe if you clued her in to what you went through, she'd understand why you're so pushy," Cash stated.

"I'm not pushy."

Cash merely raised his brows.

Pushing to his feet, Tanner looked to his two cousins. "If we're done with the demo for the day, I'm heading home."

"Does that mean we're done sharing our feelings?" Cash asked.

Tanner flipped him the bird and headed toward the door. "Neither of you shared anything, you were too busy trying to get inside my head."

"Stay and have a beer with us," Jax invited. "I promise we'll stay out of your head."

"He's lying," Cash countered. "I want to annoy you some more."

Tanner shook his head. "I'm out."

He headed through the side entrance and around the mess of metal they'd removed from the exterior outdoor patio area. They'd managed quite a bit of demolition, and Tanner knew this place was going to look a whole lot worse before it got better. The renovations would take months, but in the end, the women's vision seemed to be huge and could be a total game changer for the tiny town of Haven.

Jade had been on to something when she'd tapped in to the fact that the film industry was coming in and out of parts of Georgia nearly all the time. With the taxes on the movie and television industry so low in Georgia, it was no wonder so many things were filmed here.

And the way Bella Vous had exploded onto the scene, pulling in so many women from literally all over the country, Tanner had a good feeling about Jax and Olivia's airport.

The thought of Bella Vous had Tanner taking a slight side trip to the women's only resort and spa. Liam Monroe ran the kitchen at the place and had recently opened a bakery. Tanner's side trip before heading home would be the perfect surprise for Melanie.

She might not like the way he pushed, but he wasn't backing down. Not when the chemistry was so great, and he was set on proving to her that he was in this forever.

Wait. Forever? Is that where this was going? Raising a baby was one thing, but going full force as a couple was entirely different.

Tanner pulled into the side parking area of Bella Vous and shot a quick text to Melanie to meet him at his house later. Even though they were going to Thanksgiving at his mother's house tomorrow, he wanted to see her tonight. Maybe the more time he spent with her, the more he could gather his thoughts and sort these jumbled up emotions.

One day at a time. That's all he had to keep telling himself. Between the anxiety and the worry, he was a mess. But keeping on top of his feelings was the only way to conquer this period in his life.

His cell vibrated in his hand and he thought for sure it would be Melanie responding, but one glance and he stilled. His boss on the private security detail he'd been working on had set up another time and place to go in and extract a woman and three children.

Tomorrow. Thanksgiving. Fabulous.

Tanner raked a hand down his face and battled an instant war with himself. He'd already hit the point of having to choose his work or his family.

Damn it.

He set the phone down without a reply and weighed his decision. There were plenty of men on the team, and Tanner had never missed a rescue, but he wanted to be there. That pit deep inside him that kept him going from one job to the next gnawed at him. He had to save anyone he could. There was a need inside him he couldn't explain.

But on the other hand, he also had other obligations he didn't have before. Melanie had to come first above all else, and tomorrow should be about family and his mother meeting Mel.

By the time this baby came, Tanner needed to reorganize. He'd been loyal to his career. Hell, he'd been married to his job for so long, but now he had to take a step back and truly work on time management and make sure his personal life was taken care of first.

Ignoring his phone, Tanner headed into the bakery entrance of the women's resort. The old pre–Civil War era home had been done up to reflect the time period. It was no wonder women flocked here year round. And the story of three brothers opening the place to honor the memory of their late sister didn't hurt in drawing the crowd, either.

As soon as he stepped inside, the aroma of pastries

assaulted his senses. The glass cases were filled with everything a person could want. This was definitely a sweet tooth's fantasy.

"Hey, man."

Tanner smiled as Liam Monroe came out of the back, wiping his hands on a towel. The once mysterious Monroe brother had truly come out of his shell now that he'd married Macy, and was pretty much forced to work with the public here at Bella Vous.

So much had changed for the Monroe brothers and this home, in such a short amount of time. Tanner sure as hell wished the same success for Jax and Livie and their vision for the airport.

"Haven't seen you in here since the bakery opened to the public."

"Thought it was time I came by and saw what all the fuss was about," Tanner replied.

Liam rested his arms on the top of the case. "We've been busy, that's for sure. What can I get you?"

The wedding ring on Liam's finger glinted in the light. Tanner was thrilled Macy and Liam had found each other. They were perfect together and Tanner figured Macy had a hand in keeping Liam in town when he'd wanted to be anywhere else.

"What do you recommend?" Tanner asked, glancing through all of the options. From the looks of the full trays, there wasn't a bad option. Sugar and icing? Yeah, not a bad option at all.

"The éclairs are always a hit. I just made an apple spice cupcake, which is seasonal, and I have pumpkin tarts. There is a cinnamon pumpkin bread I'm getting out of the oven soon, if you want to wait around for that."

Hell, he had no idea what to get Melanie. Was she a

chocolate lover? Did she get wrapped up in the pumpkin craze like so many did this time of year?

There were so many things he didn't know about her. But she'd said she didn't recall the last time she'd had a cupcake, so that helped him narrow his choices down.

"I'll take two of the apple cupcakes."

"Good choice." Liam folded a small white box and carefully placed two cupcakes inside. Then he added an éclair. "On the house because I know you'll love them."

Tanner laughed as he pulled out his wallet and counted out some bills. "Is that how you get people coming back? You throw in a freebie?"

Liam set the box on the counter. "I'm a businessman. It's how we work."

"Business is going well, then?" Tanner asked. "I know the resort is always booked, but the bakery is everything you wanted?"

"It really is. I never knew this place would take off the way it did. When Chelsea passed and we found her notes . . . hell, I thought my brothers were crazy for wanting to do this."

The three Monroe boys had lost their sister a few years back, but they'd all come together to fulfill her dream of this women's resort and spa. Like everyone else in the town, Tanner had wondered how this would go over, but the guys had pulled it together, with the help of their now spouses, and Bella Vous was the biggest hit Haven had ever seen.

"How's the airport renovations coming?" Liam asked. "I've heard rumors you guys are making it something grand."

"We're hoping to," Tanner replied. "We've been working

hard on it, but time will tell if we're making a mistake or if it will pay off in the end."

Liam smiled, and the scar running along his cheek creased. "Taking a risk is the only way to find out, but I have a feeling you guys are going to be just fine."

"I sure as hell hope so. We've invested quite a bit into this project." Tanner paid for the desserts and grabbed the box from the counter. "Tell Macy I said hi."

Liam nodded. "Will do, buddy. Don't be a stranger."

"Oh, I'm sure I'll be back soon."

When Tanner got back into his truck, he checked his phone and couldn't help the sliver of relief when he saw Melanie's message that she'd meet him at his place in an hour. That gave him enough time to get home and shower, because he was a mess after working all morning at the airport.

He made his way home and left the box of tempting treats on the kitchen island while he cleaned up. By the time he got out of the shower and dressed in jeans and a tee, he knew he needed to give his superior a heads-up about tomorrow.

Tanner took a seat at his bar in the kitchen and sent a text explaining that he'd be unable to participate in the rescue tomorrow. He didn't make excuses or apologize. He'd never taken time off from this project before, and he didn't figure this would be a problem unless others had already bowed out.

He'd worry about that later if need be.

Tanner sent a coded text to the officer involved in the gym sting. Hopefully he hadn't been lying when he'd told Cash they'd wrap this up this week. They were close, so close, but Tanner and his captain wanted the name of the top dealer. This was their best chance at getting it.

Setting his phone down, Tanner raked his hands down his face. He wasn't used to bouncing between his work and family, but that's exactly the territory he was venturing into.

When his doorbell rang, he left his phone and headed down the hallway toward the entryway. Darkness had settled in already, thanks to the time of year. Tanner flicked on the porch light and the light to the foyer. With a flick of the lock, he opened the door.

"Sorry about the darkness," he stated. "I lost track of time."

Melanie smoothed her hair behind her shoulders and shrugged. "No big deal."

Tanner stepped back and gestured her inside. When she offered him a shaky smile, he reached for her arm before she could pass him by.

Her eyes darted to his, her face just a breath away.

"Tanner," she muttered.

Without giving himself much time to think things through, he closed the distance between them and covered her mouth. Feathering his lips across hers, he waited until she relaxed before he slid his hand up her arm, over her shoulder, and cupped the back of her head.

How had he gone without tasting her for nearly two months? Melanie was sweeter than he'd remembered. Her body shifted against his as she reached up and threaded her fingers through his hair. Tanner nipped at her bottom lip before easing back. As much as he wanted to completely devour her, he also wanted to take things slow until she was comfortable with his touch.

Ironic considering their current status, but he needed Melanie to feel secure.

"Why did you kiss me?" she whispered.

Tanner eased his hand around and ran his thumb over her moist bottom lip. "Because I've been wanting to since we slept together and because you looked tense as hell when you walked in here."

"I am tense," she replied with a half smile. "You ask me to come over and I don't know if you want to talk or rip my clothes off."

Tanner couldn't stop his laughter. "You're always honest. I appreciate that. And for the record, if I thought tearing your clothes off was something you were on board with, you'd already be naked."

Melanie's bright eyes darkened just enough for him to see the arousal staring back at him. Perfect. He didn't want her immune to this chemistry.

"How are you feeling?" he asked as he closed the door behind her.

When he turned, he reached for her purse and hung it on one of the pegs beside the door.

"I'm feeling good. A little tired and had some nausea this morning, but the doctor said all of that was to be expected."

Tanner didn't want her to feel anything but perfect, but he also knew she was carrying a child. There would be difficult days, he just prayed like hell nothing would go wrong.

"Hey." She reached out and touched his arm. "Everything okay?"

He wasn't ready to get into the past. "I'm fine. I asked you over because I wanted to see you, but I picked up a surprise for you."

Melanie's brows shot toward her hairline. "A surprise? What on earth for?"

"Because I wanted to."

She propped one hand on her hip, pulling her long-sleeved tee tighter across her chest. "You got me a surprise for no reason at all?"

"Why is this so hard for you to believe?" he asked. "Trust me, it's nothing major."

"Still, I'm just . . . confused."

That pretty much told him all he needed to know about the prick she'd been married to, or any other man that had come along in her life. Clearly she'd never been taken off guard in a good way, and Tanner vowed to make this the first of many.

"Maybe you should have more surprises in your life," he told her as he took her hand. "Follow me."

"Did you get me a dog? I always thought when I had kids I'd have a dog, too. I feel like they go hand in hand, you know?"

Tanner laughed as he led her down the hallway toward the kitchen. "Sorry. That can be the next surprise."

"It's not much of a surprise if you tell me, but if you get me a dog, make sure it's a rescue animal. I'm a firm believer in the adopt-don't-shop motto."

He stopped and turned to face her. "You'd want a rescue dog?"

"Of course." Those beautiful eyes held his and gave another punch of lust to his gut. Damn it, he could still taste her. "Why buy an expensive dog or one from a puppy mill where the moms are abused? There are so many precious dogs at the shelters. It's heartbreaking."

Melanie continued to amaze him in so many different ways. "I never would've taken you for a shelter shopper."

"Well, I've never had a dog," she amended. "But there's no way I'd pay for one. I'd love to rescue them all if I had the land to care for them. I definitely think I'll get at least one or two when I find my own place."

"Maybe we should go look for a dog, then."

Where had that come from? He'd invited her over for a

damn cupcake, not to get a joint pet. When the hell could he take care of one? Added to that, they didn't live together. Did he want to share custody of a child and a dog?

Tanner didn't want to share. Period. He wanted to do everything with Melanie—together. While he'd resisted all committed relationships for years, he couldn't keep denying he wanted to at least give it a try with her.

"We?" she asked, her eyes wide.

"Move in here for now until you decide what to do."

Okay, really. Why did he keep opening his mouth and letting thoughts come out before he fully thought them through? Although, he wouldn't mind one bit if Melanie moved in here. He could keep an eye on her better that way and they could get to know each other even more.

Fine, he also wanted the hell out of her and craved her in his bed. Having her close would only make sense. Why shouldn't they explore their attraction? Why was a sudden halt put on things simply because she was expecting a baby?

Melanie held up her hands. "I mention a dog and you suddenly want me to move in? Tanner, we're not some big happy family."

The knot in his gut tightened. Once upon a time he'd wanted that big happy family. Now fate was dangling the possibility in front of his face once again.

"You want a place for a dog," he justified, like this solution made all the sense in the world. "Plus you don't want to stay in Livie's old house forever."

"I said that I meant to get a place of my own." Vibrant eyes held his gaze a moment before she blinked and glanced away. "Moving in together is hardly the answer."

The more he thought about it, the more he realized it was the perfect answer, and damn if he wasn't going to fight for what he wanted.

"Think about it."

Melanie tipped her head and in a surprising move, she reached out and patted his chest as she offered him a smile. "Are you always this relentless?"

Tanner grabbed her hand and kissed her palm. Heat flared in her eyes. "When I want something bad enough," he replied.

"Maybe we should move on to the surprise and table this discussion for another time," she suggested.

Tanner released her hand and turned toward the center island. "You said something the other day that had me thinking, so I stopped at Bella Vous and picked up something for you."

"Really?" Her smile widened. "Is it a massage? Because Cora Monroe gives the best massages. I had one when Livie's dad passed and we stayed at the resort before the funeral. Man, I could seriously use another."

He'd text Macy later and have her schedule a massage for Mel at the very next opening.

"Sorry, no massage, but something I think you'll enjoy just as much." Melanie could definitely use the relaxation time. He should've thought of that already. "I actually went to the bakery and Liam hooked me up with a few pastries."

Melanie's smile faltered as she spotted the white box on the counter.

Tanner wasn't sure why she suddenly seemed so . . . hell, he couldn't even put a word to the look on her face. He lifted the lid and presented the treats, never taking his eyes off that pained look on her face.

"Liam said these were some of his favorites," Tanner stated. "The other day you told me you hadn't had desserts for some time, so I thought what better chance than from the greatest baker in Haven. Actually, probably all of

Georgia considering he worked for Magnolias, the most popular restaurant in Atlanta, before coming here."

Her eyes were fixed on the box, and for a half second Tanner feared she was going to start crying. She remained silent as she continued to stare. Tanner waited for her to say something, anything, or even make a motion. Hell, she wasn't even blinking.

"Melanie?"

She jerked and turned her attention to him. "Is this a joke?"

Confused, Tanner rested his hand on the island and propped his other on his hip. "What's wrong? I thought you'd love this."

"What's wrong?" Melanie threw her arms in the air and spun around, then began pacing like some caged animal who had nowhere to go. "What's wrong is I've been down this path before. You can't make me into someone you can control and keep on a tight leash. I won't fall into that trap ever again."

Tanner pushed away from the counter and crossed to where Melanie stood facing the patio doors, staring out into the backyard. His hands gripped her shoulders, and he didn't give a damn that she tensed when he eased her back against his chest. The war she waged with herself apparently was going to spill over into whatever they had going on, and there was no way in hell he would let her battle this alone.

"Talk to me," he murmured into her ear. "What got you so upset over seeing that box?"

Something had triggered in her memory bank. Whatever it was, he was hell-bent on eradicating the old flashes of fear and replacing them with only happy thoughts and hope for the future.

She'd yet to relax against him, so he slid his hands

down her arms and wrapped his arms around her waist. Tanner wasn't always the best at consoling, but right now Melanie needed to be held, whether she wanted to admit it or not.

"I'm sorry," she whispered. "I shouldn't have exploded on you like that."

"Don't apologize for someone else's actions, because that stems from your past, I'm sure. I can take your words, Mel, but I can't take you being hurt or shutting me out when I want to help."

She pulled in a shaky breath. "I was heavy my entire life up until about two-and-a-half years ago."

"I saw that on your blog."

Melanie twisted in his arms just enough to peek up at him. "You read my blog?"

"I wanted to find out more about you."

Now she did offer a smile that released some of her pent-up energy. She settled a little more against him as she refocused her attention out the back door. Night had fallen and the back lights had kicked on, but with that added glow, he could see her reflection so perfectly.

The image of them together, standing in such an intimate way, had Tanner growing more accustomed to the idea of her living here. He'd never invited another woman to live with him. Even his fiancée hadn't lived with him. They'd been young and in the beginning stages of planning when his life had turned to shit.

Tanner didn't want to say anything, he wanted Melanie to work this out on her own and go at her own pace. Finally, she was opening up to him about her past. He wasn't sure how far she would delve into it, but he had a feeling he was going to be pissed at what she'd endured.

"My ex was fine with me being overweight," she went on. "In fact, he was all too eager to make sure I stayed that way. He was jealous, to say the least. Anything to keep another guy from looking at me. Neville liked to exploit the fact I was a smart attorney, but he never called me pretty or seemed proud of me. I was a pawn in his game to further his political career."

Tanner gritted his teeth and struggled to find the right words. Neville was a grade-A bastard.

"What made you decide to get away?"

"One night I couldn't sleep, so I was online reading different blogs and I stumbled upon one called *Women Empowering Women*. As soon as I read a few paragraphs, I knew I wanted to motivate other women, too. But I also knew in my current state, I couldn't do that."

"Are you talking about your weight, or the fact that your ex was abusive?"

Melanie tensed and pulled away from his arms. Instantly he regretted his words.

"Mel—"

"No." She held up her hands. "Don't apologize for speaking the truth. Honestly, I knew I couldn't keep going because of all of that. Everything about my life was unhealthy, from my weight to my marriage. I started walking, which led to running. I was damn slow, but I was moving, and for the first time in my life I was doing something for me. Neville didn't know this until the weight started to gradually come off. Needless to say he was angry."

Tanner watched Mel as she glanced at the box of pastries and back to him. "That's when I told him I was leaving," she went on. "I was done living that life, being in a prison and posing as a happy couple for the sake of his political career."

"And he just let you go?"

Melanie twisted her hands in front of her for a moment,

then smoothed down her shirt and tipped her head up. "No. I blackmailed him and left him no choice."

Tanner crossed his arms over his chest. "What type of blackmail?"

Melanie circled the island and surveyed the inside of the bakery box. She grabbed a cupcake and peeled away the lining little by little.

"That's a story for another time, and right now I'm going to dive face-first into this cupcake and give the proverbial middle finger to my ex."

"You don't have to—"

She leveled his gaze. "Yes, I do. Care to join me in a celebration?"

This woman was so damn remarkable he didn't know what to expect next from her. Every part of him wanted to know the blackmail she had on Neville, though he suspected he knew. Most likely she had images of the abuse or recorded account of an act. No politician wanted that type of negativity out there for the voters to see.

"I can't turn down sugar." Tanner reached across the island and grabbed the éclair. "It's a weakness of mine, which is why I'm often in the gym."

"Oh, please," she said around a bite, "you are perfectly fine. Men carry weight better than women."

Tanner set his pastry down and waited until he caught her attention once again. "When I saw your blog, you need to know that the before-and-after pictures you posted regarding your weight were both beautiful. I'm glad your confidence is higher and I'm proud of you for encouraging other women, but you are a stunning woman. No added pounds could change that."

He needed her to know this, he needed her to see that she was beautiful inside and out, because he was confident nobody in her life had ever told her. And it was well past time she started seeing herself for the remarkable woman she truly was.

Yes, she put up amazing posts about confidence, but he saw how she still fidgeted with her hands or her purse when she was nervous and how she averted her gaze when a topic hit too close to home.

Melanie had a successful online base for inspiring women, but who was inspiring her?

Tanner felt as if each day with Melanie came with a new set of rules and goals. There was so much to take in with her, and he feared the only way to accomplish everything was to get her to see that he was completely serious when it came to wanting a relationship.

Chapter Eleven

*If you were able to believe in Santa for nine years,
you can believe in yourself for five minutes.*

—Mel's Motivational Blog

Melanie wasn't sure what to say. She was positive she had a blank look on her face and quite possibly icing on her lips, but she was utterly stunned at the passion in Tanner's tone. He meant every single word.

When was the last time someone had commanded her attention to tell her such things? When was the last time someone made her see herself in a different light?

Jade and Livie were great at such things, but they were her best friends. Tanner didn't have to tell her anything, yet he made sure she was looking at him when he laid down his claim with such conviction.

"Wow," she muttered, putting her cupcake down and brushing her hand across her mouth. "I don't even know what to say."

"You don't have to say anything. You have to believe what I'm telling you."

She wanted to. Hearing him say things that she'd said herself on her blog was strange. She'd always been the one doling out advice and reaching out to women who needed an extra lift in life. Sometimes she threw in humor to keep the daily motivations uplifting, and random times she would even feel a boost from her viewers' comments. But to have a man she cared for say something so meaningful, straight to her face . . . she had no clue how to react.

"I want to believe you." Melanie made her way around the island, coming to stand directly in front of Tanner. "I guess I never realized I lacked in that area. I mean, I'm putting myself out there every day, and I believe what I'm telling my viewers is the best advice for them."

"Do you feel that way about yourself?" he asked, reaching to take her hand in his.

Melanie weighed her words carefully. "I know that I'm a better person than I was two years ago. I know that each day I get stronger and I want to be better tomorrow than I am today. That's how I move forward."

Tanner lifted her hand to his mouth and kissed her palm. The heat from his touch, the bristle of his stubble against her skin had her trembling. Anticipation, need, arousal, all spiraled through her. She shouldn't want him. She shouldn't trust herself to fall back into a relationship, but he said all the right things, did all the right things.

How could she deny the way he made her feel? Each time she was near him, each time he looked at her, there were sensations she couldn't explain . . . mainly because she'd never felt them before. That in and of itself terrified her. As if expecting his baby weren't enough of a scare.

"Don't," she murmured.

He kissed her palm again. "Don't what?"

"All of this. The surprise, the kisses, the looks."

"What looks are you referring to?" he asked, still holding on to her hand within a breath of his lips.

"The one where you look like . . ."

A ghost of a smile danced around his mouth. "Like what? Like I want you? I do. Every minute I'm with you I want you, Mel."

"We had one night," she hurried to say because her heart was beating too fast, her emotions were threatening to overtake her. "It was great, but we can't do this, Tanner."

"Give me one good reason."

"Because. Well, we can't."

Damn it. Her reasons sounded weak and clueless. But she wasn't clueless. She was hopeless when it came to this man. For two years she'd built up a resolve and shored up her defenses, yet Tanner had pushed and pushed against each one. He forced her to open her eyes and see things she wasn't ready to see . . . like a relationship.

A slight tug of her hand and Melanie tumbled against Tanner's chest. She looked into his eyes, those dark, heavy-lidded eyes that held her captive.

"Why don't you keep trying to think of excuses," he stated. "And I'll work on every reason why this is a good idea."

Before she could question his intentions, he snaked an arm around her waist and covered her mouth with his. The sweet taste of his pastry mixed with hers, and there was no dessert that compared to being kissed by Tanner Roark. She was utterly helpless. But not in the way she'd once been. No, this was the type of helplessness that was positively glorious and made her want to rip his clothes off and go for an encore of their first experience.

Melanie threaded her fingers through his hair and opened for him. When both of his arms banded against the small of her back, he pulled her tighter against him, causing her body to arch. He tipped her back and completely took over the kiss and the amazing assault on her senses.

Being held by such a strong man, being cherished by him, was still so new and something she wanted to cling to and relish for as long as possible.

Tanner nipped at her bottom lip before easing back slightly. "If you need me to stop, say so now."

The Melanie that lived in fear of being controlled emotionally and physically told her to put an end to this, but the new Melanie, the one who ached for this man, had no words.

Leaning forward to close the gap, she slid her lips across his. Tanner obviously took that as the green light he'd been waiting for, because he lifted her up and started carrying her from the room. She wrapped her legs around his waist and marveled at his strength as he moved through the hallway and headed toward the stairs.

"You can't carry me up there."

Both his hands gripped her backside as he whispered in her ear, "Challenge accepted."

Melanie wrapped her arms around his neck and closed her eyes. Arousal pumped through her fiercer than she'd ever known. By the time they reached the top landing, Tanner still had a tight hold on her and wasn't even breathing hard. There was something to be said about a man who was strong, sexy, and determined.

Tanner moved on down the narrow hallway and turned into a room. She'd never been up here before and hadn't ever planned on it, actually.

Yet here she was in Tanner's bedroom, and the anticipation coiled tight within her.

He released her and she slid down his body until she stood firmly on her feet. The only light was the glow from the full moon coming in the window through the open curtains. He reached down to the nightstand and clicked on the lamp.

"I was fine in the dark," she said, hoping her nerves weren't showing too much.

Tanner raked his eyes over her, giving her a visual sampling that had her heating up even more. "I want to see you. The last time didn't nearly satisfy my craving."

Oh, those clever words he said. She'd never known guys actually spoke this way. To be honest, she'd never known she could feel this way, that she'd actually crave sex and not think of it as a chore or a duty. She'd only been with one other man and—

"Hey." He reached up, framing her face in his hands. "Look at me. It's just us in this room. Got it?"

Melanie nodded, pushing aside thoughts that threatened to steal their moment. "Just us."

Without looking away, Tanner reached for the hem of her tee and lifted it up and over her head. Her first thought was that she hadn't even put on her pretty bra and panties. The plain pale pink cotton probably wasn't doing much for Tanner. This was a far cry from the brazen woman he'd taken home from the bar several weeks ago.

"You're frowning." He reached for the button on her jeans. "I must be doing something wrong."

"Can we turn the light off?" she asked.

He tipped his head down slightly until she was forced to look him directly in the eyes. "Just us, remember? No worry of looks or doubts, and sure as hell no memories of your ex. Just Tanner and Melanie."

"In theory that sounds great."

He shoved her jeans down and dropped to his knees in front of her. "I'm about to show you it's not just a theory. It's a fact."

Melanie held on to his shoulders as he removed her shoes, socks, and jeans. She stood before him so exposed. This was nothing like the last time. Their first time had been flirty, frantic, and they were still half dressed, fumbling in the darkness of his foyer.

Now they were so emotionally involved, with a baby no less, lights on, and apparently getting down to the bare essentials.

Nerves curled low in her belly and Melanie had to force herself to remain calm.

"I didn't see this before." His finger traced over the small circular tattoo on her hip bone. The Roman numerals represented freedom. "What's this mean?"

Melanie watched as his fingertip continued to slide over the ink. "That's the day I decided to live for myself and leave my abusive marriage. That date symbolizes a new beginning."

His eyes came up, locking onto hers. "I've said it before, but you're so damn remarkable."

She felt that way when he said such things. Melanie felt like she couldn't possibly fail at anything when Tanner pushed his way through that wall of doubt she kept in place. How did he do that? How did someone she'd known for such a short time already get her and know all the right words to say?

Not only just saying the right words, but she knew deep in her soul that he meant every single one.

"You're still feeling okay, right?" he asked, his brows drawn in. "With the baby?"

Melanie nodded. "We're fine. No need to worry."

The worry lines between his brows didn't diminish. Melanie smoothed her thumb over the narrow area and offered him a smile. "I won't keep anything from you, Tanner. This is our child. Now are you going to undress or just stay down there on your knees?"

Perhaps that was the wrong thing to say—or the right one, considering the way his eyes darkened and he pressed his lips to the inside of her knee. He trailed up toward the apex of her thighs and she found herself clutching his shoulders once again.

Just when he came so close to the area where she ached for him most, he turned his attention to her other leg and started the process over again. Her hips shifted and the groan escaped before she could stop herself. Tanner was driving her positively mad with want and need.

"Relax," he murmured as he stared up at her. "We've got all night."

"Is that a threat or a promise?"

"Both."

He nipped at her belly just above the band of her panties. She hated that he could see the stretch marks, but she wasn't ashamed of who she'd been. Those were her reminders of the woman she never wanted to be again. The woman who let others walk all over her, the woman who didn't care for herself the way she should.

His hands covered her stomach as he placed another kiss on her. "I know this wasn't planned, but I'm not even going to pretend I'm sorry. I can't wait to meet our baby."

Melanie's heart tumbled. They were most definitely not in the right place to have a child together. They knew little about each other, but she wasn't sorry, either. If she was honest with herself, she'd much rather have Tanner as the father of her child than any other man she'd ever known.

Each day she felt she uncovered another layer of what made up this remarkable man. Which meant each day she fell a little more for him and there wasn't much she could do to prevent the inevitable.

When Tanner came to his feet, Melanie reached for him, but he stepped aside. "I've got this."

In record time he'd stripped and stood before her completely bare, without a shame in the world. Sure, if she looked like him she'd parade around with the lights on, too. Damn that man didn't have an ounce of fat anywhere . . . and she'd looked. Twice.

"Keep lookin' at me like that and you'll never leave this room."

Melanie felt her cheeks heat up as she smiled. "Well, you did put it all on display, so don't act like you're shy."

In a lightning fast move, he reached behind her and flicked her bra. She didn't want to think about how he'd perfected that move. Melanie straightened her arms and let the pink cotton glide silently to the floor.

His eyes darted down to her panties and back up as a wry grin spread across his face. Melanie slid her underwear off, kicking them to the side. Feeling more confident than she ever would've imagined, she propped her hands on her hips and tilted her head.

"Now what, hot shot?"

"Now you better hang on, because things are about to get interesting."

Tanner closed the minuscule space between them, bringing their bodies flush as he gripped her face and covered her mouth with his. Melanie curled her fingers around his wrists and sank into the kiss, her body melting against his.

He spun her around, never breaking contact, and her knees hit the side of the bed. Slowly, with more care than she'd ever been shown, he eased her down, keeping his weight off her. His hands rested on either side of her head and she eased her legs apart to accommodate his hips.

"I've never wanted this." She didn't know why those words tumbled out because she'd meant to keep them locked away.

Tanner stared down at her. "With me?"

"With anyone," she admitted. "Before we were together, I never knew sex could be . . . satisfying."

The muscle clenched in his jaw and a flash of rage came and went in his dark eyes. Melanie shivered, not that she was afraid of him, not by any means. But Tanner was a protector and she knew her admission had him thinking how he could make everything right. For her.

He kissed the tip of her nose. "I'm glad I could be the one to show you how sex should be."

So was she, but she couldn't say the words. Not right now when she was too vulnerable, too raw and feeling exposed.

"Do we need protection?" he asked.

Melanie laughed. "Obvious reasons aside, I've never been with anyone other than my ex, but I know I'm clean."

"I've never gone without, but this is your call, Mel."

She looped her arms around his neck and arched her body against his. "I just want to feel you, Tanner. Show me how this should be."

"With pleasure."

His lips feathered lightly over hers as he joined their bodies. Melanie wrapped her legs around his waist and opened her mouth to him. She wanted to feel him everywhere all at once. Finally, he settled his weight a bit more on her and she savored the moment. There was something indescribably sexy about the strength Tanner possessed, a strength she didn't fear.

With slow movements, he shifted his hips in sync with hers. Melanie's fingertips dug into his back as she pulled from the kiss and arched her neck. Eyes shut, she fell into the moment, letting each and every sensation take hold of her.

Tanner's hands seemed to be everywhere, his lips traveled down her neck and across her chest. He murmured something she couldn't make out. Her entire body tightened as she tumbled into the most blissful state her body had ever known. Even more than before.

When Tanner's fingertips dug into her hips, his body stilled. Melanie opened her eyes to watch him and was shocked to see him looking down at her. The muscles in his jaw clenched, his lips thinned, and those eyes held so many emotions Melanie couldn't even begin to describe them.

Tanner's body relaxed and he eased himself onto her and nuzzled his face against her neck. Melanie flattened her palms against his back and inhaled the masculine scent she'd come to associate with Tanner.

She wasn't sure what to say or do at this moment, but lying there, just like that, felt right. Words weren't necessary; in all honesty they would ruin the bliss they'd just shared.

The blaring of an obnoxious ringtone sliced right through the blessed peace. So much for enjoying the moment.

"That's me," he murmured, lifting himself off her. "Sorry, but I have to take that."

She nodded her understanding, instantly cold from the lack of his warm body pressing her into his bed. Melanie tugged at the comforter and wrapped herself up as Tanner walked from the room. He didn't bother with clothes, but yet again, if he looked that stellar, she wouldn't wear clothes, either.

Melanie heard him mumbling in the other room. She leaned back against his pillows and glanced around Tanner's bedroom. This wasn't how she thought a bachelor's inner sanctum would look. He had a gray accent chair in the corner with a white throw over the back. The dresser and chest of drawers matched his bed and looked like something from a magazine. There was even an area rug.

Everything was done in gray and navy, but still, quite shocking for someone like Tanner. She expected a bed with rumpled sheets and maybe a nightstand.

Leaning forward just a bit, she was able to glance into his master bath. Was that a soaker tub? Sweet mercy, what she wouldn't give for an hour in that right about now.

"Go ahead."

Melanie yelped and jerked her attention back to the doorway where Tanner stood unashamedly naked and smiling.

"The tub, go right ahead," he stated, closing the distance to the bed. "I actually have to go out, but you can stay."

He climbed onto the bed and framed her face in his hands, holding her gaze with his. "In fact, I want you to be right here when I return."

"Tanner—"

"It's getting late," he argued. "You might as well sleep here."

His fingertip ran up her arm and over her shoulder. The tremble that shook her had her nodding in agreement before she could fully consider the consequences of spending the night.

"Use the tub," he told her. "I've never used it, so you'll be the first."

Melanie quirked her brow. "You've never had another woman in that tub?"

"Never." He came to his feet and stared down at her. "Despite my reputation, I haven't slept with every woman I've dated and I never bring anyone to my house."

"You brought me twice." Way to state the obvious, but she just couldn't believe she was the only one.

"We'll discuss my past later," he promised. "Right now duty calls."

Melanie didn't know where he was going and she wasn't

sure she even had the right to ask. She trusted Tanner. He'd given her no reason not to.

He went to the chest of drawers and pulled out a pair of boxer briefs. She had to admit, watching him dress was just as erotic and sensual as watching him undress. How could she already be aroused?

"If you don't stop looking at me like that I'll never get out of here."

Melanie swiveled her legs over the side of the bed and gathered the comforter around her. She crossed toward the bathroom and offered him a smile as she passed.

"I'm going to assume you don't keep a stock of fragrant bubble bath in here."

Tanner laughed. "That would be a negative. But the tub does have jets. I assume they work just fine."

"How long will you be?" she asked, then mentally cursed herself for getting too personal. "Sorry. Ignore that. You don't owe me an explanation."

"Mel."

She glanced over her shoulder. Tanner stood with his jeans on and unbuttoned, that glorious chest with a splattering of dark hair covering his pecs. The tattoo over his shoulder captivated her, and she wondered what had made him choose a sprawling eagle with one wing that spread over his shoulder and onto his back while the other seemed to spear down his arm.

"You can ask me anything," he stated. "I've told you that before. All I can tell you about tonight is that it's work related, but I have no idea how long I'll be."

He stalked toward her and Melanie gripped the comforter even tighter against her body. "Make yourself at home, okay? Fridge is stocked, watch TV, take a bath, go to bed. Do anything. Just don't leave."

Melanie smiled. "I promise I'll stay."

"When you move in I'll buy you that bubble bath."

Rolling her eyes, she swatted at his bare chest. "I'm not moving in, Tanner. This is just one night."

He quirked one brow as if to argue, but he went back to the dresser and pulled out a T-shirt. She headed into the bathroom to start filling up the tub, and before he left he called out his goodbye.

There was something so familial about this entire night. Tanner surprising her, the amazing sex, him rushing off to work while she relaxed with a bath. Is this how a real relationship actually worked? Is this what life with someone who cared about you was supposed to be?

Melanie tested the water with her toe and then climbed on in. She sank into the warm water as she reclined against the cool porcelain. She lifted her hair up and let it fall over the back of the tub to rest on the surround.

Part of her felt a bit strange being in Tanner's house without him. She'd gone from a one-night stand to cozying up in his personal space.

Melanie closed her eyes and forced herself to relax. She was expecting his child and they had plenty of time to figure out the dynamics of their relationship. But one thing was certain, Melanie wouldn't lose sight of who she'd set out to be. She was damn proud of the woman she'd become. She wouldn't be who she was today without the help of Livie and Jade.

And it was those two women who had pulled her here to Haven. Melanie loved this quaint town, loved the prospect of the airport growing into something fabulous, she loved the idea of becoming a mother and setting down roots here for her child.

She would be remiss if she didn't add Tanner to that mix. Her feelings for him were growing, whether she was ready or not. She couldn't have slept with him twice if she didn't care.

Melanie smiled as she thought of how he'd spoken to her. There had been such conviction and determination in his tone. He truly cared. Whether or not that led to something more, well, only time would tell.

Chapter Twelve

*Taking naps sounds so childish. I prefer to call
them horizontal life pauses.*

—Mel's Motivational Blog

"This is bogus, man."

Tanner put his hand on the guy's head and settled him
into the back of the patrol car before slamming the door.
He'd yet to arrest someone who fully confessed to dealing
drugs. However, they were always so quick to squeal on
their friends.

This time the undercover officer they'd placed in the
gym had managed to get the names of the "higher ups,"
and that made for one successful bust.

Tanner patted the top of the car and the officer pulled
from the lot, heading toward the station. It was well past
midnight now and all he wanted to do was get back home
to Melanie.

Home to Melanie. Just those words sent a spiral of
emotions through him. Anticipation of what their future
held gripped his heart. Wondering where they'd ultimately
end up constantly filtered through his mind. But most of
all, there was still that fear he couldn't let go of.

As long as she was with him, he could convince himself she and the baby were safe. Not that he was a doctor by any means, but there was peace of mind in seeing her happy and healthy.

Soon her belly would start rounding out. There would be ultrasounds, kicks from growing little legs, and ultimately the birth. His arms ached to hold his child. He never thought he'd feel this way again, but damn it, he wanted this. He wanted to be a father, to raise a child in a loving, caring home.

His mother had instilled loyalty and compassion in him at an early age. Tanner owed everything to that amazing woman and couldn't wait to spend Thanksgiving with her, his stepdad, and Mel.

He headed back into the gym, where Cash was talking with another officer. When Cash glanced over, he shook the other guy's hand and made his way to Tanner. With a quick nod of thanks to his coworker, Tanner stepped closer to Cash.

"Well, that's done."

Cash nodded and slapped Tanner on the back. "I owe you a beer, man."

"A beer? Hell, you owe me a steak dinner."

Cash smiled. "Consider it done."

"I'm just glad we could wrap this up, and it was late, so the gym was empty."

With the twenty-four-hour gym access for members, Tanner hadn't been sure if anyone would be here, but thankfully no one was. The bust went off easily and quickly—which was not always the case.

"You think you'll be able to get the other guy?" Cash asked.

Tanner nodded and leaned his arm against the wrap-around check-in counter. "Positive. The force in Macon is already on it. Those guys had been shuttling pills up here for some time now."

"Bastards get whatever is coming to them." Cash raked a hand over his stubbled jaw and tugged the bill of his hat down. "You heading home now, or do you want to head on over to Taps?"

"I'm heading home."

Tanner bit the inside of his cheek to keep from smiling. The image of Melanie waiting for him in his bed was all that was keeping him going right now.

Cash's eyes narrowed. "Oh, I see how it is. I guess this has to do with Melanie?"

Tanner gave a slight shrug. "Perhaps."

"Care to tell me what's going on there? Besides the baby, I mean. You're not hovering because of—"

"No." Tanner wasn't. Well, he was, sort of, but he also cared for Melanie. "Listen, I'm scared as hell, but there's something about her that I just can't resist. I want to get to know her more and she's at my house now, so if we could put off the grilling until later, that would be great."

Cash laughed and shoved his hands in his pockets. "Go on, man. Get home to your woman."

His woman. Tanner wasn't quite sure she was ready for that label, but that's exactly how he thought of her. She was his. Not in the way that he wanted to possess her, but in the way that he wanted to cherish her and start something new and exciting with her.

Tanner let himself out of the gym and headed to his truck. Thankfully tomorrow, or really today, was Thanksgiving and he was taking Melanie to meet his mother. That thought alone had him looking forward to a future. There was only one other woman who had met his mother, so to say Melanie was special was a vast understatement.

Part of him wondered if he should tell his mother about

the pregnancy before he arrived. He wasn't sure how she'd take the news. She'd been just as devastated when he'd lost his fiancée and child so many years ago.

Springing something this monumental on her . . .

No. She would love this surprise. Tanner wanted Melanie to be part of the revealing. There was nothing his mother loved more than a joyful surprise, and Tanner had a good feeling his mother and Melanie would hit it off perfectly.

The closer he got to his house, the more anxious he became. He figured she'd be asleep, but he hoped like hell she wasn't. It had been all he could do to concentrate on the case and not the fact that a naked woman was back at his house, soaking in his tub or lying in his bed.

Tanner pulled into his drive and on into the garage. He couldn't deny he liked seeing Melanie's car in the drive. Well, the car she was driving now. He still didn't understand why she'd gotten rid of her Beemer in exchange for something that had clearly seen better days. She had money, that he was fairly certain of. If she'd blackmailed her husband so he'd let her leave, how had she not left with enough money to keep her going?

Added to that, she was an attorney. Granted, she wasn't practicing here in Haven, but she had in the past. Her online blog and social media sites brought in sponsors and so much press that she'd become quite successful.

Which left him curious as to why she'd chosen a car that looked like something a sixteen-year-old would have if they were working a minimum wage job and paying for their own ride.

He let himself into the kitchen through the attached garage. A quietness settled over the house, but for the first time in years, he was coming home to someone. Tanner never thought he'd want to have someone to come home to again, never thought he'd let himself fall to such vulnerabilities again. But here he was, exposing the very part of his soul that could destroy him.

But the flip side of that fear was the fact that Melanie was just as fragile. Actually, she was likely more so. Which was just another reason he wanted her here. Call it that protective instinct he'd always had, but he wanted to shield her from everything, including and most importantly her past, which clearly still haunted her.

As he did every night, he double-checked all the locks and made sure his alarms were set. He pulled his shoulder holster off as he mounted the steps toward his room. The fresh aroma of his soap enveloped him as he hit the landing. He smiled, knowing Mel had used his things. Call him territorial or barbaric or whatever, but the idea of her rubbing his soap over her sweet body had him feeling exactly that. He was territorial.

The soft glow from his bedroom drew him closer, and as he turned the corner, he couldn't help but freeze in the doorway at the sight before him. Melanie curled up on his side of the bed, covers drawn up to her chin. The instant punch to that vulnerable point in his soul hit him hard.

Tanner leaned against the door frame and waited for the sliver of doubt to enter in. He'd been a bachelor for so long. He'd enjoyed dating and purposely not getting attached. Yet the moment Melanie came into town, something about her had captivated his attention. Then he'd slept with her and had been completely blindsided by how much he wanted to actually get to know her. But he'd purposely tried to take things slow and back off a tad after their intense encounter. He knew she was skittish and he hadn't wanted to scare her off.

Add in the baby, and he was a damn lost cause. This right here before his eyes was his family. He wanted her here, and when he'd blurted out about her moving in, he hadn't thought it through, but he would do everything he could to convince her to stay.

Trying to be quiet, Tanner eased across the room with careful steps. He put his holster and gun on the chest of drawers and took a seat in the corner chair. He'd never changed this room since he moved in. The furniture had come with the house. He'd bought a mattress and a comforter, but that was all. The living room and dining room were the same. He wasn't much on décor, and what was here had been good enough for him.

He unlaced his shoes and toed them off, then stood to jerk his shirt up and over his head. After sliding out of his jeans, he left his boxer briefs on and started across the room to the opposite side of the bed.

Something hit his foot and he tripped, falling onto the footboard of the bed and muttering a string of curses. Melanie shot up in bed, clutching the sheet to her chest.

"Damn it. Sorry."

He turned to see what he'd fallen over, and it had been her shoes.

"No, it's fine," she said, rubbing her eyes and sitting up fully. "I was trying to stay up for you. I guess I didn't make it and took a little nap."

Even though his toe throbbed from contact with the heel of her shoe, his heart warmed at the idea that she had wanted to wait for him. Nobody had ever done that. Then again, he'd never given anyone the chance.

"What time is it?" she asked.

"Almost one."

Melanie smoothed her hair past her face. "I can go if

you . . . I'm not sure if you had a bad day or . . . sorry. I'm not sure what to do here."

Her rumpled state and awkward words had him smiling and easing onto the bed. "All you have to do is stay right where you are. Unless you really want to leave."

With the sheet tucked under her arms, she glanced down to her fingers in her lap. "I should make myself go. I'm not sure cozying up here is smart."

"But you don't want to."

"I don't," she murmured. "It's just, it's difficult to trust my instincts after a failed marriage."

Tanner shifted and propped his back against the headboard and pulled her against his side. "I don't know much about your marriage. I know enough to know you went through hell and I want to protect you from any more pain."

"I don't need to be protected," she whispered as her palm flattened against his abs. "I need to move on, which I'm doing. I need to learn to trust again, but that's the hard part, and you just happen to be on my path. Which isn't really fair to you."

Tanner turned and leaned her back against her pillows, resting his hands on either side of her face. "Did I give you a reason to not trust me?"

Melanie shook her head.

"Then don't worry about what's fair to me," he commanded. "You work on moving forward just like you have been. I'll take care of me."

Melanie stared up at him. He could hardly make out the expression on her face, but he could feel the soft beat of her heart against his side. Her hand slid up over his chest and Tanner swore right then and there that he'd go through anything to keep this woman in his life. He wanted this family, he wanted Melanie.

"I guess I'll stay tonight," she whispered as she eased on up and slid her lips over his.

Tanner wasn't going to argue, but this wasn't the only night she'd be staying.

"I can't believe you stayed all night with Tanner," Jade exclaimed.

Melanie studied the man in question as he drove toward his mother's house. Apparently she lived nearly an hour away, but Melanie didn't know much more.

"Yup," Melanie replied, obviously not wanting to say too much.

"I can hear her, you know." Tanner chuckled. "She's not exactly quiet."

"Tell him to kiss my ass," Jade stated.

Melanie rolled her eyes and leaned her elbow on the console. "I'm not relaying that message."

"Already heard it," Tanner countered.

"Listen," Melanie said, getting back on topic. "I'll be home later tonight. I forgot to charge my laptop, so can you go into the office and do that for me? I have some work to do when I get back."

"A new blog post? Let me do it."

"We've discussed this. You can do it, but I'll need to oversee and schedule."

"You're no fun," Jade complained. "I just want to take over for a week. Your followers would love me."

"I'm sure they would," Melanie agreed with a laugh. "I feel bad you're home alone on Thanksgiving."

"Don't feel bad for me. I've got a new bottle of rosé that I drove two towns over to get because I needed something with an actual cork, plus I have a whole new series on Netflix I'm about to binge-watch. It's a great day. Besides, Brad may come over for a bit."

Brad . . . some guy Melanie had yet to meet, but apparently Cash didn't like him. Who knew what was going on there.

"I'll bring you some food back," Melanie promised.

"I'm fine, really. Go enjoy meeting the mother and getting your new little family in order."

"It's not like that," Melanie stated.

Tanner's hands gripped the wheel tighter as his lips thinned. She immediately regretted her words, but she wasn't sure what to say. Yes, she was meeting his mom, but it wasn't like she and Tanner were ready to pick out china patterns or get monogrammed towels.

"Maybe not yet, but it will be." Jade paused for a second and then lowered her tone. "Mel, he's good for you. Don't find reasons to dismiss him."

Melanie continued to stare at his profile. She'd spent the night in his bed. They'd made love twice last night and once this morning in the shower before he'd taken her back home to change her clothes. Jade had been out for her morning run, so the walk of shame had gone unnoticed.

Tanner put her needs first at all times. Not just in bed, but constantly asking about her, making sure she was comfortable, asking how she felt or if she needed anything. The man was 100 percent not what she was used to.

"I'll talk to you later," Melanie said. "Don't forget my computer."

"I'm on it."

She disconnected the call and couldn't help the overwhelming sensation of awkward tension. Talking on a cell phone was never private. There wasn't a doubt in her mind Tanner heard everything.

"Do you get home often?" she asked, trying to push through the silence.

"Not as often as my mother would like. But she and my stepdad travel quite a bit."

"She doesn't know about the baby, does she?"

Tanner shook his head. "I didn't want to tell her over the phone. I'd like to think this will be exciting for her, but truth be told, she may have difficulty taking the news."

Melanie shifted in her seat, sliding her purse from her lap to the floor and dropping her cell inside. "Because she doesn't know me?"

Tanner swallowed and stared out at the stretch of road ahead. Melanie waited, watched, but he said nothing.

"Tanner?"

"I should've told you before now." He glanced in the side mirror and switched lanes to pass a truck. "Damn it. I just didn't want to talk about it at all, but you need to know something."

Dread curled low in her belly. "You're scaring me."

He reached across and took her hand before glancing her way for the briefest of seconds. "It's just about my past. I was engaged before."

"Okay. I didn't think I was the first woman in your life."

"She was pregnant," he went on. "The doctors had told her she should never try to have a baby because of her health issues, but she wanted a family. The pregnancy wasn't planned by any means, but it happened."

Fear consumed her. She saw where this was going and her heart literally ached for him.

"I lost them both," he murmured.

Melanie squeezed his hand and wondered what she could possibly say that would make this any better. Now she knew why he hovered, why he was constantly asking about her.

"Is that why you wanted me to move in?" she asked. "So you could keep an eye on me?"

She hated the question that came out, but she had to know. Did he care about her or was he reliving his past and terrified something just as tragic would happen?

"Honestly? That was part of the reason. When you first told me about the baby I was thrust back to that time, and the wind was knocked out of me."

She remembered exactly what he'd looked like when she told him. Now that she knew, his reaction was definitely justified.

"You should've told me before now."

"I know."

Melanie threaded her fingers through his. "I understand why you didn't. There's still so much of me that you don't know that I don't want to dive into."

His thumb feathered back and forth over the back of her hand. "Don't feel pressured to tell me. I'm here whenever you're ready. But I needed to fill you in before my mom said something. I didn't want you going in blind."

Melanie appreciated his honesty, appreciated that he had opened up something so painful just so she wouldn't feel lost. Could Tanner be this perfect for her?

She'd been fooled by a charming man with a mesmerizing grin once before. She'd been led astray by her emotions when she didn't know any better.

But she was different now. She had nothing to hide.

"Neville Prescott abused me," she stated simply.

"Mel, you don't have to do this."

She stared at him for just a moment before looking back to the stretch of highway before them. "I know I don't, but I'm not the scared woman I was before. He can't hurt me because I won't let him."

"You're one strong woman." Tanner released her hand

and shut off the radio before clasping her fingers in his again. "I know from working on the force it's difficult to get women to leave. They're afraid or they think they deserve the abuse because they've done something wrong. It pains me to leave them, but there's nothing I can do until they want to help themselves."

There he went again with that passion-filled tone. She'd never stopped to consider what he saw at work or what he had to deal with day in and day out. She knew he couldn't share anything with her, but knowing he'd worked with women in her situation made her appreciate their bond all the more.

"I stayed longer than I should've, but not as long as most women do," she added. "In all honesty, things could've been worse. I'm not defending him, but there were days that would go by when I didn't even see him, so that was a blessing. If he ignored me, then I knew I was safe."

"You said you blackmailed him. Has he left you alone since the divorce?"

Melanie glanced down to their hands. How strangely their relationship had formed. Bickering banter turned to a one-night stand, then a pregnancy, and now she wanted to spend more and more time with him. Oh, and she was on the way for the obligatory mother meeting.

"Not exactly," she said, slowly weighing her words because Tanner was one overprotective man. "He's contacted me multiple times. He mostly has his assistants reach out to me, but he actually texted me the other day."

"He what?" Tanner exploded. "Why didn't you tell me?"

Melanie shrugged. "It's not your problem to solve. He's always going to be a menace, I'm afraid. He's gearing up to run for the senate next year and thinks a dramatic reunion on camera will do wonders in the polls."

"He can't be serious."

Melanie eased her hand from Tanner's and adjusted her vents. She needed some cooler air if she was going to dive into this. According to the dash clock, they still had another twenty-five minutes to go.

"Neville never joked about politics," she told Tanner. "His life revolves around them. His assistants, his campaign manager, they were always at the house, and when they weren't, they all traveled like a pack of wolves to the office. I was the dutiful wife who hosted parties, smiled, pretended like we had the perfect marriage. But if he had a bad day or if I had done something displeasing, like hanging his shirts wrong in his walk-in closet, there was hell to pay."

Silence filled the truck and she knew Tanner was letting her go at her own pace. He wasn't pressuring her into details, and she wasn't quite sure how far she'd go into those, but she found that getting this out in the open actually gave her more power. She wasn't hiding behind the ugliness that was her past. She'd never posted any of this on her blog, but Livie and Jade knew every sordid detail.

"Emotional abuse is just as scarring as physical," she added. "The things he'd tell me were hurtful and I still hear those words when I fall into self-doubt. But that's not often, because I refuse to let him win."

"You walking away showed him he wasn't winning," Tanner praised. "What the hell did he say to you the other day?"

"He texted, then he had his assistant call. I ignore him, which I'm sure just enrages him all the more."

When Tanner didn't respond, Melanie risked looking his way and the first word that came to mind at the sight of his clenched jaw and thin lips was *rage*. She reached over and placed her hand on his thigh.

"Don't let him occupy your thoughts," she demanded. "He's nothing to you."

He threw her a glance. "If he's harassing you in any way—and texting you after the divorce is harassment, since you were abused—then he has everything to do with me."

Fear gripped Melanie, threatening to overwhelm her. Tanner couldn't have any idea how powerful Neville was. The man had so many law enforcement personnel in his pocket, so many government officials. There was no way Melanie would ever allow the path of those two men to cross.

"Does he know you're pregnant?"

Melanie shook her head. "No. I don't even want to know how he'll react."

"Stop answering calls from the assistants," Tanner told her. "Change your number if you have to."

"Oh, I've changed it. I give up now. It's not worth the trouble because he always finds it."

"I'll handle him if he contacts you again—him or his assistants. He's not the only one with powerful contacts and people in his back pocket. I'm pretty damn resourceful."

Melanie said nothing. She knew she'd never be able to tell Tanner if she had contact again. There was no way in hell Neville could learn about Tanner.

Besides, Tanner was busy with his own life without worrying about taking on her issues.

Her cell chimed in her purse, but she ignored it. She wasn't in the mood right now and nothing was too pressing that it couldn't wait.

"Do you want to get that?" Tanner asked.

"I'll check it later."

She moved her hand from his thigh and settled back against her seat. "Tell me about your mom before we get there. Am I going to be tackle-hugged, or is she a handshake type woman?"

"Considering I never bring a woman home, she'll definitely tackle-hug you."

Melanie laughed. "Good to know. Plus, she likes to cook. I think I'm going to get along just fine with her."

The nerves in her belly didn't cease. Now that Melanie knew more about Tanner's past, the dynamics of this meeting just escalated into a territory Melanie had no experience with. But his mother had to know what was going on. In all honesty, Melanie was glad she was meeting Tanner's mother. There was quite a bit to be said about a man in how he treated his mom, and knowing Tanner had dropped everything to spend the holiday with his mother warmed Melanie so much.

She wanted to believe he was more than a rebound, that he could be someone she could depend on. On the other hand, she worried if she'd ever fully be free of her past, because she hadn't been lying when she'd told him Neville was evil. There was nothing that man wouldn't do to get what he wanted. Unfortunately, he wanted her back in his life.

Melanie wrapped her arms around her midsection. Like hell she'd ever return to the life she'd barely escaped from.

Chapter Thirteen

Throw glitter in today's face.

—Mel's Motivational Blog

Tanner waited until the meal was over. He wasn't quite sure when to tell his mother about the baby, but now seemed as good a time as any, considering she had threatened to pull out his baby books.

"I'd love to see them," Melanie stated, giving Tanner a wide grin across the table.

"They're in the front closet on the top shelf." His mother pushed her seat back from the table and came to her feet. "Leave all of these dishes and I'll get them later. Tanner, be a dear and reach up in the closet and grab the two leather-bound picture albums."

He raked a hand across the back of his neck and blew out a sigh. "Actually, Mom, I need to tell you something."

His stepfather stood as well. "You three go into the living room and I'll get all the dishes into the kitchen."

Tanner couldn't have handpicked a better man for his mother than Patrick Bailey. He spoiled her and showed his mother she was worthy of being pampered and loved.

Melanie eyed him, her smile disappearing. Her jovial

state now replaced by nerves and fear that he was judging her taut expression correctly. He offered her a grin, trying to ease her worry.

"C'mon, Mel. Let's go in the living room."

"Why don't I help Patrick with the dishes?" she offered.

Tanner shook his head. "No way."

"You most certainly will not," his mother said at the same time. "No guest in my home will do dishes. Now, come in the living room. I want to hear what my son has to say, and then I have the most adorable baby photo to show you. Oh, and then there's that one from your junior high dance. Do you remember, Tanner? The one where you were so nervous you went for a haircut—"

"Yes, Mom. I remember."

He really didn't want to take this stroll down memory lane. Beyond the embarrassment, he had more pressing matters to deal with.

Tanner rounded the table in the narrow dining room and eased Melanie's chair out. He leaned down to whisper in her ear. "Relax."

Placing a secure hand on the small of her back, he led her into the living room and onto the same floral sofa his mother had owned for the past twenty years. She claimed they didn't make them sturdy like this anymore, so she refused to get new furniture. She also claimed she'd rather spend her money on cruises, which she and Patrick often took.

Teresa Bailey sank into her favorite tan rocker-recliner and crossed her legs. Resting one elbow on the arm of the puffy chair, she smiled. "So, what is it you want to tell me? Though I do have a pretty good idea."

From the huge smile on his mother's face, he truly feared he was about to burst that bubble his mother was floating in.

"I'm not sure how to say this other than to just come out and tell you."

His mother practically beamed. "You're getting married? Am I right? Oh, sorry. I shouldn't have ruined the announcement, but I couldn't wait."

"We're not getting married, Mom."

Melanie shifted beside him and slid her arm around his. Her silent support meant a great deal to him. He'd opened up to her about his past hurt. He'd hated doing so on the drive here because he'd felt like maybe they couldn't fully engage in what needed to be said, but he couldn't have Melanie completely off guard.

"Melanie is pregnant."

His mom's smile faltered, her eyes widened as she darted her gaze to Melanie. "Pregnant?"

"I'm about six weeks along now."

Silence settled in the room and Tanner wasn't sure what his mom was thinking, but in the next second she jumped from her seat and squealed, throwing her arms wide.

"Oh, my word, honey. Come give me a hug."

Tanner wasn't sure who she was talking to, but Melanie came to her feet and was enveloped by his mom. The weight of what seemed like years of worry slid right off his shoulders. Patrick came rushing into the room.

"What happened?"

"We're going to be grandparents," his mom exclaimed, releasing Melanie.

"That's great," Patrick stated.

Tanner found himself enveloped in his mother's tight embrace. The next second she sniffed and the slight sound pierced his heart. Tanner patted her back.

"Are those happy tears, I assume?" he asked.

His mom eased back and gripped his shoulders. "I'm

so happy for you. Are you . . . is this okay? I mean, how are you dealing with everything?"

Tanner smiled and glanced at Melanie. "We're over the shock for the most part."

"That's not what I meant."

His mother's eyes searched his and he gave her shoulder a slight squeeze. "I know what you meant, Mom. I'm okay."

"The baby and I are both healthy," Melanie was quick to add. "I'm sure this is scary for you, Mrs. Bailey."

"Oh, please. Call me Teresa. We're family now."

Tanner caught Melanie's slight cringe. That word terrified her, and knowing what she'd come from, he couldn't blame her for being overly cautious. This entire pregnancy had thrust them both into a territory neither of them had been ready for, but they were going to get through it together.

"This is the best Thanksgiving ever," his mother said, beaming. "I can't think of anything to be more thankful for than family and the promise of new life."

The chime of a cell went off, penetrating the moment. Melanie's eyes darted toward her purse on the accent table by the front door.

"Go ahead, dear," his mom said.

Melanie shook her head. "It's fine. I'll get it later."

This was the second time it had gone off and she wasn't concerned. Or maybe she was and that's why she wasn't answering. Was she worried her ex or one of his minions was calling again? Every part of Tanner wanted to get ahold of her phone and check, but he wouldn't disrespect her that way. She wanted to handle things, and that was fine, but if there was even an inkling of danger or any stress for her, he'd step in without hesitation.

Tanner's cell vibrated in his pocket and he groaned.

"Sorry," he said, pulling out his phone. "I actually do have to get this."

"I guess I can't complain," his mom stated. "I had you over for dinner and you're making me a grandma. Go ahead and work."

No doubt it was work. The extraction going down this evening had been on his mind all day. This was the first one he'd requested to sit out on.

Tanner stepped outside on the front porch and answered. "Roark."

"I know you're at your mother's, but is there any chance you can come back?"

Considering his captain was calling, there must be a damn good reason. Tanner glanced at his watch and sighed as he watched a couple kids running down the opposite side of the street. Their laughter carried through the tiny neighborhood. This is what he wanted for his life. Something simple, something pure. Which is why he had to be the one to consistently keep the evil away.

"I can be there in just over an hour." He needed to get Melanie home and get back to his house to change. "Text me the details."

"I appreciate it," his captain said. "You know I wouldn't ask if it wasn't an emergency. We've just received some intel that this is also a drug house. We are looking at a full bust."

Damn. There was no way he would sit this one out.

"I'm leaving now."

He disconnected the call and turned toward the house. The image through the wide window was one that would stay forever in his memory bank. His mother and Melanie were on the sofa flipping through what was no doubt his embarrassing youth pictures. Right now, though, Tanner didn't care. These two women held a place in his heart.

Melanie had come to be so much more than a quick hookup or even the mother of his child. She was a remarkably strong woman and his mother had been through hell, coming out on top. These two shared a parallel history and Tanner wondered just how strong their bond would grow over the years.

Yes, years. Tanner knew he wanted Melanie to be part of his life, and now he just had to mold this relationship so she could see the same future together.

He was used to saving abused women from their homes and abusers, but that had been the extent of his involvement with them. He recalled what his mother had gone through to rebuild her life, but being involved with Melanie was completely different. No matter what it took, he'd make sure she knew he cared and that he wasn't going anywhere.

Tanner let himself back in and both women looked up at him; they both had the same expression on their faces.

"Can't be helped," he stated with a shrug. "There's an emergency."

"I understand." His mother closed the album and smiled. "I'm glad we at least got to enjoy dinner together. Why don't I package some things for you to take?"

"Already done." Patrick came from the kitchen with a large basket no doubt full of plates of food. "When he got the call I had a feeling he'd have to go."

"Thanks." He took the basket then shifted his attention to Melanie. "Ready?"

"I was just getting to the good parts of your childhood," she joked with a crooked grin. "That school play where you were the back end of the donkey was priceless."

Tanner rolled his eyes. "The ass end of the ass was not my finest moment."

His mom laughed. "That was your first school play and I was very proud."

Tanner figured whenever his kid was in school he'd be proud, too. Must be a parent thing.

"We'll save the rest of that memory lane for the next visit," Tanner promised.

"Then you better hurry back. I don't want so much time to pass between visits."

"When is your next trip?" he asked.

"We'll be home through the first of the year. Plenty of time for you to come for dinner."

Melanie gave his mother a hug. "I'll make sure he comes back soon. Thank you so much for having me."

They all said their goodbyes and Tanner rushed Melanie out to his truck. He needed to get back soon and his mind was already racing to the night ahead.

"Just take me to your house," Melanie told him, breaking into his thoughts.

"Are you sure?"

"Positive," she assured him. "I can wait for you to get back."

"I may not be back until late again."

Melanie slid her hand over his on the console. "Then maybe I should just stay tonight."

Tanner couldn't believe she'd thrown that out, but he wasn't going to let this moment go. He turned his hand over in hers to lace their fingers together.

"You should stay the night. And every night after."

"Let's focus on tonight," she murmured as she stared out the window.

Tanner wasn't about to argue. This was the second night she was staying. Little by little he was wearing her down—not mentally or trying to break her strength, he was wearing her down in a way that she was learning more and more to trust.

"Tonight," he repeated with a smile on his face.

"When can I get my own plane?"

Jax laughed as he filled out his flight log for the day. "When you can pay for one."

Piper stomped her foot and turned to Tanner. "Will you buy me one for Christmas, Uncle Tanner?"

Tanner tucked his aviator glasses in the V of his T-shirt and patted Piper on the back. "I can't save money that fast, Pip."

"I have sixteen dollars and twenty-three cents in my plane bank." Those bright blue eyes peered up at him, practically begging him. "Will that help?"

"Darlin', if that's all it took, I'd have several planes. Why don't I take you for a ride later today? You can pretend to be my flight coach."

"I actually do have lessons later," Jax stated. "Livie is busy with Jade and Melanie. They went to some place this side of Atlanta to look for flooring. Apparently there was some discount outlet where Livie thought she could get a good deal for the restaurant."

For the past four nights Melanie had stayed at his house. He hadn't spoken about or questioned the obvious. If she was content staying, he was more than eager to share his space with her. He hadn't known where she was going this morning when he'd gotten dressed and left. She'd just been waking up and he'd made her a cup of coffee and some toast. He'd discovered she had a little queasiness in the mornings, so he tried to make things as simple as possible for her.

He also wasn't going to ask about her plans or try to

keep tabs on her. That she felt safe at his place was more than he'd hoped for at this stage. Even though he'd known her for several months, this past eight weeks had snowballed into a relationship he hadn't been ready for. But he was damn glad they were at this point.

And so far, she was healthy. The nausea was normal, though he hated that she felt bad. But he'd take normal, because that meant things were progressing as they should. Now if he could just keep his anxiety at bay during the duration of this pregnancy.

"Dude." Jax snapped his fingers. "You with me?"

Tanner nodded. "Yeah. I'll take Piper. We can do something this afternoon."

"You got any DIY projects?" she asked.

Jax laughed. "She's been watching HGTV like it's her job."

Tanner instantly thought about the rocker in his garage. Would Melanie even like something old and refurbished? She'd never indicated otherwise, but part of him knew she'd probably gotten used to that high-society lifestyle. Even though she'd hated her marriage, had she enjoyed the finer things that her money could buy?

Perhaps not. She did, after all, trade out her stylish SUV for a very well-used car.

"I actually do have something we can work on," Tanner stated, earning him a wide smile from his favorite five-year-old. "You'll need old clothes."

"What she's wearing is fine." Jax flipped the log and jotted down more information for the upcoming flights. "I should be done around eight this evening, but as soon as Livie is back, I'll have her stop by your house and pick Piper up. She mentioned running one more errand once the flooring trip was done. My student needs to get in a couple hours of dusk-to-dark flying."

"I can keep her busy that long." Tanner yanked on one curly blond ponytail. "You ready to go now?"

"Grab the booster out of the back of my truck," Jax told him.

Piper bobbed her head and grabbed her little blue purse from the counter. "Ready!"

When she slid her hand in his, Tanner's heart lurched. Oh, he'd held her hand and carried her plenty of times over the course of her five years, but knowing he was going to be doing this with his own child had him realizing just how precious these moments were.

"Do you like my new purse?" Piper asked as they headed toward his truck. "Mom bought it for me the other day. She said it matched my eyes."

Mom. He absolutely loved that Jax had found someone to love him and Piper so much that she flawlessly fit right into their little family. Piper had never known her birth mother. Jax's ex took off so soon after Piper was born. The woman was selfish, but in hindsight it was the best move, because Jax and Piper deserved so much better.

Tanner grabbed her purple booster seat and carried it to his truck. Once he had it in place, he lifted her up and settled her in. "Buckle up, Pip. We're going for ice cream first."

"You're my favorite uncle ever!"

Tanner kissed her on the nose. "Make sure to tell that to your Uncle Cash."

She only giggled as he closed the door. Tanner headed toward town, listening to Piper chatter about school and her friends. Then she went into how her teacher had yellow hair and wore black glasses and cool shoes.

"You like kindergarten, then?"

"It's the best grade I've ever been in," she declared.

Considering she'd only done one year of preschool, she hadn't much experience. But her eagerness was adorable. Tanner actually had hated school. He and Cash and Jax had been too eager to get out and join the air force. Jax and Cash had been in love with their girlfriends at the time of graduation, which nearly stopped them from enlisting, but Tanner had been ready.

When he'd been home on leave he'd fallen in love, and his life had spiraled into heartache he'd barely recovered from. Throwing himself into the military had been his only way of coping at the time.

"Can I call Melanie Aunt Mel?"

Piper's question completely pulled him from his thoughts. "Well, I guess that's up to her."

"Are you excited to be a daddy? I think you'll be a great dad."

"I appreciate that, squirt. I am excited."

"Is Aunt Mel having a boy or a girl?"

Tanner glanced in his rearview mirror and spotted those little eyes on him. "We're not sure yet. But as soon as we know, I'll tell you."

"I want a baby boy cousin. Boys are more fun than girls."

Poor kid. Before Livie came around, Piper had only been around men. They'd had to clean up their language real quick when the toddler started dropping F-bombs. The guys realized raising a kid wasn't going to be as simple as they'd thought.

"You know, you'll kind of be like a big sister," Tanner told her. Her brows raised, her eyes widened, and she let out another one of those squeals.

"You know what would be really cool?" she asked. "If

you could tell Mom and Dad to have a baby. Then I could be a big sister for real."

Yeah, that was not an area he was going to venture into with his cousin and Livie. Tanner pulled into the Scoops parking lot just as his cell went off in his pocket.

"Give me one second, Piper."

When he eyed the screen, he was surprised to see a message from Jade.

Delete this after you read it, but Neville just called Melanie. Thought you should know.

Rage bubbled within him. He sent a quick reply of thanks and deleted the message. What the hell did her ex want? And why was Jade telling him? If he knew Melanie like he thought, she probably brushed aside the call like it was no big deal. But this definitely was a big deal.

"You okay, Uncle Tanner?"

He pulled himself from the anger boiling inside him and nodded. "I'm good. Are you ready for a scoop of double chocolate chunk?"

"I want two scoops," she stated.

Tanner eyed her in the mirror. "If I give you two scoops then you won't eat your dinner."

"This is my dinner."

With a shrug, he smiled. "Fine by me. Let's go."

Tanner kept the call in the back of his mind. He hoped Melanie opened up to him about it because there was no way for him to ask without giving up Jade. But Jade must be concerned or she wouldn't have just texted him like that.

First things first, he had to get ice cream and get Piper back to his place so they could start sanding and painting the rocker. Later tonight, he would focus on Melanie.

Because nothing was going to threaten his family. He didn't care how powerful Neville Prescott was. Tanner was more powerful in ways Neville couldn't imagine.

When it came to protecting Mel and the baby, Tanner had no limits.

Chapter Fourteen

I am currently under construction. Thank you for your patience.

—Mel's Motivational Blog

"Whatever that smell is, make it stop."

Jade tapped the wooden spoon on the side of the pot and turned to face Melanie. "You're not looking too good."

Holding her hand over her nose, Melanie took a seat on the bar stool. "I was feeling a little nauseated, but now that smell is about to put me over the edge."

"I thought pregnant women were only sick in the morning."

"Technically I haven't been sick, but apparently my little one didn't get the memo on the time of day to make me queasy."

Jade crossed her arms over her chest and leaned back against the counter next to the stove. "Ready to talk about that phone call?"

The phone call. Might as well have its own zip code for the amount of real estate it took up in her mind. Her blog announcement regarding her pregnancy had been a hit right off the bat. She'd been replying most of the day to her viewers' congrats and excitement. Having her post go live made this all seem so much more real.

She'd known Neville would find out, but once she'd told Tanner about a portion of her past, Melanie decided she wasn't hiding anymore. She was excited for this baby and she refused to let her ex steal any more of her joy. She'd moved on and he needed to learn to do the same . . . without her. Apparently two years wasn't enough for him to get the idea she was never coming back.

"What do you want me to say?" Melanie asked. "Neville is furious, but he's ready to spin this as his child and that we're one big happy family."

The thought churned like acid in her stomach. She couldn't even imagine what Tanner would think if he knew Neville had concocted such a ridiculous plan. Anything to look like a shining star for the voters.

"He's an arrogant asshole," Jade spouted. "I hate that man."

Melanie toyed with the scalloped edge of the fall-themed place mats on the bar. "Yes, well, I think we're all in agreement there. I'm sure he'll run to tell his parents and they'll get on board, too. That won't be his last call to me."

Jade blew out a sigh, glanced at her pot of whatever smelly concoction she was making, then turned her focus back to Melanie. "He makes me nervous, Mel. You really need to consider a restraining order."

"We've been divorced for two years. He's not going to do anything to me. He knows full well I have too much on him for his threats to hold any merit."

"Still, be careful." Jade grabbed her spoon and started stirring once again. "Do you want some kale and turkey sausage soup? It's about ready."

Melanie swallowed in an attempt not to throw up at just the description. "Um, I think I'll pass."

"Does that mean you're having dinner with Tanner and staying over again?"

"I only stayed a few times."

Jade tossed a glance over her shoulder. "That's how it all starts. Do you have a toothbrush there yet?"

The instant image of a yellow toothbrush next to Tanner's green one flashed through her mind.

"I rest my case," Jade stated with a nod and a smile. "Not judging. I think it's great if you move in with him, actually. I've said it before, but you two are good for each other."

Well, they were certainly compatible between the sheets. And Melanie had to admit she adored his mother and stepdad. She'd felt so welcome and . . . loved. As crazy as that sounded to say, considering she'd only spent a few hours with them, Melanie knew they were good people. From her experience, she liked to think she was an excellent judge of character.

"He told me about his fiancée and baby."

"I was hoping you two would open up to each other." Jade moved to the cabinet next to the fridge to pull out a bowl. "You've both endured quite a bit."

"I can't even imagine losing someone you love, and a baby," Melanie murmured. "At first I thought he was trying to be controlling and possessive, but his actions and worry are completely justified."

"He's not a jerk," Jade said as she dipped out her soup. "Cash, on the other hand, is arrogant and a total prick at times, but Tanner and Jax . . . total sweethearts."

Melanie couldn't help but smile and fold her hands over the place mat. "Trouble with Cash?"

"No trouble. He keeps trying to warn me about Brad, but it's none of his concern and Brad is a nice guy." Jade rolled her eyes. "Cash just has to get over the fact that he doesn't impress me like he does the other ladies in this town. He dates younger girls who are easy to charm. I know better."

Jade definitely knew better. Her sexual harassment suit had forced her to look at things in a whole new light. Now she was more cautious than ever before. Not that she'd ever been in a long-term relationship, but Jade at one time had hearts in her eyes and marriage on her mind. The whole workplace debacle had tarnished her spirit.

"Cash isn't a bad guy," Melanie said. "He is a bit . . . confident."

"You mean arrogant, like I just said."

Melanie shook her head. "I think a certain level of confidence is attractive in a guy. Maybe you should try going out with Cash. How weird would it be if we all ended up together?"

Jade let out a snort and settled onto a bar stool next to Melanie. "I wouldn't go on a date with Cash, let alone end up with the guy. Yeah, he's hot and sexy, if you find tattoos and muscles attractive."

"Ironically, I do."

Jade laughed. "Damn it, I do, too. But still, Cash is . . . well, he's Cash. I went to school with him and even then he thought he was God's gift to anything wearing a skirt. Or nothing at all, which is how he prefers."

Melanie came to her feet and stepped back. "As much as I'd love to discuss this with you, that kale soup is making me question the lunch I had. I'm just going to get my things and head out."

Jade spooned up another bite and slurped it. "Tell Tanner I said hi."

Melanie shook her head and smiled. No need to deny exactly where she was going. She'd fallen into an easy pattern of being with Tanner and he was all too eager to get her to move in with him. Part of her wanted that, too. But was it too early? Was this just her clinging to some semblance of hope for a positive future? Could all of this between them really be that easy?

When they'd first met there had been so much tension, but looking back now she recognized it for exactly what it was. Total attraction.

Melanie gathered a small bag and headed out the front door to her car, parked on the street. She'd gotten used to the smaller ride; she was even used to the pillow behind her back. The horn, on the other hand, was still a tad embarrassing when she had to use it. But she still wouldn't change a thing. She was thrilled the sale of her overpriced SUV would help out in some small way toward the airport renovation.

The grants that were set to come through would be everything, though. Melanie smiled as she drove to the other side of town toward Tanner's house. Earlier today she, Jade, and Livie had driven to Atlanta and found some fabulous flooring that would work perfectly for the restaurant. They'd brainstormed on their mini–road trip about a vision for the menu and how to go about finding the right people to employ.

Even though this was Jax and Livie's baby, they were all taking part in making this airport something grand. This time next year, hopefully their clientele would be from the film and movie industry, coming to make blockbusters and series.

Melanie wanted to blog about the progress, but would definitely have to run this by Livie and Jax first. That would be something that readers would certainly find interesting, especially considering the publicity Haven had gotten over the last year.

When she turned into Tanner's drive, she smiled at the sight in the garage. Piper sat atop Tanner's shoulders and he was spinning in a circle. Piper's arms were out wide, her mouth open, no doubt in a squeal, as Tanner gripped her ankles.

If she ever had a doubt about the type of father he'd be, this put her worries to rest. These guys were so great with sweet Piper. Considering the little girl had been practically raised by three men, they'd all done an amazing job.

Melanie left her bag in the car and stepped out. The sun had set, but the garage lights were on, as were the porch lights. She headed up the stone drive and her footfalls caught Tanner's attention. He came to an abrupt stop and Piper's head kept bobbing.

"Whoa, Uncle Tanner. That made my belly feel funny."

"Don't puke on my head, little one."

Melanie laughed and reached up. "Why don't I help you down?"

Piper went eagerly to her arms. "Thanks, Aunt Mel."

Melanie caught Tanner's gaze. "She asked if she could call you that."

"A promotion in my name?" Melanie asked, turning her attention to the cutie in her arms. "I've never been an aunt before. I think I like it already."

"Come see what we've been working on," Piper stated, clapping her hands, then pointing to the back corner.

"Oh, honey, she doesn't need to," Tanner said. "It's getting late and your mom should be here any minute to pick you up."

Piper's brows drew in. "Why don't you want Aunt Mel to see my work? Did I do a bad job?"

"No, of course not." Tanner gestured toward the back. "Go ahead and show her."

Still holding Piper secure in her arms, Melanie moved around the truck and past the motorcycle. In the corner was an old wooden rocker covered with dust from sanding.

"I got to use the sandpaper," Piper said, beaming. "But then I got hungry because ice cream isn't real dinner, so Uncle Tanner had to make me a cheeseburger, so we didn't have time to paint."

Melanie laughed. "Sounds like you've had quite an eventful evening."

"You weren't supposed to mention the ice cream for dinner thing," Tanner murmured with a tug on her ponytail.

Melanie squeezed Piper tighter. "I won't tell a soul."

A car door slammed behind them and Piper scrambled down and yelled for her mom as she ran from the garage.

Melanie focused back on the sanded rocker, then glanced at Tanner. "Looks like you guys enjoyed some quality time."

Tanner nodded and shoved his hands in his pockets. "We did. I took her earlier while you guys were still in Atlanta and Jax had some lessons to do. She's a good kid, but, man, I'm worn out."

"Aw, poor you," Melanie mocked. "You can chase bad guys and work long shifts, but a little girl who eats ice cream and burgers was too much to handle."

Tanner raked a hand over his hair, messing it up even more and causing dark points to stand on end. "Go ahead, mock me."

"Thanks, Tanner," Livie called from the front of the garage. "I appreciate you keeping her all day."

"Nothing else I'd rather do on my regular day off."

Melanie shoved her elbow in his side, earning her a grunt. "Bye, Piper. Glad I got to see you."

Piper waved. "See ya, Aunt Mel."

As they walked away, Melanie heard Livie asking about Aunt Mel, and Piper explaining. The last thing Livie had wanted when they'd come to Haven just less than a year ago was any form of attachment. She'd wanted to sell her father's airport, take her money, and get back to Atlanta. Fate had had other plans—namely Jax, Piper, and love.

The easy way they all fell in love with each other had been so perfect. Melanie knew Livie really wanted the wedding to happen soon, but at the same time the airport was consuming each and every moment of their days.

"So, you stopped by to say good night, or were you thinking of something more?" Tanner asked.

Melanie smiled and tipped her head. "I have a bag in the car."

"Is this an overnight bag or a long-term size bag?"

He reached forward and took both her hands in his. Melanie stared into those dark eyes and wondered how she could stop herself from falling for him.

"You look tired," he told her. "That's not a ploy to get you to stay, but are you feeling okay?"

"I am tired and I do plan on staying." She leaned forward and slid her lips over his. "If the offer still stands."

"The offer is always there."

"Then for tonight, I'll stay."

He released her hands and wrapped his arms around her waist. Thankfully he didn't mention that she kept staying one night at a time. To say she was moving in was just too much of a commitment. There was still some fear of letting that last shred of control go if she relinquished her independence.

"Go on into the house," he murmured against her lips. "I'll lock up out here and get your bag from the car."

"I'll get the bag, you lock up here." She started to turn, but stopped and shifted her gaze back to the rocker. "What are you doing with that?"

Tanner shrugged one shoulder. "Just a project I've been meaning to work on."

She hesitated, thinking there was more to the story. Part of her couldn't help but wonder if this was for the baby, but she didn't want to ruin any surprise if that was indeed the case.

Melanie grabbed her bag and purse from the car. As tired as she was, she contemplated telling Tanner about the call earlier from Neville. On one hand she felt Tanner deserved to know, but on the other, she wanted to shield him from her ex and his evils.

Tonight, she figured she'd just relax and enjoy Tanner. Any issues she had would be there tomorrow, and if things got to a point she felt she couldn't handle them, then she'd fill him in.

Dueling cells went off at the same time on Tanner's dresser. He rolled out of bed, leaving Melanie as she rolled over and placed her hand where he'd been.

If both their cells were vibrating, then most likely this wasn't a work emergency.

He'd worked the past four days straight and Melanie had stayed over each night. And each time she'd gone home and come back with just enough for that night.

One day, he figured he'd come home and she'd have a full suitcase and half his closet full. He couldn't wait.

He grabbed his cell and checked the message. A group text. Those were always evil and damn annoying.

Everyone meet at Bella Vous at 2. Dress nice.

The message was from Jax. Dress nice? What the hell did that mean, and since when did Jax give a damn about what people wore?

"What's going on?" Mel murmured with her head still half into the pillow.

"We've been summoned to the resort this afternoon and—"

Melanie jumped out of bed and ran toward the bathroom, bumping his shoulder along the way. The next moment he heard her getting sick. Tanner quickly went to the kitchen to get a cold bottle of water and came back. He knew she would want privacy, but there was no way he could just stand by and do nothing.

He stepped into the adjoining bath and set the water on the vanity.

"Go away," she muttered.

Ignoring her request, Tanner opened the cabinet and grabbed a cloth and wet it. He wrung out the cold water and then pulled her hair back from her neck and laid the cloth on her skin.

"I'm not leaving," he told her. "I'm here for all of this."

"I'd rather you not see the gross parts." She grabbed the cloth from her neck and swiped at her face. "Do you care to get me a couple crackers?"

"Of course."

He went back to the kitchen. He had no idea if she truly wanted something in her stomach or if she was using the excuse to get him out of the bathroom. Regardless, he would do anything for her. Pregnancy scared the hell out of him. Obvious understatement, but aside from the worry that something could go wrong, he hated like hell that Melanie felt so miserable.

Tanner grabbed three boxes of crackers. He had no clue what kind she wanted or how many. By the time he got back to the bedroom, she was sitting on the edge of the bed sipping the water.

"I think I'm okay," she told him. "I feel a little dizzy, but hopefully the crackers will help."

Her eyes darted to the boxes in his hands. "You really do go above and beyond. Is that an occupational hazard?"

Tanner set the boxes beside her. "I just wanted to cover all my bases."

Melanie twisted the cap back on the water bottle and set it behind her on the bed. She attempted to smooth her bedraggled hair from her face, then his T-shirt she'd slept in slipped off her shoulder and she tried to right that as well.

"I'm a mess," she muttered.

"You're beautiful." He adjusted the shirt, then tucked her hair behind one ear as he sat next to her. "Which crackers do you want?"

"Any will be fine."

He opened one box and handed her an entire sleeve. She chewed on a few and then turned to face him. "What were you saying about the resort?"

It took him a minute to recall the text. "Jax said for everyone to be at Bella Vous at two o'clock and to dress nice."

Melanie's brows drew in. "That's weird. Wonder what's going on."

Tanner shrugged. "No idea. It's my first day off, so I haven't really talked to him much the past few days. Did Livie mention anything to you?"

"Nothing. We even went running yesterday, but Jade was busy discussing a guy she'd met that she's thinking of going out with."

Tanner instantly went still. "What guy?"

"Relax," Melanie said, reaching for another cracker. "No need to go all big brother. I didn't get his name actually, but she said he'd just moved here."

Tanner couldn't help but be protective of his friends. Hell, he was protective of the entire town.

"Are the crackers helping?"

Melanie shrugged. "I have no idea. I feel like I could go back to bed and sleep for a week."

"Go back to bed, then. You have nothing else to do until this afternoon, right?"

"I have several emails to answer because someone occupied my evening and I didn't get to them."

Tanner wasn't the least bit sorry they'd spent the night watching an old movie and making love on the sofa. Every time he came home from work and she was waiting for him was like receiving the greatest gift over and over.

"The emails aren't going anywhere," he told her. "At least lie back down for an hour and then get up and work."

Melanie handed the crackers back to him and nodded. "Will you wake me?"

"Of course."

He gathered the boxes and the water and waited until she was settled in before heading to the kitchen. She'd still not said a word about Neville calling, and that grated on his trust level. He wholeheartedly trusted her, except in one area. She was going to try to protect him. That much was evident. He'd finally gotten her to open up and feel again, whether she wanted to admit it or not, but he couldn't break through her determination to shield him from her past.

There was no one Tanner feared. Not one person. Neville might be powerful, but that meant nothing in the long run. The guy was a grade-A asshole. People like that had skeletons in their closets, and if Neville tried to threaten what was Tanner's, there would be hell to pay like Neville had never known.

If Melanie was insistent on protecting him, then he would just have to stay one step ahead of her, because she and this baby were absolutely everything. And nothing would wreck his family again.

Chapter Fifteen

Your comeback needs to be stronger than your setback.

—Mel's Motivational Blog

The crisp fall afternoon was perfect. Tanner had taken Melanie back to her house and she'd thrown on a simple sleeveless, knee-length dress in green, her favorite color, and she'd paired that with a cream cardigan and little peep-toe booties. She'd thrown on a gold strand with random clear beads, and hoop earrings. Her makeup remained simple, too. She had no idea what was going on, but the resort was a stunning Civil War–era home and the grounds were absolutely breathtaking.

When Melanie was changing, Jade had been getting ready as well and was equally confused. They'd both tried texting Olivia, but she'd been so vague, she just kept telling them there was a surprise.

Tanner headed up the long, curved drive toward Bella Vous. The old magnolia trees dotted all around the property demanded attention. Once he reached the top of the drive, the view of the pond and cypress trees was instantly relaxing. Melanie could easily see herself sitting in the shade beneath the trees at the water's edge and getting more than enough inspiration for her blog.

Tanner pulled his truck in next to Cash's and right behind them came Jade in her sporty car. Cash grabbed the door handle and opened for Melanie. When he reached his hand in, she placed hers in his and let him help her down.

"Go get your own damn girl," Tanner growled as he killed the engine and got out.

Cash wrapped Melanie's hand around the bend of his arm. "He really is territorial. Like a grouchy bear."

"Any clue what's going on?" Jade asked as she came around the back of Tanner's truck.

Cash stilled against Melanie and she was positive the man stopped breathing as he stared at Jade, who was adjusting her body-hugging dress and smoothing it down her thighs so she totally missed the transfixed Cash.

Melanie shot a glance to Tanner, who was trying in vain not to smile. He silently replied with a wink. Poor Cash. He had it bad, but apparently Jade was either oblivious or she didn't care. Melanie figured the latter.

It would take one very special man with patience and strength to fight through the defensive walls Jade had erected around herself.

Not that Cash wasn't special, but could he do the job? Melanie wished someone would step into Jade's life and help her get over the bitterness she let fester day after day. But Melanie wasn't about to call her out on that. At least, not quite yet.

"We're all in the dark here," Tanner stated. "You ladies look nice, whatever is going on."

Melanie elbowed Cash to get him out of his trance before drool started down his chin. He blinked and shook his head as he turned his attention toward the house.

"No clue what's going on," he stated. "Ready?"

Melanie smiled and he simply raised his brows. Yeah, he'd totally been caught checking out her best friend, but Jade was a stunning woman, with all of that auburn hair waving down her back and that deep sapphire blue dress she wore. The woman would always turn heads, no matter if she was dressed up or in her running gear. Melanie wanted to hate her, but it was impossible not to love someone who was so loyal and kind.

They headed up the sidewalk that curved out around the lush landscaping and led them toward the wide porch with thick white columns. The oak door swung wide and Sophie Monroe stood there with a wide smile. She'd cut her dark hair since Melanie had last seen her. Now it lay in a classy cut just below her chin. She wore a pale pink dress with silver flats and as always was the epitome of charming.

"Hey, guys. So glad you could come." She opened the door wider and gestured them inside. "Go on out back through the study. Everything is set up on the patio today."

Sophie Monroe was just as cryptic as Jax and Livie. What in the world was going on?

Leading the way toward the back of the house, Sophie ushered them into the den. Any other time Melanie would take a moment and appreciate the beauty of the way they'd managed to bring the old and the new together with the décor and the built-in bookcases that ran from floor to ceiling.

But right now Melanie was more intrigued with all the secrecy.

Cash released her arm and moved forward to hold open the French doors. Tanner stepped up next to her side and palmed the small of her back.

The moment they stepped onto the patio, Melanie

couldn't suppress her smile. There were three outdoor benches on each side with a small aisle in the middle. The white petals on the stone running from the doorway, down the aisle, and to the beaming couple at the end told the entire story.

"Surprise," Piper shouted, wearing the blue dress Livie had purchased for the wedding. She stood between Jax and Livie, holding their hands. "We're getting married."

"We didn't know when we'd have time to plan everything, so we decided to just do it," Olivia stated. "Also, Melanie, you don't have to worry about a dress fitting."

Melanie laughed. "Well, then, congratulations to both of us."

"We've closed this section off to the guests for the afternoon, so it's all ours." Sophie went to stand next to Zach and wrapped her arm through his. "We're so excited everyone could make it."

"We had no idea what was going on," Cash stated, stepping forward and slapping Jax on the back. "Good for you guys. I'm happy for you."

Jade moved in on the other side of Melanie. "I can't believe you kept this a secret. How did you manage that? And by the way, you look stunning."

Livie glanced down at her simple floor-length lace dress and then to Piper, who stared up at her with that little girl sparkle in her eyes.

"Piper and I may have been doing some behind-the-scenes work to make this happen," Livie explained. "That's another reason Tanner had Piper the other day. I was picking up my dress and Jax's suit."

"This is the only occasion she'd ever get me in a suit," Jax chimed in.

The always masculine Jax could typically be found in jeans and a tee or a flannel shirt. Work boots were always the shoe of choice. But today he had on a charcoal gray suit with matching shirt and black patent shoes. Melanie had to admit he looked handsome, even with the scruff along his jawline and the unruly hair he attempted to fix.

"Eyes over here, darlin'," Tanner whispered in her ear.

Melanie squeezed Tanner's hand and threw him a glance. "Just taking in all the scenery."

He leaned over against her ear, his lips brushing the sensitive skin. "All the scenery you need is right beside you."

Her body trembled and she couldn't figure out how the man could turn her on so simply and with all these people around.

"If you guys are ready to get started, just take a seat." Sophie gestured toward the benches. "The minister is inside talking with Liam. I'll go get him."

Piper headed down the aisle toward Melanie. "Do you like my dress, Aunt Mel? I've never had a dress so fancy, but Mom said it was perfect for the wedding."

Melanie's heart melted. "It is perfect. But you know, you're just as beautiful in your overalls helping your daddy in the hangar. You know what makes a girl beautiful?"

"Her heart?" Piper asked with a slight wrinkle of her nose.

Melanie nodded. "That's right. Did Livie tell you that?"

"She tells me all the time that being nice is more beautiful than what I wear or how my hair is."

Melanie looked to Livie, who stood with tears swimming in her eyes. "Your mom is one smart lady. You're a lucky little girl."

"I changed my mind about the boy. I want you to have a little girl," Piper added. "We'll be best friends and I'll teach her about planes."

Melanie tapped her finger on the end of Piper's button

nose. "No matter what I have, you are going to have to teach this baby all about planes, because you know way more than I do. Is that a deal, Pip?"

Piper nodded, her curled hair bouncing around her shoulders. "It's a deal."

She ran back down the aisle toward Livie and began chatting, no doubt telling her about the new deal.

Melanie took a seat on one of the garden benches that had been moved to the patio for the ceremony. When she sat next to Tanner, he placed his hand on her knee and leaned in.

"Thank you for loving her like we do."

Melanie settled her hand over his. "She's so easy to love."

And so was the man beside her. There was no denying the truth any longer. She'd started falling for him when he'd pulled her over for a speeding ticket on her first day in town. She'd been angry, but he'd been so damn attractive in that uniform and those dark aviators, with that Southern drawl and the way he'd said *ma'am*. Her heart had fluttered right there on the side of the road as he wrote her up a hefty fine for going nearly twenty over the limit.

And now they were starting a family.

Fear niggled deep in her belly at the veiled threat from Neville the other day. She'd yet to tell Tanner. He needed to know, it was only right to tell him. Yet she didn't want him to get involved. Neville had tarnished so much of her life, Melanie didn't want him anywhere near Tanner.

The minister stepped out and went to stand in front. With everyone all smiles and hopeful, Melanie pushed the concerning thoughts from her mind.

As the ceremony progressed, Melanie's mind filled with what-ifs. What if this were her and Tanner one day? What if he wanted to make this something permanent?

What if she let her guard completely down and let him into her once battered heart?

Could she? Would Tanner want to take on someone with so much baggage? Because as much as she wanted to protect him from her past, if they were indeed looking at long-term as a couple, he'd have to know everything, and there was a good possibility Neville would cause trouble for them.

Tanner's thumb stroked the back of her hand. Just that slight feathering touch had her pulling back to the moment and calming her fears. She was here now, with her friends, with her lover, and the most precious wedding ever.

After Jax and Livie exchanged rings, the minister presented Piper with a ring as well. Melanie instantly teared up. Had she known she was coming to a wedding, she would at least have brought tissues. Her emotions were all over the place lately, and this was just too much.

Tanner wrapped his arm around her shoulders and pulled her against his side. Melanie swiped at her cheeks and spotted Jade across the aisle. Even she had let a tear escape. Melanie hadn't known that woman could cry. Whenever she got upset, she bottled up her emotions and went into pure badass mode.

Weddings, especially with an angelic little girl, would clench anyone's heart. Finally, the minister had Jax kiss Livie, and Piper jumped up and down, clapping her hands. Jax released Livie and reached down, picked up his daughter, and kissed her cheek. They all turned to face their friends, and Melanie loved this picture of the little family Livie had now.

Sophie stepped to the front of the patio, her smile still beaming as it had since they'd all arrived. "There is cake and some food in the main dining area. We'd love to have you all stay as long as you need. We've made other arrangements for our guests, so this time is all yours."

At the mention of cake, Melanie couldn't help but recall the amazing cupcake Tanner had brought her from Liam's pastry shop here. She'd been watching what she ate with this baby, not just because she was health conscious, but because the baby needed proper nutrients.

They all made their way into the dining room, which looked like something straight from a Southern magazine. There was no doubt in what era this home was built. With the narrow floor-to-ceiling windows, the intricate detailing in the crown moldings and the medallion surrounding the base of the chandelier, Melanie couldn't take in all the beauty at once. The Monroe boys had definitely put in a vast amount of money and time on this project. Melanie had heard how run-down the place was when they'd taken over.

Seeing how magnificent they'd made this home and the business they'd created, gave Melanie a new burst of hope for the airport. They definitely had a vision, and with all the determination among the six of them, there was no way they'd fail. They were all fighters, each having their own skills to aid in making the newly revamped airport a success.

A beautiful lace cloth covered the long, oblong dining table, and in the center was a simple pale pink cake with two tiers separated with flawless white roses. A gold initial M sat atop the cake, symbolizing the new Morgan family.

Along the sideboard were various finger foods, and Liam brought in another tray of some type of wraps that smelled heavenly as he passed by.

"This all looks so amazing," Livie stated. "I can't thank

you all enough for helping throw this together last minute, and while guests are here."

Sophie waved a hand in the air and shook her head. "We are thrilled to help. Besides, you're giving my husband work with the renovations. It's the least we could do."

"If you all need anything else, let me know," Liam stated before he headed back toward the kitchen.

Melanie didn't know the Monroe brothers well, since she hadn't grown up here, but she'd had some dealings with Zach since the start of the airport project. Liam was the quiet one, but Braxton was the one brother Melanie had never seen. She knew he was married to the fabulous masseuse here at Bella Vous.

Three power couples ran this place, and flawlessly so far. Melanie had heard nothing but amazing things about it. She knew firsthand the pastries and the massages were top-notch, and those were reasons enough to want to come here. Who wouldn't want to get away and escape reality when Bella Vous offered so much?

"If I ever lose my mind and get married, I want it to be simple like this," Jade whispered as she took a seat next to Melanie.

"You'll marry one day," Melanie assured her friend. "The right guy will come along and you'll be helpless against your feelings for him."

Jade smirked and raised one brow. "Is that what's happening to you?"

Melanie pursed her lips, then grinned. "Maybe."

"Good." Jade gave a firm nod of approval. "You deserve to be helplessly in love with a man who isn't an asshole."

Melanie swatted at Jade's arm. "I never said I was in love, and you shouldn't say *asshole* at a wedding reception."

"Why not? These guys have said worse, trust me."

Tanner's hand slid over Melanie's thigh beneath the table, drawing her attention to the fact that he sat so close, the entire side of his body brushed against hers.

She tipped her head and found his gaze locked onto hers.

"Feeling alright?" he asked.

"I feel fine. Stop worrying."

This morning she'd been mortified that he'd been there to witness her first bout of morning sickness, but he'd been so attentive and caring, she was sort of glad she hadn't been alone.

They all ate and raved over the finger foods and the fabulous raspberry and vanilla torte. And Melanie had thought that cupcake was divine. This slice of cake was positively heavenly. No doubt her little one would be enjoying this.

Hey, it was fruit, so that totally counted as a day's serving.

What seemed like hours later, Melanie stretched and came to her feet. Jade was across the room talking with Sophie, and Tanner had congregated in the corner with Jax and Cash. After all she'd eaten, she seriously needed a nap. Who knew growing a child took so much energy? She'd read in several places that the second trimester brought on less sickness and more energy. She couldn't wait to hit that twelve-week mark.

"Can I feel your tummy?"

Melanie turned around to see Piper with her wide eyes glued to Melanie's midsection. She couldn't help but laugh.

"You can, but there's not much to feel right now. My belly hasn't gotten any bigger yet. The baby is just the size of a raspberry."

She gasped. "Like the kind we had in the cake?"

Melanie laughed. "That's just the comparison. My baby will grow, and as she does, my belly will grow. It won't be long and you'll be able to feel her moving around."

"You think it's a girl?"

Melanie shrugged. "I really have no idea. That just came out."

"I'm going to guess a boy." Piper laid her little hands over Melanie's flat belly. "Just don't name him Austin. There's a kid in my class and he always pulls my ponytails. His name is Austin and I hate him."

Melanie bit the inside of her lips to keep from smiling. Piper was passionate about everything she ever discussed. That's what made her so special and perfect. Melanie hoped she never changed.

"You about ready to go?" Tanner asked, coming up to her side. He wrapped his arm around her and smiled down at Piper. "You feeling for the baby?"

"I think it's a boy, but Aunt Mel said a girl."

"I think it's a girl, too," Tanner said, surprising Melanie.

"You do?" she asked.

"I've just had a feeling." He gave a slight shrug. "I guess when I think of the baby, I instantly think of her having your blond hair and bright green eyes."

The fact that he'd given so much thought to the way their baby would look had her heart lurching even more toward him. There was no way at all to keep her heart from becoming involved. Tanner had made it impossible.

Which made her wonder just exactly how he felt about her. He'd asked her to move in, but that could have more to do with the baby. He'd said at first that's why he was so protective, but now, did he truly care for her on a more permanent level, or did he just want to keep a closer eye on her?

"We should say goodbye to everyone," Melanie stated

before turning her attention back to Piper. "Maybe when the time comes, you could help me decorate the nursery. You're the only kid I know."

Piper's eyes lit up. "Could I really? No matter if you have a boy or a girl?"

"No matter what," Melanie promised.

Piper threw her arms around Melanie's waist, her little head resting on Melanie's belly. "You're the best, Aunt Mel."

Melanie squeezed her back and met Tanner's eyes. "I think you're pretty special, too. You've had a pretty exciting day. I'm glad my best friend is your mom now officially."

Piper eased back and held up her hand with the sparkly gold band. "We're married forever. The minister said so."

"That's right, Pip." Tanner gave one of her curls a tug. "You're a perfect family now."

"Are you going to be a family like Mom and Dad?"

Piper glanced back and forth between Melanie and Tanner. The silence grew beyond uncomfortable and there was no way Melanie was going to answer that.

"We are already a family," Tanner explained. "Melanie and I are having a baby."

"But are you going to put a ring on her finger like my daddy did?"

Tanner raked a hand over the back of his neck, and his eyes darted to Melanie as if silently asking for help. Melanie held her hands up and shook her head. Hell no, she wasn't about to answer.

"I'd like to know the answer to that, too." Jade stepped up next to Melanie and gave her a wink. "Melanie has always been partial to emeralds, but she'd never tell you that. Green is her favorite color, though."

Melanie recalled one night when they'd had girls' night

in and she'd had too much to drink after her divorce was final. Okay, fine, it was a divorce party, but only her, Jade, and Livie were in attendance. Anyway, she remembered stating if she ever married again she never wanted to see another diamond. Neville had bought her the most obnoxious stone, all for the show and the drama. The last thing she wanted in a relationship was flare. She wanted honor, loyalty, love. Was that too much to ask?

"Emeralds are pretty," Tanner agreed slowly. "Anyway, I need to say bye to the bride and groom and get Melanie home. She's tired."

"That dodge wasn't so slick," Jade muttered toward Tanner.

"I thought it was."

He stepped away and went over to hug Livie. Piper was right on his heels and held up her arms to her father.

"You think this little wedding has prompted the two of you to make a major decision?" Jade whispered.

Melanie crossed her arms and watched Tanner from across the wide dining room. "I'm not sure that I'm ready for that."

"You're having the man's baby. You mean to tell me a ring scares you?"

Melanie glanced at Jade. "All of this scares me. I've already been thrust into one life-altering factor, I'm not sure I can handle another right now."

"You better prepare yourself, because that man has more feelings for you than just as his baby mama."

Melanie couldn't describe the emotions that rolled through her at Jade's bold statement. Jade must've seen things that Melanie hadn't. Tanner was a blunt man and he was honest. But he'd never hinted at marriage.

And she needed to get those thoughts out of her head anyway. Yes, one day she wanted to marry and live the dream of happily ever after. She firmly believed love existed. She'd seen it—case in point the happy couple across the room.

Just because she had made a wrong choice and her first marriage was a living hell, didn't mean she didn't hold out hope for a man who would love and cherish her.

Was that man Tanner? Only time would tell.

Chapter Sixteen

There's no way I was born to just pay bills and die.
                                        —Mel's Motivational Blog

"Then the other office could go over in the opposite corner instead of making that a lobby area."

Melanie rubbed her head. Livie and Jax opted to not go on a honeymoon, and got right back into the renovations. Time was money, literally. They were paying contractors and Zach was overseeing everything, so they didn't want him tied up any longer than necessary.

"You can't keep changing things," Jax told Livie. "We don't need another office, so let's stick to the original plan and have this front area open for the lobby. We all liked the idea of some leather sofas and a few desks and chairs along the wall for work spaces."

Melanie listened to their bantering back and forth and was glad she'd waited until her stomach settled before she came in. Tanner had left for his shift early and she'd been on her own for her morning sickness. Thankfully, he'd left water and crackers next to her side of the bed.

Her side of the bed. That was the point they were at in this relationship. Was that a label?

"Zach said he was going to start the heavy work in the kitchen today because that's where the bulk of our renovations will be." Jax shoved his hands in his pockets and rocked back on his heels. "He had to run out and get a few more things, but when he comes back, we need to go over anything you want changed now, because once he starts, there's no going back."

Livie nodded. "I know, I know. I'm just nervous and I don't want to make a mistake in this. We've tied up so much of our money and now we have these grants."

Melanie took a seat on the old, worn plaid sofa in the current lobby. "There's nothing to worry about. Anything worth having is worth the risk, and I believe you guys are going to make this airport something your father would most definitely be proud of."

Livie smiled. "I hope so."

Melanie's cell chimed from her purse. She reached across the sofa and pulled it out, only to find Neville's assistant's name staring back at her.

"Still having issues?" Livie asked. Apparently the heavy sigh and the eye roll gave away the unwanted caller.

"Nothing I can't handle," Melanie assured her. "Excuse me."

Melanie stepped outside and around the corner where the building hadn't been touched yet. No debris or equipment there, and complete privacy.

She swiped the screen. "Hello?"

"Melanie, so glad I caught you. Neville has scheduled a meeting with you next Tuesday at eleven."

Taken aback, Melanie pulled the phone away and glared at it as if she'd heard the demand completely wrong.

"I'm not meeting with Neville."

"He said you'd say that," his assistant stated. "He did

say he'd let you choose the meeting place, but Tuesday at eleven is his only opening for quite some time."

Melanie snorted. Arrogant son of a bitch. He demands a meeting and acts like he's doing her a favor by carving out this time.

"I'm not coming to Atlanta or anywhere else to meet," Melanie reiterated. "I'm not going to answer any more of your calls or his. You can pass that along to him."

"Um, he says that he has some information that you will want to know."

Melanie stilled. "What type of information?"

"I'm not at liberty to say, but trust me when I tell you that you'll want to hear him out."

Melanie weighed her decision. What the hell was he up to now? This little impromptu meeting sure as hell wasn't for her benefit, and he wasn't giving her this supposed information because he was concerned about her. No, whatever game he was playing would benefit one person. Neville.

However, if she went and met with him face-to-face, maybe she could put this part of her past to rest once and for all. Perhaps he just needed to see that she was a different woman now. She was stronger, more determined than ever to own her life and put him behind her for good. He was used to the weak Melanie. He wouldn't even recognize the woman she'd become.

"Fine," Melanie conceded. "I'll text him with the location."

Melanie disconnected the call before his assistant could argue or ask for the location of the meeting. Pulling in a deep breath, Melanie had a knot of tension in her belly. Had she just made a date with the devil?

No matter. She wanted to get this over with. She wasn't doing this for Neville, she was doing this for herself. To face her past one final time, to prove that she'd come out on top despite all she'd been through. To face the monster one last time.

Melanie gripped her phone and headed back inside. Livie and Jax were still discussing the office versus lobby, but Livie quickly turned her attention to Melanie.

"Everything okay?"

With a slight nod, Melanie smiled. "Fine. What can I do for you guys today?"

"I'm going to be in the kitchen with Zach when he arrives," Jax stated. "I have no scheduled flights or lessons today."

"I plan on picking Piper up from school in a bit and we're going to do a little shopping. Care to join us?"

Melanie hadn't been shopping for herself in some time, but she was also saving every last dollar that came in through her sites. Eventually she was going to have to get a place of her own and save for her baby.

"I think I'll sit this one out," she told her friend. "I have some work to get done if I'm not needed here."

Livie tipped her head to the side. "What happened with the phone call?"

"Are you having trouble?" Jax asked, taking a step toward her.

"No, no trouble. I'll just head back to the house and get some things done. If you need me, just text."

Melanie turned to grab her purse from the sofa.

"Mel."

Livie's firm tone had Melanie turning back around. "I swear I'm fine. Go shopping. I'll catch you the next time."

Melanie headed out of the building to the car that she'd become used to. Her simple life here in Haven was clicking into place one portion at a time. She didn't want anyone to know about the meeting with Neville. They'd try to talk her out of it.

But she needed to go. She had to, for herself. There was something therapeutic about knowing he held no power over her anymore, and a thrill of strength shot through her because soon he would realize it as well.

She had greater things planned for her life, for her baby's life. And quite possibly a future with a man she'd fallen in love with.

Tanner pulled his patrol car up next to the curb a block away from the bank where currently a deranged man inside was waving a gun around and demanding money. The alarm had come through only six minutes ago, but those six minutes must seem like a lifetime to the innocent bystanders inside.

Ducking alongside his car, he moved toward one of the other officers on the scene. "How many hostages?"

"We have a teller inside the boardroom. She closed the door and the blinds as soon as the guy started yelling demands." The officer pointed toward one of the windows. "That's the room right there. She's in the utility closet in there on her cell phone. She can hear a little, but she's been giving us updates."

Well, at least they had someone inside. But damn it, things like this didn't happen in Haven. Tanner stared at the building, blinking against the bright afternoon sun despite having his sunglasses on.

"Just one armed gunman?" he asked.

"Yes. Other than wanting the money from the vault, he hasn't made demands to us or tried to contact anyone outside."

He would. No doubt the guy would try to use an innocent

as a bartering ploy to escape safely. Tanner's main objective here was to make sure each and every person got out of that bank safely.

So far there were four deputies and three officers on hand. Over his radio he heard requests for more backup from neighboring towns. The place needed to be completely surrounded.

"Captain is calling in now," the other officer said.

Making contact with the gunman was imperative from the start. Any good negotiator could get him talking, play to his sympathetic side, and try to pretend to understand where the suspect was coming from.

Tanner's gut tightened. He didn't like the waiting game, it only made his anxiety that much worse. He focused on his breathing, on looking ahead to an outcome where everyone remained safe and unharmed. He refused to think any other way.

He glanced down the row of police cars lined up against the curb facing the bank. His captain was on the phone and it was only a matter of time before they knew more and could make a plan of action.

"Damn it." The other officer pointed over Tanner's shoulder. "The media is here."

Not what they needed right now. Having even more innocent people around was never good. Besides, they didn't need this on the news or all over social media because the trickle effect would be hell. Once family members realized their loved ones were inside, then they'd come down, too.

Tanner remained crouched behind the car, but patted his buddy on the shoulder. "I'll go to them."

Someone had to field them and keep them at a safe distance. Already two other officers were sectioning off the area and pushing the journalists back.

"If you all could hold the photos and reporting for just

a bit," Tanner yelled to the growing group. "We promise to give a full statement shortly, but we don't want to cause more havoc than necessary and we need to focus on the situation inside."

"So there is a gunman with hostages?" one young female reporter asked. She had her cell pointed toward him and Tanner had to resist the urge to jerk it from her hands. She was only doing her job; unfortunately it interfered with his.

"No comment. A statement will come shortly, like I said. We need you to stay back."

Without another word, he headed back to the shield of cars and hunkered back down. "What did we learn?"

"Captain says the guy is slurring his words, most likely strung out or drunk." The officer kept his attention on the building as he spoke. "We learned he recently lost his job at the factory over in Silas and he needs money for his family."

Tanner couldn't even imagine the desperation that guy felt, but there was a right way and a wrong way to go about fixing your life when you were thrown for a loop. Breaking the law was definitely not the right way.

Added to that, if he'd been drinking or using any substances, he was most certainly unstable and they needed to get the hostages out of there now.

"Captain asked for him to release one hostage in good faith, but the gunman hung up," the officer went on. "We have learned his name is Marshall Malone. We're trying to reach his wife now, and hopefully she can call in and talk him out."

Another way to appeal to their compassionate side. All they had to do was get someone down here who knew him personally and could hopefully use the right words to end this situation.

Despite its being December, between Tanner's uniform and his Kevlar vest, the afternoon sun was starting to take its toll. Sweat rolled down his face, but he never took his eyes off the bank. He wondered what the situation was inside, prayed that they'd all go home at the end of the day.

Dread curled inside him as he thought of Melanie. If she saw this on the news or through social media . . . damn it. She lived on social media, and there was no way to prevent her from seeing this robbery in progress. He couldn't exactly take time to text and assure her he was fine.

The last thing he wanted was for her to be stressed, and this would no doubt terrify her.

Tanner had to remain focused, though. Those people inside were his top priority. He would have to worry about Melanie later, and this was the first time he truly hated putting his job ahead of his family.

This was also the first time he could truly admit that he was falling in love with her. He'd never wanted to put anyone ahead of his job before, but he'd give anything to reassure her right now. Anything to alleviate the fear she no doubt had, or would soon when she discovered what was happening.

As the crowd gathered along the perimeter of the roped-off area, he willed himself to remain in the moment and make it his mission to bring every single hostage out safely.

Then, once he was home safe himself, he'd tell Melanie how he truly felt.

Melanie couldn't tear her eyes from the screen. The news report had a camera pointed right toward the bank in town, and she'd already spotted Tanner. He hadn't moved in so long, but at least he was safe. For now.

She'd been in the middle of finishing up her scheduled blogs for next week when she'd scrolled through her phone to check on something from her social media page. That's when she'd seen the images from random folks who stood in the crowd and had uploaded phone pics of the events.

Her stomach had dropped and everything else had been forgotten. The blog, her work, literally everything ceased to exist.

She sat right on the floor of Tanner's living room with her legs crossed and her eyes glued to the television. Her heart raced like mad, but she tried to tell herself that as long as she could see his back on the screen, then he was fine.

But at some point this would all come to an end and she hoped he came home safe. Just the thought of something happening to him ripped her heart in two.

How had she ever compared him to Neville? When she had first met Tanner, she assumed he used his position on the force to be controlling and powerful. But that couldn't be further from the truth. This man put his life on the line every single day, and she hadn't realized until now just how valuable he was in her life.

Her cell rang, but she ignored it. She didn't care who was calling, she needed to keep her eyes on this screen.

Melanie wasn't sure how long she'd watched, but the next thing she knew the front door opened and closed.

"Mel."

Livie's voice pulled her from the screen. "The living room."

Moments later Livie and Jade took a seat on either side of her. Of course they'd be here. She hadn't even thought to call them for help so she wouldn't be alone. All her thoughts had been on Tanner.

"He'll be fine," Jade assured her. "This is his job."

Yeah, that's the part that scared Melanie the most.

"Jax and Cash are heading down," Livie said, taking Melanie's hand in hers for support. "They're staying back, but they wanted to be there to help crowd control."

"Why is this taking so long?" Melanie muttered. "Can't they just go in and get the guy?"

"In theory that sounds great." Jade rubbed her hand up and down Melanie's back. "This will take some time, but we're right here for you. Tanner is going to be fine. He's a smart cop."

The instant burn in her throat and nose gave Melanie about a minute's warning before the tears started falling. She had no clue how to keep her emotions at bay, so she opted to just let them go.

"You're going to need to remain calm," Livie said. "Think of the baby. Think of Tanner. He wouldn't want you getting this upset, right? Wouldn't he tell you there's nothing to worry about and he'll be fine?"

Melanie sniffed and nodded. "He would. Damn it, I just feel so helpless doing nothing but waiting and watching."

"Honestly, that's all the cops are doing, too," Jade added. "They're waiting and watching for this guy to make a move or give himself up."

Melanie concentrated on breathing slowly, on remaining as calm as she could for the baby. "I just want to do something."

"What were you doing before the news broke?" Livie asked.

"I was working on my blogs and getting them scheduled for the next week, and then I was going to attempt to make dinner."

Jade laughed. "Wow. You really are getting into this whole domestic life. What were you going to make?"

"Well, I'm usually only good at throwing things together and winging it for experiments to use on my blog. But I thought I'd make an actual dinner that didn't involve kale or spinach." She smiled, thinking of how she'd been so eager to surprise Tanner. "He's more of a meat-and-potatoes type of guy."

"Most Southern guys are," Livie chimed in. "It's how they were raised."

Jade patted Melanie's knee. "Why don't we start dinner. Tanner is going to be tired and hungry when he gets home."

Melanie stared at the television. "I should call his mom," she muttered. "I'm sure she's heard, but I feel like I need to call her."

"You go call her." Livie came to her feet. "Jade and I will start dinner, and you need to remain calm. Okay? Everything will work out and Tanner will be home before you know it."

Melanie nodded. At least there was a plan.

Jade stood up and extended her hand to help Melanie to her feet. "Thanks, guys," Melanie said, looking from one concerned friend to the other. "I'm glad I'm not alone."

"We wouldn't let you be alone," Livie told her. "Now go call his mom."

With Teresa living an hour away, Melanie wasn't sure if she'd heard the news or not, but she needed to be informed. Melanie used her cell and sat on the sofa, making sure to keep her eyes locked on the television for any new updates.

She waited, but the phone just kept ringing. Ultimately, Melanie ended up leaving a message to call back. She really didn't want to discuss the situation over voicemail.

Soon, tempting scents started wafting from the kitchen. A news anchor stood in front of the camera and gave an update that the cops were in negotiations with the gunman. Moments later in the background, Melanie saw two women running from the front of the bank. Tanner and another officer ran up to meet them and escorted them to safety.

The sun was starting to set. Who knew how much longer this would go on, but Melanie would be right here waiting for Tanner to come home. Because as soon as he walked through that door, she was going to tell him she loved him. There were no doubts and there was no promise of another day. If she wanted him to know how she felt, she couldn't hold off any longer.

Chapter Seventeen

Broken crayons still color.

                    —Mel's Motivational Blog

"She's asleep."

Jade whispered as she came to her feet from the over-sized leather chair and folded the throw blanket.

Tanner wasn't a bit surprised to walk in and see Jade and Livie in his living room. Livie sat on the sofa with Melanie's feet in her lap. Livie's head tipped back against the cushion as she slept, Melanie's head rested on the arm of the couch, and Jade rubbed her eyes and shoved her hair back from her face. This had definitely been a long night for everyone, and he was relieved to know Melanie hadn't spent it alone.

The muted television flickered, showing some late night infomercial about knives.

"She's been rooted to this spot all night, but she finally couldn't take it anymore," Jade explained, then placed a hand on his arm. "How are you? You look ready to drop."

Tanner rolled his shoulders and blew out a sigh. "I'm exhausted, but relieved the events turned out the way they did. Things could've gone so much worse."

When the gunman's wife had come onto the scene, she'd called her husband and hours later she finally managed to talk him into giving himself up. He was now in custody. His poor wife and children not only reeled from their main source of support losing his job, but now he also faced criminal charges. It was a tough situation, but all in all the day could've ended tragically. At least everyone was safe.

"Thanks for staying with her," Tanner whispered. "I worried she'd be stressed, but there was no way I could call her."

"She knows." Jade reached around to the table by the door and grabbed her keys. "Livie and I will get out of here and let you get some rest."

Jade walked over and nudged Livie awake. When she glanced up and saw Tanner, she smiled and then eased out from under Melanie's legs. Livie crossed the room and wrapped her arms around him, giving him that brotherly squeeze he'd come to love from her.

"Glad you're safe," she murmured before easing back. "If you're hungry, dinner is in the fridge."

"Thanks, guys. I mean it. I don't know where Melanie would be without you."

Jade smiled. "We think the same about you."

Tanner didn't question her reply. Melanie definitely didn't need him, but he sure as hell needed her.

After Melanie's friends left, Tanner locked the door and reset the alarm. He turned back to look at the woman on his sofa. Even in her sleep her brows were drawn in, her fist clenched up by her cheek. The worry she must've experienced had obviously carried over into her nap.

To know she had been here pretty much holding vigil for him, worrying for him, had Tanner feeling so . . . well, relieved. He'd never had someone waiting like this. Oh, his mother always fretted about his job, but to have Melanie in his life was something he couldn't explain.

He removed his holster and his gun and took them upstairs to his room, placing them in the safe in his closet. He grabbed a quick shower and threw on a pair of shorts and came back down to the living room. Melanie slept on.

The soft light from the television flashed shadows onto her face. Her long lashes feathered over her porcelain skin. The worry lines between her brows remained and he wished he could've shielded her from any stress.

After all she'd been through this evening, would she even want to be with him? Would she see this as a reason to push him away and safeguard her heart? Would she want to have a family life with a man who put his life on the line? He'd never thought about it until now, but there were no guaranteed days of ease on his job. Yes, the crime rate in Haven was low for the most part, but that didn't mean there wouldn't be danger.

Had this night changed Melanie's heart? He knew she was falling for him. There wasn't a doubt in his mind. She trusted him, she stayed with him, they were having a child. Their bond had only grown stronger over the past month. Hell, his mother was in love with her. Every piece of the puzzle lined up perfectly for a dynamic future if she was ready to discuss their future.

Tanner couldn't imagine coming home without her here now. He'd gotten so used to her, had gotten in the routine of making sure her water and crackers were on the nightstand before he left for work. He'd gotten used to discussing their days when he came home in the evenings.

Still, she brought one outfit at a time in her little bag, claiming just one more night. She slept in his shirts, in his bed . . . and took up a heavy portion of his heart.

Tanner bent down and scooped her up into his arms, careful not to jostle her too much. Her head lolled over to his shoulder. Her bare cheek rested against his chest and her soft, warm breath tickled him as he carried her up the staircase.

Never before had he been one to think poetic thoughts, but he literally felt his heart clench at the idea that he was carrying his entire world right here. The baby, Melanie . . . he'd do anything for them and he wanted them to stay here. Forever.

Hell, he hadn't even told her he loved her yet and was already wanting to put that ring on her finger.

Between Livie and Jax's wedding and the turn of events today on the job, Tanner looked at life in a whole new light. He wasn't waiting any longer to go after what he wanted.

The moonlight cast horizontal slivers through the blinds in his room. The pale glow slashed across the bed like stripes as he laid Melanie on the covers. The moment he let go, she stirred, her lids fluttered and he waited as he watched her come to.

When she focused in on him, she shot straight up and came to her feet. In an instant, she threw her arms around him. Tanner took a step back as the weight of her body knocked him off balance.

"Hey, I'm fine," he assured her, squeezing her tight.

Relief radiated off her as she turned her head toward his neck, needing to inhale that familiar, masculine scent that only belonged to Tanner. Her fingers lacing through his hair and trembled against him.

"You scared the hell out of me," she muttered.

"I can take care of myself," he assured her. "Nothing to worry about."

Melanie eased back, her hair an absolute mess around her face, but she was stunning and he loved her. Damn, he didn't want to wait another moment.

Pushing her hair back, Tanner framed her face with his hands and forced her eyes on his. "I want you to move in," he started. "None of this just one night at a time. I want you permanently in my bed. I love you, Mel."

She pulled in a shaky breath and gripped his wrists. "As in, you love me or you're in love with me? Or that you want to love me so we can try to make this family work?"

Tanner laughed and kissed her hard before releasing her. "All of the above. I love you, I'm in love with you, and we will make this family work."

She slid her hands over his shoulders, trailing the tips of her fingers down over his pecs. Instantly his body stirred. Moments ago he was ready to fall into bed. Now, well . . . he was definitely ready to fall into bed.

"I have a secret I've been keeping," she whispered.

He thought for a second she was going to fill him in on something about her ex. That was the only gap between them, but he was determined to close it.

"I love you, too."

Tanner reached around and gripped her backside, pulling her flush against his body. "Is that right? I've known for a while."

"You have not," she stated, swatting his chest. "I just figured it out the other day."

"Maybe you just came to the realization, but you wouldn't be here with me if you didn't." He nipped at her lips and spun her around so the back of her knees hit the bed. "You don't trust easily. You were heartbroken and left wondering if you could open your heart again. So the fact that you're with me told me all I need to know about your feelings."

"You think you're so smart," she murmured against his lips.

"It's my job to assess the situation."

She rubbed her body against his before pulling him down with her onto the bed. "Then what am I thinking now?"

"That you have on too many clothes."

Melanie laughed and raked her nails over his back. "You are good at your job, Officer."

"I'm about to show you how good I can be."

Tanner stripped her of every shred of clothing and removed his shorts. She reached up for him, welcoming him into her arms. This turning point in their relationship was everything to him, to their future.

Tanner traced his lips over her collarbone and up her neck to finally land on her parted lips. Melanie wrapped her legs around his waist and he didn't hesitate to join their bodies. He swallowed her groan, welcomed her arched body against his, and took his time in pleasuring her.

He didn't care that he had to be up in a few hours for work. All he cared about was that this woman he loved, loved him right back.

When her fingertips bit into his back, he thrust fast, harder. Her heavy panting against his ear had him turning to capture her mouth once again. He couldn't get enough, didn't think he'd ever have enough of Melanie.

Her body tightened all around him as his own release hit. She trembled beneath him, letting out a soft moan when he slid his lips from her mouth along her jawline. After a few moments, she'd gone lax and Tanner's body calmed. He shifted to the side and pulled her right with him into the crook of his arm.

"I was scared for you tonight," she said, breaking the silence.

Tanner trailed his fingertips up and down her bare arm. "I knew you would be. I'm trained for situations like that. I can honestly say Haven doesn't have much major crime, like robberies, but we are ready when it happens. The waiting is the hardest part, for everyone."

"I was so afraid something was going to happen on live TV and I'd have to see it . . ."

Her last word came out on a hiccup as he felt moisture on his chest. Tanner rolled her onto her back and hovered above her, swiping away at her tears. The moonlight slanted right across her face.

"We had the situation under control." Tanner kissed her tear-tracked cheeks. "You need to know that I also work some evenings that aren't with the precinct. I'm not supposed to tell anyone, but I don't want you to worry when I have to leave."

Melanie blinked away the moisture. "I know you disappear randomly. Do you have a second job?"

Tanner pulled in a breath and rolled over on his back. Resting his arm across his forehead, he stared up at the ceiling.

"I'm part of a small operation that consists of former military and former law enforcement. We work undercover to pull women and children out of abusive situations and set them up in a safe place until they can get on their feet and move on."

Melanie lifted up onto her elbow and stared down at him. "That's where you've been all those times we had no idea?"

He nodded and glanced her way. "This is all top secret, so you can't even discuss this with Jade or Livie. Even

Cash and Jax are unaware. They've speculated it's for work, so I just go with it."

Melanie's hand settled over his heart. "And you trusted me with this?"

"I trust you with everything."

Please open up, Mel. Tell me about Neville and the calls.

She fisted her hand on his chest and rested her chin. "I've never known anyone like you, Tanner. You're constantly giving and caring. Our baby is so lucky to have you as her father."

"Her?" he asked, though part of him cracked a little that she still wasn't giving him 100 percent of herself.

"Until we find out, I'll be referring to the baby as her."

He slid his hand up her back. "Fine by me. Who knows, maybe the next one will be a boy."

Melanie stilled. "The next one?"

Tanner smiled into the dark and wrapped his arms around her. "Get some rest, Mel. We've had a long day."

"Well, this looks like shit."

Tanner stepped over the boxes of still-wrapped flooring in the lobby as he attempted to get into the front entrance of the airport.

Dripping sweat and holding a crowbar, Jax looked up and flipped him the finger. "Shouldn't you be working and actually earning the taxpayers' hard-earned money instead of harassing me?"

"I already earned my paycheck." Tanner watched as Jax took the crowbar and hammer and tapped at the old tile on the floor. "I have a bag of clothes in the car if you need help. But if you're going to bitch about my job, I can just go home and have a beer."

"Kiss my ass and change your clothes."

Tanner laughed. "I knew you couldn't do this without me."

He headed back out to his truck and grabbed his bag. Within minutes he was changed and had his own crowbar and hammer, working on the other end of the lobby area.

"Where's Cash?" Tanner asked.

"He has a date."

"When doesn't he?" Tanner tapped at another tile, cursing when only the corner piece chipped away. "He may have to reschedule that social life until we make some headway here."

"He swears he'll come by on Sunday and Monday."

"He's also buying the beer for the workdays."

Jax laughed as he tapped away at more of the tile. Thankfully the lobby area wasn't overly huge. They were opening some walls and changing out the flooring to provide a better flow and definitely something more updated for their future high-class clientele.

"What do you think about me asking Melanie to marry me?"

Jax's tapping came to a halt. He stood straight up, wiped his forehead with the back of his arm, and stared at Tanner like that was the last topic he ever thought would come up.

"What?" Tanner asked, tapping the hammer lightly to the curve on the crowbar to chip at the tile. "It's a legit question. How did you know when you wanted to ask Livie?"

"Hell, I don't know." Jax held both tools in one hand and swiped his hand over the back of his neck. "The thought of her leaving and going back to Atlanta made me so angry. I couldn't just let her leave without a fight."

Melanie hadn't mentioned leaving; she actually went on and on about how much she loved Haven.

"Are you only thinking of asking because of the baby?" Jax asked.

Tanner set his tools at his side and shook his head. "No. What Melanie and I have is completely different than what I went through before. Mel and I have both been through hell, but she's so strong and resilient. I just—I want her to always be there, you know?"

"So when are you asking?"

Tanner sighed and wished like hell he had all the answers or someone to give him clear insight. "I'm not sure now is the time."

Jax's brows drew together. "Why not?"

"I know she's had contact with her ex," Tanner explained. "Not that she's getting back with him, but I think he's still a threat and she hasn't opened up to me about it. It's like she hasn't trusted me with that final piece of her life."

"I can't believe you haven't called her on it." Jax crossed the room and opened a cooler, pulling out two bottles of water. "You afraid she'll lie about it?"

Tanner took the bottle Jax offered. "I don't think she'd lie if I said something, but I want her to come to me on her own. I know her well enough and she thinks she's protecting me. She's mentioned several times how powerful her ex is and how she doesn't want me to have any involvement with him. She's not afraid for herself at this point, she's afraid for me."

Jax twisted the cap off the bottle and tossed it into the large trash bin in the corner. "You need to confront her, man. This has nothing to do with her not trusting you. That may be how you see it, but as an outsider, I'm telling you she's afraid. She wants a future with you, that much is evident. But she's worried her powerful ex will ruin it."

That's exactly what she thought, no doubt. He would have to confront her, but he didn't want her to feel like he was accusing her of anything.

"Livie has told me some about him," Jax went on. "The guy is a certified asshole. You need help with anything, you know Cash and I have your back. Mel is like family to us, too."

"Appreciate it." Tanner finished his water and tossed the empty bottle into the trash. "I just need to figure out how to approach Melanie first without making her even more scared or close in more on herself."

"You've got one strong-willed woman on your hands, that's for sure." Jax let out a bark of laughter. "I'm still stunned she sold that shiny new Beemer and gave the money to us."

Tanner stilled. "What?"

"The money she gave for the renovations." Jax's face fell and he muttered a curse. "I figured you knew. Melanie told Livie she didn't want anything more to do with her ex or that life, so she sold the car, bought that clunker she has now, and gave the rest toward the renovations."

Tanner couldn't believe this. Well, he could. This was such a Melanie move. He shouldn't be surprised at her selfless act, but what shocked him was that she had blown off the reason she'd sold her car. Why didn't she just come out and tell him the truth?

Just add *humble* to the list of mysteries surrounding the woman he loved. Some people might think she'd kept that secret because of a lack of trust, but a little secret like this wasn't an area where she had trouble with trust. No, his Mel didn't want praise or accolades, she just wanted to help where she could.

"Maybe I shouldn't have said anything."

Tanner waved his hand. "No, no. It's fine."

Jax grabbed his tools and tapped the crowbar against his side. "You should probably have a long talk before you think about buying a ring. But that's just my opinion—which you asked for, by the way."

Tanner swallowed and hunkered back down to get to work. "I did ask. I just don't know why things can't be easy."

"Dude, with women they never are. But if you love her, then she'll totally be worth it."

Chapter Eighteen

No one is you and that is your superpower.

—Mel's Motivational Blog

Atlanta was just as stifling as she remembered. All the buildings, the people bustling to and from offices. Melanie had been here all of ten minutes and was already missing the open park in Haven, the wide town streets dotted with lampposts and evergreens with holly flowing from the pots. The holidays in a small town were quite different than in the city.

Melanie pulled her navy blue cardigan around her and waited just outside the small café where she'd chosen to meet Neville. The place was next to his office building, but public enough she felt safe. He wouldn't cause a spectacle where any of his voters could possibly see what was going on.

"Melanie."

She cringed at his voice and took just a moment before she spun around. Melanie hadn't seen her ex in two years, and he hadn't changed a bit. Obviously still getting Botox to ward off the wrinkles in his forehead. His dark hair still had the same perfect part on the right side. Those dark eyes still looked like they belonged on the devil rather than the mayor.

The old Melanie wanted to shiver with fear, but that woman had been revamped. She'd been made new, and now she was about to show them both what she was made of.

"Let's get this over with."

She headed toward the café entrance, but his hand shot out and gripped her elbow. Melanie eyed the way his fingers curled around her sweater, then she glared up at him.

"Get your hand off me."

His eyes widened as he slowly released her. "My Melanie has gotten a backbone, I see."

"I was never yours," she retorted.

He gestured to the sleek black town car on the street. "We'll talk in here where it's private."

Melanie gave the car a quick glance and laughed. "You're delusional if you think I'm going to be in private with you anywhere."

"If you want to talk about your officer boyfriend out in the open, we can." Neville's smile turned into a sneer. "But I'm sure you'd rather keep things quiet."

Melanie hated this man. She hated him with a passion she couldn't even explain. Once upon a time she'd believed he was her salvation out of the poverty she lived in. She'd rather live back in her trailer park with a car that barely ran and a father who worked his ass off and a mother who was an alcoholic than to be with this man ever again.

Hindsight didn't change the past, but it was a hell of a lesson for future decisions.

"If I get in that car, it stays parked right there," she demanded. "Understood?"

Neville merely nodded his head and extended his arm toward the car. She clutched her purse over her shoulder and stepped forward. When he brushed against her to open the door, she cringed, but didn't say anything. Giving in to his games would only excite him. She knew how he played, knew how he thought. And he was absolutely right. She did have a backbone now and she damn well was going to use it.

She slid into the back seat and Neville moved in right next to her before closing the door. The driver up front remained facing forward, no doubt paid very well to keep his eyes and ears to himself. This wasn't the same driver Melanie recalled, so who knew what happened to the other poor guy.

"Will, drive around the block."

Melanie jerked her attention to Neville. "That wasn't what we agreed upon."

"I didn't agree to your demands," he countered.

She should've known he'd never let anyone better him. All the more reason she needed to end this once and for all.

"Say what you have to say and then have your driver circle back around to my car."

"I didn't see your car parked anywhere."

Melanie smiled and adjusted her cardigan over her lap. "I sold it and gave the money to a charity."

She didn't need to say what type of charity, and contributing to Livie and Jax's restoration project was a charitable move on her part. Oh, the look on Neville's face made driving her clunker so completely worth every embarrassing horn honk and sitting against a pillow to reach the pedals.

His freshly shaven jaw clenched, nostrils flared, lips thinned. "I don't even recognize you anymore," he spouted. "You get rid of the nicest thing you owned, you're dressing like trash again, and you're mouthy as hell."

And here she'd thrown on her nice jeans today. Actually, her belly was getting firm and she was afraid to wear her other jeans because this was the pair that was a little loose. She was already approaching the tenth week. Hopefully only two more to go and the nausea would be gone. Fingers crossed.

Melanie blew out a sigh and crossed her arms. "Just say what you have to say and let's be done with each other."

"You're going to move back in and remarry me. I've set everything up, the wedding will be at the New Year and the press has already been given a heads-up."

Melanie listened as he rattled on about some fantasy world he'd created. She just let him go—maybe he'd feel better once it was all out in the open. She knew she'd feel better once he was finished and she'd sliced and diced his words to smithereens.

"We will raise this baby as our own," he went on. "As for the boyfriend, he's not going to be an issue. I've come up with a nice amount that I think will please him to stay out of our lives."

Melanie waited a moment, making sure he was finished with his preposterous plan.

"First of all, I'd rather die than marry you or ever let a child around you. Second, you don't know Tanner at all if you think even for one moment that he would take any amount of money in exchange for his child. You're even more of an arrogant ass than I thought."

Neville's smile slowly spread across his face. "I couldn't care less if he takes the money or not. He can either stay out of the baby's life, and yours, or I'll have his badge and he won't work in law enforcement ever again. Not even as a mall security cop. Is that what you want?"

Her blood chilled at the very idea of Neville ruining Tanner's career. This is exactly what she'd hoped to avoid. She'd never wanted Tanner involved, didn't want him harmed or even threatened.

"Did you forget I have pictures and documentation of our marriage?" she reminded him.

"You won't go anywhere with those photos," he countered. "Not if you want your boyfriend to keep that tiny town badge of his."

The car turned another corner and Melanie stared down to her lap as she weighed her next move. If she talked to Tanner, confided in him, maybe they could pull together and fight this. She would never marry Neville, no matter the threat. But how did she prevent him from destroying Tanner's life?

"Neville." She glanced back up at him, ready to fight right back. "There will be no wedding, so you might as well—"

The car lurched as metal on metal crunched, glass shattered. Melanie screamed as she was flung across the seat an instant before her world faded to black.

Where on earth was she?

Tanner eyed the clock above the mantel and couldn't believe Melanie hadn't texted or called. It was already six o'clock and he hadn't heard a word from her since this morning when he'd left for work.

Worry started forming deep in his belly. This wasn't like Melanie at all. He pulled his cell from his pocket and tried calling hers, only to get voicemail . . . again.

The second he hung up, his cell vibrated in his hand. The screen lit up with Jade's number.

He swiped to answer. "Hey, Jade. Are you by chance with Melanie? I can't find her."

"There's been an accident."

Tanner's world tilted. He placed a hand on the back of the oversized chair and clutched his phone. In that instant, the worst possible scenarios flooded his mind. Being in law enforcement, being in the military, he'd seen some scary, horrific things.

"Where is she?" he barely choked out.

"She's in a hospital in Atlanta," Jade stated.

"Atlanta? What the hell—"

"You need to listen to me and not explode," Jade warned, then he heard her push out a sigh. "She was in a car accident . . . with Neville."

Fury, confusion, rage, terror . . . so many emotions rolled through him. Hell, they all rolled over him, causing his knees to go weak. He leaned further onto the back of the chair.

"I don't know the specifics," she went on. "I happened to be talking to a colleague on the phone and when it came through on the news, she told me. The media only mentioned that the mayor and his ex-wife had been involved in an accident downtown when a bus ran a red light and hit their car. They've both been taken to St. Mary's."

"I'm leaving now."

"You can't go alone," Jade claimed. "You're not going to be in any position to drive."

"I don't have time to wait for anyone."

"I texted Cash and Jax. They should be at your house any minute."

Tanner gripped the chair, fighting back the nausea rolling through him. Damn it. He couldn't lose Melanie and the baby. Right now they could be getting checked out and doing fine, or they could be . . . hell, he couldn't even think of all the what-ifs.

"Livie and I are staying back with Piper, but you better let us know something the second you do."

Tanner realized this waiting would be just as much hell for Melanie's friends as it would be for him.

"I promise."

His front door opened and closed. Turning around, he disconnected the call as he caught the worried gaze of his cousins.

"I'm driving," Jax stated.

"You better do it fast enough or I'll take over," Tanner warned, already heading out the front door.

As they all settled in Jax's SUV, Cash reached up from the back seat and placed a hand on Tanner's shoulder. "She's going to be fine."

"I can't lose her."

Damn it, his voice cracked and he was barely hanging on here. Losing one family had been pure hell, but to lose another . . .

Tanner honestly didn't think he'd recover again.

Jax started down the road and shut off the radio. "Jade only said that Mel had been in an accident in Atlanta. That's all we know. Do you know anything else?"

Tanner filled them in on the little bit of information he had.

"What the hell was she doing there with her ex?" Cash asked.

"I have no idea," Tanner muttered. "I can't even think about that right now. I just . . . I can't. I need to know she and the baby are okay. That's all that matters."

"She'll be okay," Cash repeated. "You know she wouldn't

have been meeting with him if she weren't blackmailed or threatened. Once we find out the situation, we'll handle it."

"Damn right," Jax added.

Knowing his best friends had his back was absolutely everything. They'd been there before when his world had crumbled. Each of them had faced their own hell. Jax when his wife left him with a new baby, Cash when his wife cheated on him and left with every dime in their bank accounts. But they'd all persevered.

Tanner just hoped like hell this day wouldn't turn out to be another frozen moment in time, locked in his mind, when his world had shattered again.

Only ten minutes had passed according to the dashboard clock, and already this was the longest drive of his life. The closer they got to Atlanta, the more his anxiety increased. He swiped his damp palms over his jeans and stared out the window. The guys remained silent, knowing he needed the peace and quiet.

Finally, the hospital came into view. Jax didn't even ask, he just pulled up to the front to drop Tanner off. The SUV had barely rolled to a stop when Tanner clicked off his seat belt and was out of the car.

The woman at the information desk informed Tanner that Melanie was in room 311. Another layer of dread seeped through him. If she was in a room, then this wasn't something as simple as getting looked over and sent home. They were keeping her.

His hands shook as he reached for the elevator button. When it didn't immediately open, he spun around and found a door with the sign for the stairs. He raced up to the third floor and marched past the nurses' station, staring at each room number and ticking them down until he stood in front of Melanie's.

The door was closed. There was no noise coming from

the other side and Tanner wanted to bust through, but at the same time fear gripped him and he wasn't so sure he was ready to face his fate on the other side.

Pulling in a deep breath, Tanner gripped the handle and gave it a tug. The curtain was pulled, and he closed the door with a soft click behind him. He reached out for the striped curtain and eased it back.

Melanie lay on the bed. Her face pale, a bandage on her head, her arm in a sling. Her heart monitor beeped a steady rhythm. Another monitor beeped and he studied the screens. Two heartbeats. Wires ran beneath the stark white blanket toward Melanie's midsection.

Tanner collapsed onto the chair at her bedside. The baby was okay, Melanie was okay. Well, except for the obvious injuries, but he had to believe everything was going to be fine.

He reached out and took her hand, dropping his forehead to where they joined.

"Tanner."

Her groggy voice had him jerking his head up, still clutching her hand. He needed to touch her, needed to feel that she was indeed alright.

"What are you doing here?" she asked as she shifted in the bed, then winced.

"Don't move." He came to his feet and placed his hands on her shoulders. "What can I get you? Water? The nurse? Are you in pain?"

Melanie shook her head. "I don't need the nurse. I just want to go home, but they said I had to stay."

"The baby . . ."

"Is fine. I fractured my collarbone and have a few stitches in my head. I have a concussion, so they're monitoring me."

Her eyes welled up with tears and she looked down at their hands. "You know why I was in Atlanta," she whispered.

Tanner swallowed, hating how her voice sounded so shameful, so full of guilt. "I know you were with Neville in a car when this happened."

She pulled her hand from his and covered her face. When her shoulders shook, Tanner eased onto the side of the bed.

"Talk to me. What's going on?"

"You shouldn't be here," she cried into her hand. "He can't know you're here."

The curtain behind him slid aside and Tanner glanced over his shoulder to see Cash and Jax. He held up a hand and the two slowly stepped back outside and closed the door.

"Neville can't know I'm here?" Tanner clarified. "Did he threaten you?"

Melanie shook her head and dropped her hand back to her lap. "No. He threatened you."

Tanner laughed. "Honey, I'm not afraid of your ex-husband."

"You don't understand." Her watery eyes practically begged him. "He'll ruin your career. He wants to buy you off to keep you out of the baby's life and mine."

Rage filled Tanner at the thought that some low-life politician thought for even a second that money could buy him.

Tanner reached up to wipe her damp cheeks. "It will never happen."

"I told him you'd never take money," she assured him. "But maybe if you stay away from me, maybe he won't feel threatened? I don't know. I have no clue what to do to save you at this point. He's worked up some preposterous scheme to remarry me—"

"Like hell."

Melanie shook her head. "No, I'm not marrying him. But if he thinks you're a threat at all . . . Tanner, please listen. Just go."

Part of him wanted to shake some sense into her, but the rest of him couldn't get beyond the pain that consumed him. She'd tried to do all of this on her own. She'd not trusted their relationship enough to let him in, to let him take over and protect her.

"Why didn't you come to me?" he asked, unable to keep the anger from his tone. "Why were you so adamant about keeping me locked out of this?"

Melanie dropped her head against the pillow and stared up at the ceiling. "I never wanted this for you. I wanted my old life separate from my new. I was doing a good job of it, too, until he discovered the pregnancy. I mean, he was texting and sending messages through his assistants, but the pregnancy put him over the top, and when he threatened you . . ."

Melanie turned her head and stared at him once again. "Do you not get that I trust you with my entire heart, Tanner? My life is yours, but I couldn't let you get hurt."

"You don't trust me with your life." Those words no doubt hurt her . . . they hurt like hell to say out loud. "Maybe you want to, maybe you even think you do, but you would've been completely up front with everything if that were the case."

Melanie's chin quivered as she bit down on her lip and turned her head away. "Just go," she whispered. "I'm tired."

Damn it. This was not how he wanted to leave her. He *wouldn't* leave her like this.

Tanner reached for her good hand and stroked his

thumb across her knuckles. "You're done doing things alone," he vowed. "I've said this before, but you're going to see that I don't scare easily. You're tired because you've carried the weight of this burden for years. It's my turn."

She jerked her attention toward him, her entire body tense. Eyes wide, she shook her head. "Tanner, when I said go, I didn't mean from the room. I meant from my life. I won't keep our baby from you. I'd never do that, but you and me . . . we just can't do this anymore."

Another round of rage rolled through him. He braced his fists on either side of her hips and leaned forward until he was a breath away from her face.

"Like hell we can't. You already told me you love me. There's no going back, Mel. We're a family and I'll be damned if someone, anyone, is going to destroy that."

He kissed her for the briefest of moments before releasing her. Tanner came to his feet and shoved his hands in his pockets as he stared down at the woman he loved lying in the bed.

"Rest up, Melanie. I'll finish this fight."

"I don't want you in my fight, Tanner." Her voice cracked, but she tipped her chin and stared across the space without blinking. "We can't be together anymore."

"Because you're scared?" he demanded.

Melanie pursed her lips and blinked. She pulled in a deep breath as she squared her shoulders against the stark white pillow.

"I'm not scared anymore. I'm finally doing what is right . . . for both of us."

Tanner couldn't believe what he was hearing. "And the baby? What about what's right for our child, Melanie?"

"Our baby will know love, from both of us," she assured him. "We just won't be living together."

Tanner wasn't going to stand there and argue with her.

He wasn't going to let her give up, either. He wasn't lying when he said he'd finish this fight.

Neville Prescott was about to meet his match, and not in the form of a woman he could blackmail, abuse, or threaten.

Without another word, he stepped from her room. Leaning on the wall across from him were Cash and Jax. They met his eyes and Tanner gripped his fists at his sides and crossed to them.

"We need to talk privately."

Because he needed the help of his best friends, and there was no way he was going to let Melanie go through this alone. She was going to need Livie and Jade as well.

Chapter Nineteen

*It's not who you think you are that holds you back,
it's who you think you're not.*

—Mel's Motivational Blog

"I'm really fine," Melanie stated for the fifth time in what seemed as many minutes. "Just do whatever you guys would normally be doing."

She settled back on the sofa in her house. Well, Livie's old house. Jade and Livie had picked her up once the doctor had given her the all-clear earlier that morning. She'd be lying if she didn't admit a piece of her heart had utterly crumbled when Tanner had walked out and hadn't come back today. He hadn't called or texted. Livie and Jade hadn't mentioned him, either.

Melanie had pushed him out to keep him protected—isn't that what she wanted? Above all else, she had to protect Tanner and their child. Neville didn't just toss around idle threats. He would ruin Tanner the first chance he got. But Melanie only hoped that if she proved they weren't together, then there would be no more threats against him. And if Neville couldn't use Tanner against Melanie, then he wouldn't have any way to blackmail her into another hellish marriage.

Because, in the end, Melanie would go public with her pictures and documents if she had to. That was the last thing she wanted. Yes, the harm would be on Neville, but she'd be putting herself out as a victim, and she'd sworn she'd never be that woman again. Showing such vulnerability wasn't something she wanted to do, but again, she'd do anything to protect Tanner and the baby.

"I'm actually going to send a few résumés out later today," Jade stated. "I found several places where I think I'd be a good fit, and I need to move on with my life. I can't be here forever."

Melanie sat up straighter. "You're leaving Haven?"

"Well, there's not much here for me to do." She lifted one slender shoulder in a shrug and plopped down in the leather accent chair. "Not as far as work. I need to get back to feeling like I'm contributing, and the longer I go without a job, the more I feel like I'm mooching off Livie."

Livie laughed and propped her hip against the opposite end of the couch, where Melanie sat with her feet propped up.

"Don't be ridiculous," Livie stated. "This house needs to be lived in. I can't bear the thought of selling it."

Melanie recalled a time not so long ago when that was exactly Livie's intention. She'd wanted to sell anything to do with her past, but instead she'd chosen to embrace it.

"Well, I'm staying." Melanie attempted to find a comfortable spot, but with the damn sling she just looked like a bug on its back trying to maneuver. "So this house won't go empty as long as you don't care I'm here. I don't care to mooch."

Jade rolled her eyes. "You're not mooching. You're pregnant and you'll be at Tanner's when—"

"When what?" Melanie asked.

Jade and Livie exchanged a look as silence joined their party. Melanie's stare volleyed back and forth, but her friends remained tight-lipped.

"Spill it," she demanded. "What is going on?"

"I don't know what you mean." Livie stood up and grabbed her keys from the table by the front door. "I need to get back home."

"Sit down." Melanie pointed to the couch with her good hand. "Nobody is going anywhere until I know what you-all know. I should've realized something was up when neither of you mentioned Tanner this morning."

"What you need to focus on right now is getting better," Jade said as she reached over and patted Melanie's leg.

"I'm not sick," Melanie growled. "I'm sore and pregnant, with a broken collarbone and a few stitches on my forehead. What the hell is going on with Tanner?"

Dread consumed her at the thought that Tanner was indeed going to fight her fight. The thought of him confronting Neville made her nearly nauseous.

"Please, tell me he's not in Atlanta."

Silence once again settled heavily in the room. Melanie closed her eyes and pulled in a slow, deep breath.

"And Cash and Jax?"

She was almost afraid of the answer to that question, but she knew where one went, the others followed to provide backup and support.

"Why don't I make you something to eat?" Livie suggested. She remained by the door as if she was ready to dart out at any moment. "You've got to be hungry."

"I'm not hungry." Damn it, she was, but that wasn't the issue right now. "Tell me what they've got planned."

Melanie waited, then when her friends continued their silence, she smacked her hand on the arm of the couch.

"Damn it, tell me. I never wanted all of you guys to get involved in my mess."

Jade immediately came from her seat and crouched down in front of Melanie. "Calm down. Getting worked up isn't good for you or the baby."

Livie instantly sat at her side and rested her hand on her knee. "The guys are meeting with Neville. Do not say a word, just hear me out."

Endless scenarios spiraled through her mind. She'd done her absolute best to keep Tanner from Neville, but instead she'd thrust all three guys, whom she'd come to love and respect, right at his door.

"Tanner knows what he's doing," Livie went on. "He's not going to do anything that will compromise his career. That's one of the main reasons he's taken the guys with him as witnesses."

Another reason being the three of them together looked threatening, which was exactly what Tanner would want. Neville would either be terrified of the menacing men or he'd go through on his threat of demolishing Tanner's reputation and badge. Though unless he had something really dirty from Tanner's past, Melanie wasn't sure how he'd pull off such a ruse.

"I just can't wrap my mind around everything," she muttered. "I need to talk to Tanner. Can you get my phone from my bag?"

Livie and Jade exchanged yet another look, but nobody moved.

"Come on, guys," Melanie pleaded. "You know I'm not going to just sit back and let him do this, right? I just want my phone. I won't rat you two out for telling me."

Muttering beneath her breath, Jade got up and went to the corner by the door where Melanie had dumped her purse when she got home. Jade searched around and pulled it out, but didn't come back with it. She held the phone against her chest.

"If you call him, text him, whatever, do not blast him for trying to protect you. That man loves you and he'd do anything for you."

Melanie's eyes burned as her throat clogged. She simply nodded. "That's what I'm afraid of," she whispered.

She held out her hand and waited until Jade came back and handed it over. Without a word, she laid the phone in her lap so she could use her one good hand and pull up his contact.

Melanie held the phone up to her ear and waited as it rang. And rang. And rang. Finally, his voicemail came on and Melanie ended the call without leaving a message. She had no idea what she wanted to tell him anyway, and given the option of having only thirty seconds wasn't going to cut it.

She dropped the phone back to her lap and stared at it as if the device would give her some magical answer. She shot off a quick text for Tanner to call her as soon as possible, but she knew he'd do whatever his intentions were in Atlanta first. Then he'd call. Maybe.

"Get in touch with Jax," she told Livie.

Livie offered a soft smile. "Let them do this, Mel. It's past time for someone to step in and end all of this. You have a family now to think of."

"That's exactly who I'm worried about," she cried.

Livie came to her feet and smoothed down her cardigan. "I'm going to go make you some lunch. Jade will be here, but I need to get home in about an hour for Piper. She's next door at the sitter's for now."

Melanie knew she was fighting against five people who truly cared about her. Part of her was exhausted and she wanted to turn over the reins of this fight. But the other part worried that someone else would get hurt. Someone she loved.

Tanner and company marched right into Neville's office building. With his guys behind him and fury fielding his actions, there was nothing standing in the way of saying what he came to say. This game he played with Melanie was over, because now that Tanner was in her life, for good as far as he was concerned, there was no room for Neville and his ego.

Tanner charged right toward the closed door with Neville's name in capital gold letters.

"Oh, um, excuse me, you can't go in there." The twenty-something receptionist came to her feet. "Do you need to make an appointment?"

"No," Tanner replied as he kept walking.

"Sir, I'm sorry, but—"

"What's your name, darlin'?"

Tanner smiled as Cash's question shut the receptionist right up. He reached for the door handle and shoved the heavy door open. As soon as Tanner and Jax stepped through the door, Neville jumped to his feet, which was saying something considering he'd had a busty redhead sitting on his lap. Thankfully they were dressed, because Tanner really didn't want to see any of Melanie's ex's bits and pieces.

A nasty bruise covered the left side of his forehead, presumably from the crash. Tanner wouldn't have minded seeing a few more marks on the vile man.

"What the hell are you guys doing in here? Who are you?" Neville demanded.

The redhead adjusted her dress and stepped back toward the wall of windows.

Neville reached for his phone. "My assistant will have security up here—"

"She's busy right now," Jax replied with a chuckle.

Neville narrowed his eyes. "You're Tanner."

"I'm glad to know you've admired me from afar. I'm flattered."

"Get the hell out of here before I have you arrested."

Tanner crossed his arms over his chest. "You can call the cops, but this is a public building and I'm only here to talk."

With a nod toward the woman hovering behind him, Tanner said, "You may want to consider making this more private."

Neville didn't even turn around, he simply gave a gesture toward the door and the redhead scurried away. Once the door was closed and they were alone, Tanner seriously called on every single bit of willpower he'd ever known not to reach across that desk and put his fist through Neville's face.

But he was an officer of the law and he also respected Melanie. He would get this done the right way and not pull more violence into the mix.

"Who's this?" Neville nodded toward Jax.

"Jackson Morgan," Jax replied as he came to stand next to Tanner.

"So, what, are you guys here to beat me up? Give me a warning?" Neville asked. Clearly the man was terrified, but he remained behind his desk. "I'll press charges if you touch me."

"Don't flatter yourself," Tanner replied. "The last thing I want to do is touch you. But I will tell you this, Melanie is off-limits. You're divorced. Focus on your political career, as pathetic as it is, and let her go."

Neville stared for a moment, then laughed as he shoved

his hands in his pockets. "Get the hell out of my office. Whatever is between Melanie and me is none of your concern."

Tanner took a step forward, but Jax put a hand on his shoulder. Just another reason he'd brought his small army with him.

"Melanie isn't anybody's business," Tanner clarified. "She's her own person and she's decided you are no longer part of her life. You will be respectful of her decisions or you will be removed from your position."

"Bullshit," Neville spat. "You have no power over me. Nobody will remove me, and not only that, I'll be the next senator, so you're the one who will be removed from your position."

Tanner took a half step forward, keeping his eyes locked on Neville. One of the most important lessons he'd learned in the military and through his years on the force was never back down. And of all times in his life, his relationship with Melanie and their future was the most important thing he'd ever fought for.

"I'm not spending my day here arguing," Tanner went on. "This is your warning that you can either stay out of Melanie's life, mine and our baby's as well, or face the consequences."

Neville's nostrils flared as his eyes narrowed. "Is that a threat?"

"Think of it as a promise." Tanner was so done. He didn't want to be in the presence of this jerk another second, but he needed to drive the point home. "You're not the only one with powerful contacts. The state attorney general went to school with my stepdad, and they've remained friends. I know Melanie has several pieces of evidence that support her claims of abuse, but I'll pull those as a last resort."

When Neville's eyes widened and his jaw clenched, Tanner knew he was finally hitting the man where it hurt.

"So your options are to back the hell off," Tanner went on, "or take your chances with your ugly skeletons coming out for all your voters to see. Your choice, but I think we both know who will win this fight."

Silence settled into the room. Jax remained at Tanner's side and Neville was no doubt weighing his options. He was stuck and he damn well knew it. Nothing pleased Tanner more than to know he was the one putting Neville out of Melanie's life. She tried, she'd put up every ounce of fight she had, but she and the baby were his family now, and he'd be damned if he ever let anyone harm what was his.

"Did Melanie send you?"

"She doesn't know I'm here," Tanner stated. "She's home recovering from the accident you got her into. So if you have anything else you want to say, now is the time. When I walk out of this office, your contact with me, Melanie, or anyone else in our lives is over. Are we clear?"

"How dare you threaten me."

Tanner squared his shoulders and shifted his stance. "You did a hell of a lot more to your wife, so don't hide behind your political power now. You're nothing but a lowlife who gets off on manipulating those weaker than you. You wouldn't have a clue how to handle a fight against someone stronger than you. You'd do best to remember that. I'm not weak and I sure as hell am ready to fight for what's mine."

Neville's gaze darted from Tanner to Jax and back to

Tanner. His shoulders slouched just a touch as he shook his head.

"I never should've let her go to begin with," he muttered.

"You didn't let her go," Tanner growled. "She was strong enough to leave, and there wasn't a damn thing you could do about it. If you think she's hard to handle, you've never had to deal with me. So your threats to me are laughable."

Simply because he couldn't control himself another second, Tanner swiped his hand across the stack of papers on Neville's desk, sending them fluttering to the floor.

"We're done here."

He marched out the door, Jax at his back. Tanner couldn't help but roll his eyes and keep walking at the sight of Cash resting a hip on the edge of the receptionist's desk. The poor girl shouldn't be working for an ass like Neville, but that wasn't Tanner's problem.

"Time for me to go, darlin'," Tanner heard Cash say. "I'll give you a call if I'm in town again."

Tanner knew full well his womanizing cousin wasn't going to call, and he hadn't actually lied. He would call if he was in town, but he never came to Atlanta. Cash was too much of a homebody, and Haven was definitely his home.

They all remained silent until they were outside and safely in the privacy of Tanner's truck.

"I take it things went well." Cash fastened his belt in the passenger seat and reached up to adjust his vents. "I didn't hear any glass breaking or screaming."

"We have a mutual understanding," Tanner stated as he pulled out into the late afternoon traffic. "But you bet your ass I'm keeping my eye on him."

"I only had to hold him back once," Jax stated. "I'm not sure if Neville believes us or if he was just playing stupid, but either way, we're keeping watch on Melanie, and Tanner has everything else covered."

"Nobody is touching my family," Tanner murmured.

He couldn't get back to Haven fast enough. He wanted to push forward with the next chapter in his life. He wanted Melanie to know that he'd taken care of everything and she had nothing to worry about.

But most of all, he wanted to move her into his house, permanently, and start their life together.

Chapter Twenty

Actually . . . I can.

—Mel's Motivational Blog

Three days had passed since Tanner and the guys had gone to Atlanta. In those three days, Melanie hadn't heard a word from him . . . nor had she heard a word from Neville or any of his assistants. Perhaps whatever had transpired had made an impact on her ex.

Still, Melanie was going absolutely stir crazy, because the whole typing-with-one-hand thing was a pain in the ass. This was why she always kept reserve blogs. Life and emergencies always came up. Granted this was a first with being unable to work like she was accustomed to, but still. She had plenty of plan B blogs, and she could always repost one of the more popular topics that had generated the most traffic. The more her blog grew, the more new faces came along, so it was always smart to leave snippets of information about her journey so her followers felt that connection with her.

But not being up to her full potential was frustrating. Wondering what Tanner had said to Neville was frustrating. Waiting for the stubborn man to say something to her was frustrating.

She could handle having her arm in a sling and a few stitches in her forehead. Her baby was safe and that's all that mattered to her. Well, that and Tanner. He mattered. He mattered so much, she had begged Jade to take her to Tanner's house to confront him. There was only so much irritation she could handle.

If Tanner wasn't coming to her, then she was damn well going to him. He thought she hadn't trusted him enough to tell him the truth, but what she'd felt was just the opposite. Why had he been so hurt? So angry at her actions? Everything she did had been for them . . . just the same as him going to Neville without telling her. She wanted to be angry, she wanted to pull on her feminist panties and be pissed. But she couldn't be. How could she let anger in when he was doing the exact same thing she did?

Melanie stood outside Tanner's house, but he hadn't answered the door after her three attempts at knocking. His truck was in the driveway, so she knew he was home. She'd even sent Jade on with a wave and a smile. Melanie wasn't going anywhere until she spoke to him, and she didn't need an audience for it.

Melanie tried the front door, but the knob didn't turn. Where was he?

She stepped down off the porch and made her way around the sidewalk toward the back of the house. That's when she heard the old eighties rock blaring from the garage. Melanie pulled in a deep breath and charged in that direction. She'd geared up for a fight since he'd left her hospital bed in Atlanta days ago.

If Tanner thought for one second he could play the white knight and then disappear or go silent, he was sorely mistaken. They could be a team or she could be on her own, but he wasn't going to just charge to her rescue and then dodge her. She deserved answers if he was

going to barge into her life and smooth every path she
had to walk down.

Damn it, why did she find that so appealing?

Melanie crossed to the open side door and stopped
short. Tanner had his shirt off, sweat glistening on his
muscles, and while that was a heart-stopping sight in itself,
the object in front of him is what truly caught her breath.

He squatted down at the side of the same old wooden
rocking chair he and Piper had been working on. But now
the piece of furniture had taken on a completely new look.

Melanie watched as Tanner took his paintbrush over the
curve of the base. She watched as he did each brushstroke
with care, blending the seams of the pale yellow all together.

Folding her arms over her chest, Melanie leaned against
the door. She must've made some sound because Tanner
instantly jerked his gaze over his shoulder.

Just like every other time he caught and held her gaze,
Melanie's heart clenched, her stomach curled with nerves
and desire. He was that deeply embedded into her soul,
because all he had to do was look her way and she was
completely under his spell.

Without a word, Tanner kept his gaze on her as he
slowly rose to his feet. He held the paintbrush in one hand
at his side as silence settled heavily between them. After
a moment, he moved over to the workbench along the far
wall and turned down the music before he came back to
stand next to the chair.

"Is that for me?" she asked, nodding toward the rocker.

Tanner gave a slight shrug. "At first I wanted it to be
for you. Piper and I were sanding it and that was my intention from the start of the project." He glanced down at the
paintbrush, then tossed it onto the plastic drop cloth on the
garage floor. "I figured you'd want something to rock

the baby to sleep with, but then I realized you could probably buy anything, and this is so old. I mean, it was used by my mother when I was a kid, so . . ."

Melanie's heart clenched once again. The chair took on an entirely different meaning now. When she'd initially seen it, she'd assumed he was going to give it to her, but she had no idea this was the very chair he'd been rocked in as a child. She hadn't realized how family heritage could mean so much. She had nothing like this, no special memories to pass down or anything she wanted to hand to her child.

"I wouldn't want any other chair to rock our child in," she murmured through the emotions clogging her throat.

Melanie took a step into the garage. "How long were you going to hide from me? Or are you still angry that I wasn't honest with you?"

The muscles in his jaw clenched. She had no idea what he was thinking. Part of her wondered if he even had a clue what he was feeling. No doubt he was trying to sort everything out just like she was. But she wasn't backing down.

Finally, he raked a hand through his messy hair and down along his stubbled jawline. "I'm not hiding," he admitted. "I just had no idea what to say to you and I needed time."

"Have you had enough?"

He hooked his thumbs through the belt loops on his paint-stained jeans. "Probably not, but I'm glad you're here. Are you angry with me for going to your ex?"

"Depends," she stated. "Does he have anything he can use on you to blackmail you or ruin your career?"

"Nothing."

Relief settled deep within her. "Then I'm not upset."

Tanner's lips twitched as if he was holding back a grin.

"I figured you'd be pissed with me for trying to protect you. I was trying to come up with a good defense."

Oh, this man. He was as frustrating as he was lovable.

"Because you wanted to protect me? That would be a bit hypocritical wouldn't it, considering I did the same for you?"

Tanner blew out a sigh and took a step toward her. "So where are we now?"

Melanie's palms dampened the closer he got to her. "Depends on what you want. It also depends on how much of my past you're ready to take on."

"All of it."

"To which part? What you want, or what you're willing to take on?"

"Everything." He took another step. "I want it all, Mel. I want our future, I want the present, I want your past. I want every damn thing I can take from you because I don't see a scenario where you aren't in my life. You came to me, which means you're not walking back out. I need you."

Melanie couldn't help the tear-infused hiccup she let out. The swell of emotions had finally caught up with her and she couldn't hold back.

His raw, honest words were more than she ever thought she'd hear from any man, let alone a man who loved her so much.

"Ironically, I can't leave," she said, laughing through her tears. "Jade dropped me off."

Tanner closed the last bit of distance between them and slid his arms around her waist. "I guess that means you're finally staying for more than just one night at a time?"

Melanie looped her arms around his neck and rested her forehead on his. "Looks like I'm staying for good."

Tanner lifted her against him and spun her around. His mouth covered hers in a quick, heated kiss.

"I have two questions," he muttered against her lips.

Melanie eased her head back and waited. As she stared back at this man she was head-over-stilettos for, she wondered how she'd gotten so lucky.

"Which spare room do we want to put this rocker in for the nursery?"

"The one right next to ours." She threaded her fingers through his hair. "And the other question?"

"How soon can I make you my wife?"

Melanie stilled for a half second before she rained kisses all over his face. "Tonight, tomorrow. A Christmas wedding has a nice ring to it."

Tanner turned and started walking. He hit the lights and closed the door behind him, all while carrying her. She circled her legs around his waist and dropped her forehead to his shoulder as he headed toward the back door of the house.

"I'm going to start getting heavier and you won't be able to carry me," she warned.

Tanner stopped at the back door. "I've told you before, I don't care about the weight and I will carry you, Mel. I'll always carry you."

As he took her inside, she knew he meant those words in every way. He wasn't just referring to physically. No, this man would carry her through life, and she was just independent yet stubborn enough to let him. Because they were a family now, they were a team.

And she'd finally come home. For good.

Connect with U s

Visit us online at
KensingtonBooks.com
to read more from your favorite authors, see books
by series, view reading group guides, and more.

for sneak peeks, chances to win books and prize packs,
and to share your thoughts with other readers.

facebook.com/kensingtonpublishing
twitter.com/kensingtonbooks

Tell us what you think!

To share your thoughts, submit a review,
or sign up for our eNewsletters, please visit:
KensingtonBooks.com/TellUs.